Barbara Abercrombie grew up in New York, where she worked as an actress, and now lives in California with her family in a house overlooking the ocean. She has written poetry and an introduction to contemporary poetry for children. *Good Riddance* is her first novel.

Barbara Abercrombie

Good Riddance

Futura Publications Limited

A Futura Book

First published in Great Britain by
Raven Books in association with Macdonald
and Jane's Publishers in 1979.

First Futura Publications edition 1980

ISBN : 0 7088 1748 5

Made and printed in Great Britain by
Hunt Barnard Printing Ltd., Aylesbury, Bucks.

Futura Publications Limited,
110 Warner Road,
Camberwell, London SE5.

For my mother and father

GOOD
RIDDANCE

1

THEY WERE IN A BAR at Los Angeles International Airport, sitting at a small Formica table. She tapped her finger on the tabletop. It was warm and very faintly sticky, as if the entire surface would smear if she pressed hard enough.

A voice over the loudspeaker system announced arrivals and departures. The light in the bar was dim and Robert's face had a bluish tinge. It was the first time she had seen him in two months.

"Well," said Robert, and took a sip of his wine. White wine, the only kind he drank anymore. She wondered why it had become fashionable to drink white wine and unfashionable to drink red. She was drinking a daiquiri, a drink no one she knew had ordered for the past decade.

"Alix," Robert said, letting her name hang in the air, then he looked at his watch and ran a finger across one eyebrow. She had seen him do that a thousand times. Or rather, she had looked. She considered the difference between seeing and looking and continued to tap her finger on the slightly sticky surface of the table.

Perhaps Robert was sending a signal. At one time she had been an expert at interpreting his signals, like a seismologist waiting for the earthquake.

"Do you have to do that?" he asked.

"What?"

"Tap your finger like that."

"I'm sorry." She folded her hands.

"Well," Robert said, "the children will be landing in Phoenix in forty-eight minutes."

"Oh, God," she said.

"Listen. Don't start that. Don't get that way."

"What way?" She frowned. "What are you talking about?"

"You're going to say something about jinxing the plane. About a plane crash or something."

She finished the last of the daiquiri and chewed the chopped ice at the bottom of the glass, and thought that someday when she was very old she would drink daiquiris all day long and not have to worry if she threw up or made an ass of herself. Aloud she said, "I wasn't going to say that at all, Robert."

"Oh?"

"No." She smiled at him.

After a few seconds he said, "All right, Alix. Why did you say 'Oh, God' like that?"

"You said the children would be landing in forty-eight minutes. Normal people don't talk that way, Robert. Normal people would round it off to an hour, or even forty-five minutes. But normal people don't say forty-*eight* minutes. All the way to the airport I kept thinking, The airport is forty-three minutes from the house during rush hour and twenty-seven minutes when there's no traffic; that's what Robert says."

"Lower your voice."

"The point being," she whispered, "that this habit of yours is indicative of a certain meanness of spirit. In other words, you are petty."

"But that's neither here nor there, is it?" he said. "The largesse or meanness of my spirit is no longer the point, is it?"

She pressed the empty daiquiri glass against her cheek, thinking how cool it was, even without ice in it, and why was the glass so cool and the table so warm? She was having trouble with objects again. Tables, chairs, spoons even, were assuming too great an importance; developing personalities, histories.

"You're right, Robert," she said. "There is no point anymore."

"Then we can be friends."

"Yes; then we can be friends." She held out her glass to him and he ordered another daiquiri for her and more wine for himself.

When the drinks came, she said, "You'll call your parents tonight and see that the children arrived safely?"

"Of course," said Robert.

"Remind your mother that Mark lies about brushing his teeth,. and would you ask her to please check and make sure that Cindy brought her new bathing suit? I'm so afraid I forgot to pack it. It has very small yellow ducks marching all over it."

"Yes."

"Actually they're orange. The ducks."

He nodded and took a notebook from the breast pocket of his jacket. With his gold-filled Cross pen he wrote: "M's teeth. C's suit? Ducks."

"Ah," she said.

He put the pen and notebook back in his pocket.

"Notes for everything," she said, "and about everything."

"The children will have a wonderful time in Phoenix," he said.

"Doesn't it ever take some of the joy out of life to always be taking notes?"

"Phoenix has splendid weather in June."

"Yes," she said, and sighed.

"Hardly any rain."

"And so awful here in June."

"Foggy."

"Yes."

3

"Of course, it'll be very hot there in July."

"Children adjust more easily to extremes of temperature than adults do."

"And they can spend most of the time in the pool."

"Oh, Robert."

"What?"

"We're discussing the weather."

He twirled the stem of his wineglass between his fingers.

"Do you remember the Ficketts?" she asked.

"The fellow I knew in the army? His name was Pickett."

"That's right. Ray Pickett. And what was her name? Something like Gladys or Gloria. They discussed nothing but weather that entire weekend they stayed with us. Two solid days of the weather in Europe and Asia and all the army bases in the United States, and she kept telling me what happened to her hair in each climate. As I recall, her hair became totally unmanageable in the Philippines. And after they left, you accused me of being a snob and being rude to the Picketts, and I denied vehemently that I had picked on the Picketts. And when I said that, we both started to laugh and then did imitations of the Picketts all evening."

She had begun to cry. "There's no point to that. It's funny the things you remember. Nothing important, just silly things."

Robert handed her his handkerchief.

"I'm sorry," she said.

"That's all right."

She clutched his handkerchief, wondering where he had gotten it and then realizing she must have bought it for him herself. The handkerchief was very white and smelled of Clorox. "Last June the sun didn't come out for three weeks," she said.

"How's the house?" asked Robert.

"The house is fine."

"I mean, does anyone want to buy it? Have there been any offers?"

She shook her head and carefully folded his handkerchief. Certain objects were charged with more emotional weight than other objects, she was thinking. Men's white handkerchiefs, for in-

4

stance, especially those that smelled of Clorox. Her father had never been without a white handkerchief.

"Have many people looked at it?" Robert went on.

"I don't know, Robert. I don't count them."

"The realtors leave cards, don't they?"

"Yes."

"You could count the cards."

"I never thought of that," she said, and handed him back his handkerchief.

"Have you made any plans?"

"Plans?" She looked puzzled. "For what?"

He shifted in his chair. "Well, plans for what you'll do when the house sells."

"Nothing definite," she said, and thought, I'm having a little difficulty planning what I'll do ten minutes from now. The fact is I can't plan a meal or what to buy at the market, and I can't decide what clothes to wear or what shoes, or when to water the lawn or anything. Aloud she said, "I'm going to play it by ear."

He nodded and sipped his wine.

"I don't know what to do about the windows," she said.

"What's wrong with the windows?"

"I can't cope with them anymore."

"Why not? What's the matter with them?"

"They're dirty."

"Clean them."

"I can't. They're enormous. We don't have any ladders."

"Alix," Robert said slowly, "I meant hire someone to clean them."

"The windows haven't been cleaned since you left."

"This is no big deal, Alix. When you get home look up window washers in the Yellow Pages. Or call the fellow who cleaned them last time. Is that so difficult?"

"It's the waiting that's so difficult," she said.

"What waiting?"

"Waiting for the window washer to arrive. They never tell you the exact time they'll arrive. It's like the repairmen and telephone

5

and gas people and deliveries. They never give you an exact time and so you just have to wait and you're afraid to even go to the john for fear you'll miss hearing the doorbell—"

"Look, I understand you're under a strain, Alix. I know what you're going through. I'm going through it, too. . . ."

There was not an ounce of excess flesh on Robert's face, she realized with wonder. His face was a testimony to his devotion to discipline and schedules and exercise. Even the lines across his forehead and running from his nose to the corners of his mouth looked *right,* as though they should be there, as if he had planned them.

He had beautiful hands. It had something to do with the way the bones showed through the flesh. His nails were cut straight across and were very clean. She distrusted men who got manicures and had their nails buffed, and she did not like hands that were pale, with too much flesh on them.

"Oh, Robert," she said.

He looked worried, as if she might start crying again and make a scene.

"I should never have given up ballet," she said.

"You were never serious about ballet until after you gave it up."

"I could have been a great ballerina."

"You said you were too tall."

"Aren't you going to ask me if I want another drink?"

"No."

"You think I've had enough."

"You've had sufficient."

"Go on, Robert, say it. Say I've had enough."

"*I've* had enough. And I didn't mean it that way, so don't look so goddamn hurt. I want to work tonight and I can't if I have any more wine."

"Two glasses of wine? Since when can't you write if you're drinking wine? There are some things you can't do if you've been drinking, but I was not aware writing was one of them. I remember when you couldn't write until you had wine. And it was red wine in those days, Robert."

6

"What the hell is that supposed to mean?"

"I don't know."

She watched him open his wallet and take out a ten-dollar bill and place it on the small tray the waitress had left at their table.

"Come on," he said, standing up.

"Aren't you going to wait for your change?"

"It's for the tip."

"I forgot to tell you something," she said. "It's marvelous. It'll just take a second."

He paused, sat down again and looked at her. "What?"

She shrugged. "It's just something I read in this morning's paper. It's not really all that important."

When they were first married she kept files of newspaper clippings for him; any story or article in the paper that might have a kernel of a plot or character, she would clip out for the files. Character, Plot, Location, Statistics, General Information—she was very proud of the files. Later, when Robert started writing for television, he told her not to bother with the files anymore, but by then it was such a habit she couldn't give up clipping stories from the paper.

"Alix, tell me what you read."

"It's about a woman in Florida," she said. "Every morning before the sun comes up, for four hours, she collects beer cans, and sells them to a recycling company for forty dollars a week. This woman is seventy-two years old, Robert, and she rides around on her bicycle in the dark collecting the cans in plastic bags attached to the handlebars, and she's doing this so she can save enough money to take an ocean voyage like she used to do with her husband when he was alive. She said, 'Just one more time before I die, one more time, I'd like to dance again on one of those big ships.' "

"Alix—"

"And you know what else she said, Robert? She said, 'I'm not just a dilapidated old woman who collects beer cans. I'm a sensitive woman, an educated woman. This garbage, these beer cans, they are only means to an end.' That's what she said."

Robert stared at her for a long time. "You memorized what

7

that woman said. Do you realize that? And you think I'm crazy for being exact about the time? Well, Alix, what's crazy is memorizing the goddamn newspaper every morning. Normal people don't spend half the morning memorizing what some freak in Florida said."

"She wasn't a freak, Robert. You missed the whole point."

A couple who had just sat down at the next table were trying not to look at Alix. They were in their early twenties and had the brand-new look of people who are about to take a trip. The woman had a sweet face and enormous breasts. Alix could tell that Robert was torn between staring at the breasts and leaving immediately because she was making a scene.

I'm a sensitive woman, thought Alix. An educated woman.

Going down on the escalator a few minutes later, she asked, "Did anyone ever call you Bobby?"

"What?" He was standing on the step below her.

"Nothing. It's not important." She had always meant to ask his mother what they had called him as a baby. Could you call a baby Robert? But then she couldn't imagine Robert as a baby.

She remembered struggling up and down this same escalator in the American Airlines terminal when the children were toddlers and how difficult it was to get them on and off it. She and the children were always meeting someone at the airport in those days. Robert home from location, Robert home from New York, grandparents visiting from Phoenix, her sister Lucy arriving after a fight with Brian, Lucy separated from Brian, Lucy recovering from her divorce from Brian. And now Lucy was married to Peter, and she had stopped making her hysterical flights to Los Angeles. There's always a woman on coast-to-coast flights, thought Alix, who wears very dark glasses, drinks too much, carries a hard-cover best seller and /or a fashion magazine, and a large, expensive handbag into which she has stuffed one nightgown, underwear, a toothbrush, cosmetics, and all her husband's credit cards. That was Lucy. The Lucys were always in perpetual flight, like birds whose migratory patterns had somehow been knocked out of kilter by the confusion of the modern world.

Maybe she'd call Lucy tonight and invite her out for a visit.

They stood on the moving sidewalk which took them to the front of the terminal, accompanied by voices over the loudspeakers, first in English and then in Spanish, instructing them to stay to the right so that those who wished could pass on the left. Robert stayed to the right and walked. She followed, the moving surface bumpy and unsteady under her feet. The sidewalk reminded her of a conveyor belt, as if they were to be sorted and packaged at the other end.

She thought of telling Robert about Lucy and Brian and Lucy and Peter, and the problems of getting the children on and off the escalator, but she didn't. Robert was a juggler; always in action, always keeping the various parts of his life in balance and at the proper distance. The past was neatly catalogued in his mind, and it only confused and upset him when she brought up memories that he had not already dealt with and catalogued. Maybe that was why he was a writer; he needed to have everything organized and tidy and in the right place. Like his green socks. Sometimes she thought that maybe they would still be married if it hadn't been for his green socks.

In front of the terminal, Robert said, "Where's the car?"

She noticed he said "the" car, not "your" car. He seemed to have adjusted more easily to divorce than to the loss of his Mercedes.

She pointed to a parking lot. "Row D. Fourth from pole. Left side." Once she had lost the car at the airport and it had taken her three hours to find it.

"You're improving," said Robert.

"I try, Robert. I do my best." She was no longer losing cars, this was a fact, but was she *improving*? And if so, what exactly did this mean? Another fact: She had been doing very well in ballet class until she'd become pregnant with Cindy.

"It wasn't because I was too tall; I was too pregnant," she said, and waited for the moment this took to make sense in Robert's mind. She understood the delay. She, too, was having problems with connections.

"Oh," said Robert.

"You missed the whole point about the woman in Florida."

"How's the car running?" he asked.

"I had the oil changed last week."

"Very good."

"I try, Robert, I really do."

"Well." He put his hands in his pockets. "If you need anything . . ."

She wondered what color socks he was wearing.

She sat behind the wheel of the burgundy Mercedes and cried until a car waiting for her parking space began to honk.

"Oh, hell," she said, and opened her purse for parking money. The money spilled out of her wallet, down between her legs and onto the floor. With one hand she turned on the ignition and with the other she groped for a dollar bill between her legs. The car behind her, driven by a woman wearing rhinestone-trimmed sunglasses, honked again. A small poodle on the seat next to the woman began to bark.

Alix thought of a comedy routine she had heard years ago—Bob Newhart? Shelley Berman?—about dropping a lighted cigarette between his legs while driving and then having a bus pull up next to him, full of people peering down at him while he frantically groped for the cigarette.

She leaned out the window, held up the middle finger of her left hand, waved it at the angry woman and her poodle, then backed out of the parking space.

I'm a sensitive woman, she said to herself.

2

THE WINDOWS WERE ROLLED UP, tightly shut, and the music so loud that if a fire truck or ambulance came up behind her she would never hear the siren. She had recently read an article that said people who drove with their windows up and the air conditioning on and the radio turned full volume were becoming a serious problem for emergency vehicles. She thought of all the millions of drivers in Los Angeles, sealed off in their cars, and knew that the article had somehow missed the point. The danger went much deeper than not hearing sirens.

" 'What the worllld neeeds now . . .' "* She sang along with the radio. Muzak. She loved it. Bland, beautiful, romantic movie music. Robert called it the junk food of the music world. Robert's favorite music was the Brandenburg Concertos. Precise, cool, mathematical Bach.

" '. . . love, sweet love . . .' " She imagined Robert saying "tacky." "That's really tacky, Alix." Or odious; that was another of his favorite words. One of the positive points about being divorced was that she would never have to hear Robert say, "That's really tacky, Alix," ever again.

At a red light in Manhattan Beach, a surfer with a blond beard, and his surfboard tied to the top of his Porsche, grinned at her. She smiled back. Maybe she would try a younger man next. Or a much older man. But not a man approaching forty; never again. Robert had turned forty in November and it was all he had thought about the year previous. "I'll be forty soon, Alix." "So will I, Robert." "Not for four more years. And women live longer than men." Robert had begun to think that death was a viable, so to speak, possibility shortly after his thirty-ninth birthday.

She drove south on the Pacific Coast Highway and thought about his question: "Have you made any plans?" Robert always made exact, logical, realistic plans. Precise plans. Her plans were amorphous; cloudlike structures filled with ifs and maybes, contingent on other people, the weather, moods. She tried to think of a plan for her evening; a simple, realistic plan. She would take a hot bath. A hot bath. She was a thirty-six-year-old woman who couldn't think of anything else to do but take hot baths and go shopping.

Maybe I'll stop at the drugstore on the way home and buy bath salts or something. She realized she had said this aloud, and though she was alone with the windows rolled up, she was embarrassed.

She'd call Lucy when she got home and ask her to come out for a visit.

She'd call her mother and drive up to Brentwood soon to spend the night with her.

She'd take dancing lessons again.

She'd take charge of her life.

She wondered if Robert had ever found his green socks, and started to cry again.

In Hermosa Beach she blew her nose at a red light and tried to think calmly about Robert's green socks; perhaps there was a clue, something she had missed that would explain why everything fell apart. Why Alix Stoughton, dutiful daughter, devoted sister, who always followed directions and did what was expected of her, was now Alix Kirkwood, who wore fifty-two-dollar jeans and was divorced and drove around in a burgundy Mercedes, crying all the time and unable to find directions, let alone follow them.

Robert had lost his green socks on a Monday morning shortly after the Christmas holidays. The children had already left for school and Robert had a ten o'clock story conference at the studio. She could hear him yelling up in the bedroom, and then the angry *thud, thud* of his feet coming down the stairs.

"What's wrong?" she asked when he came into the kitchen. She was frying bacon for breakfast.

"I'll tell you what's wrong," said Robert. "I can't find my goddamn green socks. Where did you put them?"

"I don't know. The maid must have put them someplace," she said. "Are they in your top drawer?"

"If they were in my top drawer would I be asking you where they are?"

She placed the bacon on two layers of paper towels and then covered it with a third, thinking that if Robert did drop dead at forty she would never have to fry bacon again. "Maybe you didn't look hard enough," she said.

"Didn't look hard enough?" Robert repeated. "I emptied the goddamn drawer. I just looked through fourteen fucking pairs of socks."

She poured the bacon grease into an empty Hunt's tomato sauce can and placed a cube of margarine in the frying pan, then took a carton of eggs from the refrigerator. "Maybe they're in the laundry room."

In the laundry room Robert dumped a basket of clean, folded clothes on top of the drier. "If you could get yourself organized we wouldn't have this problem," he said.

"We?" said Alix softly, and then in a loud voice "You're having this problem about your goddamn socks, Robert. I'm not having a sock problem. *You* are having the sock problem." She cracked the eggs into a bowl and beat them until they were foamy and pale. "Look, Robert. Can't you wear beige socks?"

"No."

"How about gray?"

He stood in the doorway between the kitchen and laundry room and said slowly, "If I could wear another color I wouldn't be looking for my green socks, would I?"

"I don't know. Maybe."

"What do you mean by that?"

"Nothing." The margarine was sizzling and beginning to turn brown. She lowered the gas and poured the beaten eggs into the pan.

"You have a maid. Can't you at least keep track of the socks, for God's sake?"

She put four pieces of bread into the toaster and stirred the eggs.

"Do you think I enjoy living like this?" said Robert.

"Living like this?" she repeated. "Living like this?" She kept stirring the eggs. "What do you mean, 'like this'? What is 'like this'? And what's wrong with living *like this*? I never know what the hell you're talking about."

Robert just stood there in his bare feet, bobbing up and down slightly like a prize fighter about to go into the ring. He was wearing gray slacks, a cashmere turtleneck sweater and a sports jacket. He smelled of English Leather.

The toast popped up, startling both of them, and she buttered it and divided the eggs on two plates. "Breakfast is ready," she said.

"I can't eat until I find my socks," said Robert.

She placed two strips of bacon on each plate. "Breakfast is ready," she said again.

"I really don't ask for much, Alix. What the hell do you do all day?"

She stared at the plates; the bacon had a thin, opaque glaze and the eggs were beginning to harden and looked rubbery. "What do I do all day? Is that what you're asking me, Robert? I'll tell you what I do all day. I get *through* the day. And you know what, Robert? Sometimes that's a big deal—just to get through the goddamn day."

"You're crazy, you know that? You're really crazy. You can't even keep track of the goddamn socks. You can't even train the maid to keep track of my socks. What the hell do you do all day? What do you *want?* I really don't know what your problem is, Alix. Maybe if you *did* something—took up painting or went back to school or got a job. I mean, what do you do all day?"

It was at that point she threw the plates at him.

Clues? None. Just the tip of his discontent. A variation of all the scenes and silences they had gone through during all the years of their marriage. It had nothing to do with his green socks. He had stopped loving her. It was as simple and complicated as that.

Robert had moved out that day and she had gone to I. Magnin's and bought four new nightgowns, two beige bras and an Hermès scarf. The following day she had her hair frosted. The first week Robert was gone she had taken twenty-two hot baths.

She thought of having an affair. She thought of never having an affair. If she didn't have an affair she'd probably go out of her mind one of these days. An affair. That was the word her mother always used when discussing social functions. (A charming affair, divine food, everyone was there.) She didn't want to have an affair. She wanted to get laid.

She'd take dancing lessons.

She'd call Lucy.

She'd take control of her life.

She thought of the old lady collecting beer cans in Florida and started to cry again.

In Redondo Beach she turned off the Pacific Coast Highway and onto the road that continued along the ocean. As she drove out on the peninsula that lay south of Los Angeles and just north of San Pedro, the flat slope of beach turned into cliffs. On clear days the cliffs, two hundred feet high, rose out of the surf surprisingly rugged and beautiful in the easy, rolling, smog-softened landscape of Southern California. This evening the fog billowed in from the ocean like huge damp sheets as she drove farther out. She turned on the headlights and drove more slowly, concentrating on the double line of yellow bumps in the middle of the winding road.

One of the first things she would do when the house sold would be to move out of the damn boonies. Somewhere without fog; someplace where June did indeed bust out all over with sun and heat and flowers, instead of slithering in with fog and mildew. Someplace without Robert.

You could go crazy here in June; she was convinced of this. She had read once about the long, dark winters in Scandinavia, sunless months when the suicide rate soared, and she wondered if anyone had ever studied the suicide rate along the coast in California during the month of June. The hot, dry Santa Ana winds got all the publicity, but someone ought to check out the June fog, because if one really wanted to know what made the people in Los Angeles crazier than the rest of the country, that was the answer. One month of fog.

Stopping at the drugstore for bath salts was a mistake; she realized this immediately. There were twenty-seven different products to put into a bath, and each product came in a variety of scents and sizes. What did she want? That was another of Robert's questions. Sometimes he asked it in a slightly high-pitched monotone in which he ran all the words together, and sometimes in a basso profundo in which he emphasized the word "do" or the word "want." What did she want? She didn't know. Did she want the little eight-dollar bottle of dark-green oil, or the box of brightly colored capsules full of different-scented oils which cost two dollars and would leave a blob of goo in the tub after her bath, or did she want lavender bubbles for a dollar fifty? All she knew was that her decision would be meaningless. If she paid eight dollars for green oil or two fifty for colored capsules, it would make absolutely no difference to anyone. Especially herself. It was the same when she went to the market or turned on the television set or picked out books at the library. What difference did her choices make, and were they choices or simply illusions of choices? She felt faint whenever she started thinking like this and she clasped her hands together to keep them from shaking. The last thing in the world she wanted to do was collapse in the bath item department at the Village Pharmacy. How long had she been standing there staring at the shelves? A minute? Fifteen minutes? Time kept getting away from her lately. Instead of going from second to second and minute to minute, a few seconds could turn into an hour, or what seemed like an hour could be a few seconds. Time was turning slippery.

Someone touched her arm and she jumped. Her next-door neighbor, Milly Drew, stood behind her, smiling and holding a bag of groceries, wearing her blue track suit and Adidas. "I've been trying to get you on the phone all afternoon," said Milly.

"I was at the airport," said Alix. She always felt oddly guilty around Milly, as if she wasn't trying hard enough. But trying hard enough for *what*, she could never figure out. Milly worked part time at a travel agency, had three children and a husband, and every night at five o'clock she jogged two miles along the cliffs. Alix had always wanted to ask Milly if she was happy, but she had never gotten up the nerve.

"What were you doing at the airport?" Milly asked. She had the ability of making personal questions flattering. Rather than sounding as if she were prying, Milly's questions appeared to be the result of an overwhelming interest in whomever she was talking to.

"We were seeing the children off."

"Oh."

"Yes."

"Where are they going?"

"To Phoenix," said Alix.

"Phoenix? Why on earth are they going to Phoenix?"

A woman with a sharp wedgelike hairdo, skinny arms and perfect faded jeans was leafing through magazines and eavesdropping on their conversation.

"They're visiting Robert's parents for a month," whispered Alix.

"Oh," said Milly, the word starting up the scale, then plunging downward.

"It's no big deal," said Alix. "They're visiting their grandparents, that's all."

The woman at the magazine rack sighed and drifted to the cosmetics counter.

Milly patted Alix's shoulder. "It's good they're seeing Robert's parents. It'll make them feel more secure. The extended family and all that. I really think it's a super idea that they're spending a month in Phoenix." She shifted the bag of groceries to her other arm. "I was calling you this afternoon to invite you to dinner Sunday night. Very informal. BK and Sidney are coming, Paul and Greta, and the new couple down the street, the young ones with that enormous black dog that looks like a bear?"

Alix nodded.

"And, Alix, guess what."

"What?"

"I have a man for you!"

Alix had a sudden vision of Milly hiding behind her myoporum bushes with a large net, capturing unsuspecting men for her.

"He's divorced," Milly went on, "is living in an apartment at the Marina, and just called out of the blue the other night. Jim went to college with him and said . . ."

Alix watched Milly's mouth move up and down and realized that Milly was not talking to her but at her. But was this Milly's fault or her own? She wondered what Milly would say if she broke into this monologue and said, "Excuse me, Milly, but I seem to be falling apart right here in the middle of the Village Pharmacy and I was wondering if you could pick out something for me to put into my bath because I am incapable of making decisions now that I know the secret." "What secret is that, Alix?" "The secret, dear Milly, is that nothing makes any difference; whatever you

18

decide doesn't mean anything or change anything and once you discover this secret it becomes very, very difficult to make decisions or plans."

"Alix?" Milly looked puzzled. "What do you think?"

"What do I think?" said Alix.

"About the fondue."

"Fondue is super, Milly."

"You don't think three courses of fondue might be too much of a super thing?"

"You can't have too much of a super thing, Milly."

Milly stared at her. "Are you okay?"

"I'm fine," replied Alix. The corners of her mouth felt peculiar, as if she couldn't control the muscles required for a smile, as if her mouth, her whole face, might melt away. "Really, I'm fine. What time on Sunday?"

"Sevenish. Casual."

"See you then, Milly. I'm looking forward to it." Alix picked up the box with the colored capsules of bath oil and took it to the cashier's counter. The woman in the mirror behind the counter didn't look thirty-six. But what did thirty-six look like? Alix stared at herself in the mirror and thought about that while she waited for her change. *She* was what thirty-six looked like. Half her face was hidden behind her dark glasses, and her hair hung to her shoulders. For as long as she could remember her mother had told her that she could be a beauty if only she'd eat more and gain some weight, and do something about her hair.

She was, in fact, a tall, thin woman with a great deal of brown hair, good cheekbones, brown eyes and very small breasts, who wore a size 8B shoe and a size 6 dress, and whose mascara was usually smudged under her eyes because she cried a lot. She had always felt she looked grotesque in a leotard.

The phone was ringing when she got home. For a moment she was tempted not to answer it, but then thought of the children and rushed to pick it up before it stopped ringing.

"Mrs. Kirkwood?"

"Yes."

"This is Betty Lee of Coast Realty and I was hoping I might be able to show your home this evening."

My home is not for sale, thought Alix. As a matter of fact, I'm not sure I have a home. What I have is a very large house with dirty windows.

"That would be fine," Alix said aloud.

"Oh, marvelous. My clients won't be here for another hour or so. Would seven be too late? They've seen the home before, so it won't take long."

The home. As if it were filled with sick people or poor people or orphans. Or crazy people.

"Seven would be fine," said Alix.

"Super. See you then."

Super. Neat. Peachy keen. Alix made a desultory check of the house and hid dirty laundry under the bed; the maid was coming only once a week now and the clothes hampers were stuffed with dirty clothes. She hid a week's worth of old newspapers (lacy and ribbonlike from all the articles she had cut out of them) in the drier. She hated having the house on the market and not being able to hide things in closets or cupboards. Every place was fair game. "Goddamn Lookie-Loos," she said aloud. She had noticed, however, that no one, not even the nosiest Lookie-Loo, ever looked into the drier or under the bed.

She picked up Mark's baseball cap from the dining room table and brought it up to his room, picked up playing cards, a pen, one sock and a roll of Scotch tape from the floor and put it all in the top drawer of his dresser. Being in his room and touching his belongings made her feel like crying again.

She went down to the family room and opened a package of instant daiquiri mix into the blender, added rum, water and an ice cube and turned it on. As the blender crunched and then whirred, she read every word on the package the mix had come in. She was addicted to reading labels and packages and boxes. It was a safe, impersonal way of passing time; it kept her mind busy. Sugar, citric acid, lime juice powder, sodium citrate, dried egg whites, calcium phosphate, lime oil, BHT and /or BHA added as a preservative. She puzzled over the "and/or" for a moment—she had never read a list of ingredients that had equivocated before—then turned off the blender, poured her daiquiri into a glass that was too large, and sat on a stool and stared at her family room. The same family room that was being described in an ad in the Los Angeles *Times* as "Fabulous family room for large, active family!" What a misnomer, Alix thought. There was no family. She missed the children. Why had she ever said that Robert's parents could have them for a whole month? And it was longer than a month. It would be five weeks minus one day.

She felt sad and abandoned and decided to call Lucy in New York.

On the sixth ring the phone was picked up. "Mmm?" said a voice.

"Lucy?"

"Uh huh."

"You sound funny."

"Who is this?" said Lucy.

"Your sister."

"Oh. Hello, Alix."

"Such warmth, Lucy. My God."

"Well . . ."

"I have the feeling that I called at a bad time."

"No, Alix, not at all. Really."

Alix knew it was a bad time because Lucy always sounded like their mother when she was in a difficult situation and pretending not to be.

"I'm sorry, Lucy; I forgot about the time change. You're in bed, aren't you?" And the minute Alix said that, she realized just exactly what the difficult situation was. "Oh, God, Lucy, I am sorry. And tell Brian I'm sorry."

"Peter," Lucy hissed across three thousand miles.

"Peter. That's right. Oh, I am sorry, Lucy. What awful timing, but of course I had no way of knowing—"

"Alix, you sound drunk. Are you all right?"

"I saw Robert this afternoon at the airport. The children left for Phoenix."

"That's nice," said Lucy, sounding distracted.

"Lucy, remember what Daddy always told us—that if we were consistent and made the right decisions and saved ourselves for the man we married, we'd live full and useful lives?"

"Alix, I don't remember him saying that. Except for the part about us being virgins when we got married. Poor Daddy never counted on us getting married and then married again."

"Well, he did tell us we'd live full and useful lives. I remember that very distinctly."

"Every time you're with Robert you drink too much," said Lucy.

"Today was the first time I saw Robert in two months."

"You sound funny. Why don't you call Mother? She can help you through this better than I can. I mean, she's right there in Los Angeles, not more than an hour away. I don't understand why you don't call her."

"Fifty-two minutes."

"What?"

"Mother's house is fifty-two minutes away from this house when traffic is moderate," said Alix. "Robert timed it."

"Well, give her a call, Alix. You shouldn't be alone when you're feeling down. And take care of yourself."

"Say hello to Peter for me." After she hung up, Alix realized she hadn't asked Lucy to come for a visit.

She went downstairs and fixed herself another daiquiri and thought of Lucy's gold bracelets and the fine gold chain Lucy always wore around her neck. She thought of the way Lucy always smelled of Calèche; even the summer she had visited Lucy and Brian in the Hamptons and they didn't have a maid, Lucy scrubbed the bathrooms of the beach house smelling of Calèche and wearing her gold bracelets and the gold chain around her neck. Lucy in a million years would never stuff dirty laundry under the bed or hide old newspapers in the drier. She thought of Lucy going to her office every day, even during the bad days after she divorced Brian, writing her ads, making money, being in charge of something. Keeping busy. She thought about Lucy lying on her Bill Blass sheets from Bloomingdale's in her apartment on East Seventy-third Street, and telling Peter about her younger sister in California who was going through a traumatic divorce from a television writer.

Lucy changed husbands but never apartments. It's a lot easier to find a husband than a decent apartment in New York, she had said on her last trip to the Coast.

Alix finished her drink quickly; then put *Giselle* on the stereo. She turned the volume very loud and rolled her jeans up to her knees. She kicked off her shoes and began to dance.

3

"AND YOU KNOW, of course, that the view is spectacular." Betty Lee opened the draperies in the living room and the fog, like a gray wall, appeared. "When it's clear you can see Malibu, city lights and just a peek of Catalina." She spoke loudly so she could be heard over *Giselle*.

Larry and Eve Cardiff stared out into the fog.

Alix, panting slightly and flushed from dancing, apologized for the volume and turned off the stereo.

The Cardiffs looked like brother and sister. They had dark curly hair, wore tinted glasses with metal frames, and clothes that were just a shade too fashionable to be elegant. Eve Cardiff looked bored. Larry Cardiff looked impatient. Alix tried to imagine them making love and couldn't.

Larry Cardiff turned and looked at Alix, staring at her rolled-up jeans and bare feet. After a moment he said, "What are the taxes?"

"Taxes?" said Alix.

"Taxes on the property."

"I have no idea."

"The taxes are . . . just one second." Betty Lee thumbed quickly though the multiple listing book, found the page with the listing and handed him the book. "Forty-one hundred," she said, and then to Alix, "Are you moving out of the area?"

"I'm not sure," said Alix, wondering what the perimeters of the area were exactly. "I'm not sure what my plans are."

"How many square feet?" asked Eve Cardiff.

"Three thousand eight hundred," said Betty Lee, "and did you notice the tile in the entrance hall?" She walked out into the hallway and tapped a small foot on the terra-cotta tiles. "Absolutely no upkeep at all. And, Eve, isn't this wallpaper divine?" The two women walked across the hallway to the dining room, Betty Lee's little breathless phrases floating out behind them like exclamations from a real estate ad.

Larry Cardiff examined the fireplace. He was the president of a small family-owned business and had political ambitions. He was a gynecologist popular for his understanding of depression and liberal prescriptions for diet pills. He was a stockbroker getting rich from a clientele of Beverly Hills divorcées and Pasadena widows.

For a moment Alix considered asking him what he did, but then decided she didn't care enough to make the effort.

"There is a pool, isn't there?" he asked.

"Yes," said Alix, bending down to unroll her jeans.

"Jacuzzi?"

"Yes."

"And loads of closet space," said Betty Lee, returning with Eve Cardiff trailing behind her. "The storage closet in the hallway is so enormous it could be made into a sewing room."

"I don't sew," said Eve Cardiff.

"Well, there are endless possibilities for it. Now, as you may recall, the house is built on three levels. We'll go downstairs first and then I'll show you the kitchen and pool area." They went off like tourists.

Alix closed the draperies and thought of the first time she and

3

Robert had seen the house. It was a hot, sunny August morning, and the house was not quite completed. Their footsteps echoed on the uncovered floorboards and there was a film of sawdust covering everything.

"It looks like a motel," Robert had said.

"It has a view," she said. "You're always talking about wanting a view."

"And space," said Robert. "God knows it has enough space."

"Yes."

"Do you like it?"

It had been clear that day; they could see the coastline curving northward thirty miles to Malibu. The ocean was even bluer than the sky; she had never seen a shade of blue like that before. "I love the view," she said.

"What about the house?"

"It's not bad." And because they had been house hunting for months, and the apartment in town was cramped and hot, and Mark had colic and cried so much that the neighbors were complaining, and Cindy needed a yard to play in, and Robert had just sold a film script, she said, "I don't care. Buy it if you like it." And the next day they bought it. But it had always remained a house in which they didn't have their hearts.

The phone rang and Alix answered it in the kitchen. "Your sister tells me you're having a problem." It was her mother, who believed that the telephone was an instrument for transmitting messages and not small talk. "Lucy just called me from New York and said that you sounded very peculiar, couldn't even remember her husband's name, and that you had just seen Robert."

"Hello, Mother."

"Alix, what is going on?"

"Nothing."

"Well, then, why did you call your sister and get her all upset? You know how emotional she is."

To be mean, to get everybody pissed off, thought Alix, staring out the kitchen window at Betty Lee and the Cardiffs, who were trying to see the swimming pool through the fog.

"Lucy is very worried about you, Alix."

"Mother, I didn't call her to get her upset. As a matter of fact, I called her to invite her to come out for a visit, but then I realized I had called at a bad time, which got me so rattled that I forgot why I called her."

"What do you mean, a bad time?" asked her mother.

"They were in *bed.*"

"Of course they were. It's three hours later in New York."

"That's not exactly what I meant, and it was only nine o'clock there when I called."

"Oh." There was a pause. "Did your sister tell you this?"

"I'm a sensitive woman."

"What?"

"Nothing, Mother."

"Lucy's right. You do sound odd. I think you ought to come home for a few days while you adjust to life without the children."

Her mother had considered Alix as "away from home" ever since she'd married Robert, as if "coming home" were a constant possibility. Home was a two-story white house in Brentwood, two blocks from Sunset Boulevard, with avocado trees and fruit trees in the garden and jacaranda trees in front of the house, and the smell of jasmine and honeysuckle by the pool on summer evenings. Alix's bedroom was painted powder pink and a starched organdy skirt was still tacked around the top of her dressing table and her Nancy Drew mysteries were in the bookcase along with her high school yearbooks; her strapless net ballerina-length prom dresses still hung in the closet because her mother was convinced they would someday come back in style.

"Did Robert say anything to upset you?" her mother asked.

"No."

Her mother sighed.

Alix always felt guilty when her mother sighed like that. The reasons for the guilt were so complex that she had never explored her own feelings. There was too great a risk involved, even though she never discovered just what the risk entailed.

"Robert has changed so," her mother was saying.

27

Alix closed her eyes and saw her mother young, her mother in her mid thirties. She remembered a February morning, during a Santa Ana, the temperature up in the eighties and the air so dry you had to lick your finger and touch a doorknob fast before actually taking hold of it so that you wouldn't get a shock of static electricity. She was in first grade and her mother had arrived at school, very serious, very dignified and solemn, and had taken her and Lucy out of their classes, telling the teachers there was a family emergency. In the car her mother had said, "Hooky! Girls, we're going to play hooky today," and they found their bathing suits in the car and a picnic lunch packed, and they spent the entire wonderful sunny day at the beach in Santa Monica, swimming in the icy ocean, eating, collecting sand dollars and laughing.

Over the years it seemed that her mother had filled up with serious things—grown-up worries and pain and being angry—and bit by bit all the enthusiasm and excitement got pushed out. And what was she herself filled with? What filled her inner space? As her mother went through the familiar litany of why she shouldn't have married Robert, Alix stood in her kitchen with her eyes shut, trying to envision her inner space.

"The ovens are self-cleaning, aren't they?" Betty Lee's voice was suddenly next to her.

Alix opened her eyes. "Yes, they are."

"And the floor is no-wax?"

"Yes; all it requires is damp mopping," said Alix.

"What on earth are you talking about?" came her mother's voice over the telephone wire.

"Some people are looking at the house, Mother."

"Such a charming kitchen," said Betty Lee to the Cardiffs, and then whispered to Alix, "May we look upstairs now?"

Alix covered the mouthpiece of the phone. "Of course."

Eve Cardiff took one last look around the kitchen. "I hate to cook," she said.

"What I don't understand," her mother was saying, "is why Judson and Virginia get the children for half the summer. Really,

28

Alix. Half the summer. It hardly seems fair—or right."

"Judson and Virginia are the children's grandparents, no matter what you may think of their son. Please, Mother, don't put me on the defensive about this. I'm just trying to do the right thing. They'll have a wonderful time in Phoenix."

"Really?"

"Yes."

"I hope so."

Alix realized that most conversations with her mother were actually in code. They used ordinary words, but the way they said the words—inflections, spacing, duration of certain sounds—all this was a language of their own, a secret language just between her and her mother.

"The extended family is important for children," she said.

"What does that have to do with anything?"

Alix didn't answer and the line between her house and her mother's was silent for a moment. Alix thought about her inner space again and how quiet it was—as silent as the connection between her and her mother.

"Well, I didn't call you up to bicker, Alix. Promise you'll come up to see me soon."

"Soon, Mother, I promise." When Alix hung up she fixed herself another drink and then took the phone off the hook.

"They are *very* interested," said Betty Lee, coming into the kitchen alone. "I have a hunch they may make a bid tonight. How do you feel about a short escrow?" She was wearing a pale-green pants suit and one pearl earring. Alix wondered where she had lost the other earring and if she realized it was missing.

"I don't know about escrow," said Alix, reaching up to check the gold hoops in her ears. "I'll have to ask—I'll have to think about it."

"I'll be in touch," said Betty Lee, and then, pausing at the front door, "Oh, are you leaving the pool equipment?"

"Yes."

"And they were wondering about the large potted plants around the pool area. Are you planning to leave them?"

"I don't know. I hadn't thought about it."

"I'll be in touch," and she hurried down the steps to join the Cardiffs, who were waiting in the car.

While the bathtub was filling, Alix plucked her eyebrows, trimmed her toenails and set her razor by the side of the tub next to her drink.

If you look good, you feel good. How many times had her mother told her and Lucy that? If she had started when Alix was five and said it at least once a week, that would be over fifteen hundred times. And there had been periods in her life when her mother had said to her every day, "If you look good, you feel good," so it was perfectly possible she had heard her mother say that ten thousand times.

Lucy had taken this maxim of their mother's very seriously. Lucy always looked good. Alix remembered the last time Lucy had come to Los Angeles—her Laszlo complexion and her Kenneth hair and her Halston-Gucci outfit—and after the fourth martini Lucy had started to cry and said, "You know, you can look good and still feel like shit."

That had a profound effect on Alix at the time.

And now Lucy was lying in her Bloomingdale's bedroom making love to her latest husband, having told Alix that she sounded as if she had had too much to drink and to please call Mother for any help needed.

Alix sat in the tub, watching a green capsule of bath oil slowly deflate and disperse a tiny trail of oil into the water. She turned the hot-water faucet on and off with her foot and sipped her drink. She realized two things: she had indeed had too much to drink, and life at some point had to get better; it was simply a question of hanging in there until it did.

She wondered where Betty Lee's other earring was and if she had discovered yet that it was missing. She wondered how she would manage without her children. She decided to call BK Morrison in the morning and ask her if she wanted to go to the sale at Bullock's.

4

BK HELD IN HER STOMACH and looked at herself in the dressing room mirror. "What do you think?"

"It's fine," said Alix.

"Fine?" BK wrinkled her nose. "What do you mean, fine? I want something sensational. Something that'll knock Sidney's eyes out." BK studied the dress, which was black and cut on the bias. "Oh, I don't know." She turned her back for Alix to unzip her and then reached for another. "I'm doing sit-ups now. Twenty-two bloody sit-ups every night. You want to know something interesting about sit-ups?"

"What?"

"We were taught to do sit-ups the wrong way. All those hours in gym class were wasted."

Alix sat on a spindly gilt chair with her packages in her arms and watched BK try on another dress.

"You see, if you hook your feet under something," BK said, "or have someone sit on them, and keep your knees bent—that's the secret, bent knees—you're using your stomach muscles. With

31

your legs straight, you're just exercising your back and all the parts of you that weren't even fat to begin with."

"I see."

BK fluffed out her short blond hair with her fingers and considered the dress she had just put on, a soft paisley print. "The problem—the bottom line, as Sidney always says—is my thighs. I keep telling myself priorities, think of the priorities in life, but the fact remains that if one third of my thighs would disappear I would be a very happy woman. The French ivy leaf extract didn't work, so now I go into town once a week for algae cream and thermal sheet treatments. I wonder what age you just say the hell with it all."

"Probably never," said Alix.

"You're so skinny you don't even have thighs. I should be so lucky to have your problems."

"BK, you're not fat."

"Well, there's fat and there's fat. The thing is I feel fat." BK arched her neck and squinted at her reflection. "What do you think of this one? The Allens are having a dinner party tomorrow night and I also need something for Milly's fondue fiesta. Are you ready for that? Three courses of fondue. We'll be so busy. We'll spend the whole evening hanging on to those damn forks."

"Don't be bitchy."

"Speaking of being bitchy, guess what about the Allens?"

"What?"

"She is now making more money than he is. Or so I hear. And you know what a leaky ego he has."

"I didn't know."

BK unbuttoned the paisley dress. "But the marvelous part is he is having a thing with *her* secretary."

"Oh."

"You don't find that slightly interesting?"

"Male or female secretary?"

"Female."

"Oh."

"Alix, you're becoming jaded in your middle age. Doesn't anything shock you anymore?" Their eyes met in the mirror for a moment.

"Not much, BK. Not much," said Alix softly.

"Well, see if I share any more goodies with you." BK stepped out of the dress and looked at herself in her silk underwear. "Do you think they are too fat?"

"Who?"

"My *thighs,*" said BK. "Sidney said I've got to get my thighs in shape."

"Sidney said that?"

"Yes."

"I wouldn't worry about it, BK."

BK sighed and began to put on her own clothes. "Maybe I'll just wear something out of my closet. I always think that I'll discover the one dress that will make Sidney find me so irresistible that he'll become romantic and dashing again."

Alix tried to imagine Sidney Morrison romantic and dashing. He and BK had been married for six years. Could Sidney have possibly been romantic and dashing six short years ago? Sidney with his ex-wife and teen-age daughters and alimony payments and his bad back and passion for growing tomatoes?

"The thing is he never even notices," BK was saying.

"Notices?"

"What I'm wearing. He never notices, or if he does, he doesn't say anything. So what the hell. I'll wear something old. Do you have any more shopping you want to do?" BK grimaced at the mirror and examined her front teeth.

"No," said Alix.

"I have to see the dentist tomorrow and I haven't flossed my teeth in weeks." She tied a scarf around her neck and then fastened it to her shirt with an enameled pin. "How did it go yesterday when you saw the kids off?"

"Fine."

"Was it hard?"

"Of course it was hard saying goodbye."

"I don't mean that. I mean, was it hard seeing Robert?"

Alix hesitated and then said, "Not particularly."

"Did he say anything about that actress?"

"What actress?"

"That new one on his series. Joyce somebody with the big tits. Sidney met her at Robert's apartment when he dropped off some papers for Robert to sign."

"No, he didn't mention her."

"You want to have lunch out or at my house?"

"It doesn't matter."

"Alix, don't be so easygoing. It isn't healthy. Where do you want to have lunch?"

"Really, it doesn't matter, BK."

Her father had collected stamps. That was one of her two most vivid memories of her father. The second one she didn't want to think about; that was later, when he had cancer and was dying in the hospital.

When she was young she would sit in the chair with the chintz slipcover next to his desk in the den and watch him as he worked on his stamps. He would soak the canceled stamps in water and meticulously remove old stamp hinges or pieces of envelope with tweezers, then he would look up the stamp in his Scott's catalogue, attach a stamp hinge to it, or if it was mint, place it in a glassine stamp mount, and then enter the stamp in one of the huge albums above his desk. By each stamp entered he would carefully note the catalogue number and, if it was worth more than a dollar, the value of the stamp. There was a sense of order and peace in her father's study when he worked on the stamps. She had the feeling that nothing very awful or unexpected could happen in a world in which her father took such care and interest in something as small and fragile as a stamp.

Her father had been a lawyer and he understood people and all the intricate and strange ways they lied and were truthful. He also knew how things worked, whether it was a machine or a purring cat or cream turning to cheese. Alix wondered at what point she stopped caring and being curious about how things worked. At what point did all her energy get used up in simply getting through her days and listening to her own noise? On her eighth birthday her father had given her a magnifying glass and they had spent the entire day examining the garden. He taught her to see it for the first time. Not just look at it, but see it.

And at some point she had stopped seeing things. Now she simply looked.

She drove through the afternoon, driving simply for something to do, and thought how sad it was that she no longer cared how things worked, and how long ago it had been since she did care.

She remembered an evening when she was a sophomore in high school, standing in her father's study, feeling awkward and inarticulate, trying to explain to him how much ballet meant to her and why she wanted to go to New York to study after high school. He had said it was out of the question, she had to have a college education. But it was never explained to her why a college education was important. She still wondered about this.

To please her father, more than anything else, she enrolled in UCLA as a liberal arts major and lived at home because UCLA was only four miles from the house in Brentwood. She worked hard, got good grades, and went to a dance class three times a week. But other than pleasing her father, she didn't know why she was there. It was just something that had happened. She didn't say no, so she went to UCLA instead of New York to become a dancer, and when she met Robert she didn't say no, so she had babies and a house that looked like a motel.

She drove through the afternoon and wondered if she would ever say no. And if she did, what would happen to her life.

There was a note from Betty Lee Scotch-taped to the front door. "Please call! Trying to reach you about offer on house. Your phone is off the hook."

Alix rolled up the note and tossed it behind a camellia bush. The fog had cleared but the sky was heavy and gray with low clouds. Wishing it would either rain or clear up, she knew it would probably do neither.

The gardener was spraying the roses by the side of the house. He saw her and waved, a clenched-fist sort of salute which she never understood but thought must have something to do with his ponytail and the way he dressed. Today he was wearing army fatigues with ironed-on patches featuring Andy Warhol soup cans. "Hi, Alix," he called.

Alix was not clear why or how the gardener came to call her by her first name; she certainly had not initiated the practice, but she felt that in some indirect way she was at fault. And the fact that she felt at fault for another human being's calling her by her first name made her feel guilty.

His name was Sam; she had never learned his last name. He worked for a local nursery and every month the nursery billed her for his services. He was thirty-two years old and had once told her that he wrote poetry. She had not pursued the subject.

She waved back to him—"Hello, Sam"—and hurried into the house. If she could only turn off her feelings, or at least turn down the noise they made.

Alix stood in her front hallway and concentrated on the sounds that were coming from outdoors—an occasional car, the hum of a helicopter flying close to the cliffs, the surf, birds—and thought you could go mad in an empty house in the suburbs on an overcast afternoon. She imagined all the millions of women alone in their houses, listening to their clocks tick and refrigerators hum, wondering what was happening out there in the real world. But where exactly was the real world?

Without bothering to remove her jacket, she took a small canvas bag from the shelf over her closet and set it on her bed. The bag had a zippered outside case for a tennis racket, and her initials, six inches high, covered the other side of the bag. She hadn't played tennis for two years.

She tossed underwear, a nightgown, toothbrush and cosmetics into the bag, snapped it shut, went downstairs into the kitchen, replaced the telephone receiver on the hook, and went outside and into her car again.

When the car had been in the shop last, she had tried taking a bus shopping, but it was like being without her purse, or shoes, or clothes even. She felt naked without her car, vulnerable. She never took walks anymore; she was never outdoors, in fact, unless she was in a car.

She headed for the San Diego Freeway, humming along with the Muzak.

5

"I ALWAYS THOUGHT they mixed up babies at the hospital," said her mother.

Alix stared at her mother's throat and wondered if a camera—the kind of camera that focuses for days on a flower bud and then shows the flower bursting into bloom in ten seconds—could do the same with aging flesh. Reverse bloom.

"You didn't look like your father, you didn't look like me, and you didn't at all resemble your sister when she was a baby." Her mother snapped the pillow into the pillowcase and then smoothed the pink bedspread over the pillow. "There! I do wish you had called first so I could have canceled my plans for tonight."

"I'll be fine. Really."

"You don't look fine. You look worn out. Are you eating properly?"

"Yes," said Alix.

"You are what you eat. You know that, don't you?"

"Yes, Mother."

"Are you eating a decent breakfast? You can't run an engine without fuel and you are just as skinny as a rail."

Alix wondered if there was an exact point—a day, an hour, a word—when one's body began the decline. When one stopped growing, blooming, even maintaining the status quo; when one's body began to fall apart. Did it all begin to go at once, or did different parts go at different times? At what moment, what word, did her mother's neck become etched with lines and then gradually, gently, loosen into soft folds?

"I don't remember what I had for breakfast," said Alix. It was either a Twinkie or leftover pizza. She couldn't remember and it didn't matter because her body was gently, quietly, beginning to fall apart and nothing she could eat for breakfast or any other meal could stop the process.

In the bathroom her mother set out fresh towels and unwrapped a new bar of soap. "Promise me one thing tonight, Alix."

"What's that?"

"You won't watch that silly show of Robert's. It's on at eight. It'll just depress you."

"I know when it's on, Mother, and that silly show, as you call it, keeps a roof over my head."

"Nonsense. You and the children could always come home."

Alix sat on the stool to her dressing table and ran her fingers over the organdy skirt, which her mother had the maid wash and starch regularly. "Or I could get a job," she said.

Her mother stood in the doorway of the bathroom and looked at her. "What on earth would you do?"

Her mother had gained twenty or thirty pounds since Alix had grown up. The added weight was like a soft suit of armor, as if life hurt less if one was slightly padded.

"I don't know what I'd do," said Alix. "I seem to be rather ill .equipped for life."

"You are not ill equipped for life, Alix. You are wonderfully equipped to be a wife and mother. Unfortunately you married the wrong man."

And you, Mother? thought Alix. Did you marry the right man? What is the *right* man anyway? Something has happened to the center. Mother, everything is falling apart. It's become unstuck, unglued. I'm an adult woman sitting in a pink bedroom with absolutely no purpose in life. I could stay in this bedroom until my children come home next month and no one would notice or care. It wouldn't change anything. I followed directions. I did what Daddy told me to do, I did what Robert told me to do. And here I am.

"Alix?" said her mother. "Don't sulk. Say something."

"I don't have anything to say," said Alix. "But please stop telling me that Robert was the wrong man. Something went wrong with *us*, the marriage went wrong. I'm tired of being treated like a victim."

"No one is treating you like a victim, and you were a perfect wife. I know what was going on. I'm not deaf and blind, Alix; it was all perfectly obvious."

Alix took a deep breath. "What was obvious?"

"The sort of man Robert was."

"What sort of man was he, Mother?"

Her mother sat down on the foot of the bed. "He fooled around with other women."

"Fooled around? What exactly do you mean by 'fooled around'?"

Her mother twisted her rings and centered her diamond engagement ring. "You know what I mean."

"Do you mean he fucked other women, Mother? Is that what you're saying? He fucked other women. Say what you mean, Mother."

Her mother looked pale. "Don't use that word in my house."

"Then for Christ's sweet sake don't tell me what my husband did behind my back."

Silence filled up the room; Alix felt as though she might choke on it. The effort it took to keep her face blank and emotionless kept her from crying.

Her mother was wearing a soft blue cardigan and very slowly

40

and meticulously she began to button it, not looking at Alix, just button by button fastening her sweater. "Well," she said when she had finished, "I don't want to be late for my bridge game and I promised Elsa I'd pick her up at seven. There's some lovely white chicken in the icebox and potato salad. Please fix yourself a proper supper. And there are strawberries for dessert, the giant ones you like so much. You'll find some confectioners' sugar in the cupboard to dip them in and there may even be some sour cream left."

"Thank you, Mother."

"I'll be home about eleven." Her mother kissed her forehead and left.

When she heard the car leave, Alix went downstairs. The house was her mother's house now. Once it had been the family's, her parents' house, but now in some subtle way it had become her mother's house. The furniture was the same furniture she had grown up with and the paintings and etchings on the walls hadn't changed; only little things indicated that her mother had finally gotten her own way, finally won. A slightly different arrangement of chairs, the placement of lamps, even the wattage of light bulbs. Her father had preferred soft lighting and her mother believed "Better light, better sight." The lights were bright in the house now and there were no untidy piles of magazines or mail or papers. Her father had saved everything; her mother believed in perpetual discard. These were the things her parents had disagreed about. Alix had never once heard her parents fight or yell or mention any problem deeper than whether one could read properly with a sixty-watt light bulb.

She fixed herself a double Scotch on the rocks for supper and then watched Robert's television show at eight o'clock. The series was about a family of doctors who lived and worked in a small town in the Midwest, an area that Robert had flown over many times on his way to New York but to Alix's knowledge had never actually visited. The show was a nighttime soap opera of infidelities, abortions, divorce, distant cousins going mad or turning gay, plus a great deal of what Robert described as meaningful dialogue between the generations. Grandpa was a GP who still made house calls, his son Jason specialized in cardiology, had problems relating to his patients and never made house calls, and Jason's daughter Cassie had become a GP like Grandpa, but Grandpa was having problems accepting a woman as an equal in medicine even if it was his beloved little granddaughter Cassie. And so on. Alix was convinced it was the worst series ever to appear on television, and in spite of Robert's euphemisms about meaningful dialogue, she thought he must realize this also.

Alix sipped her Scotch—her father's Black Label—and studied Joyce somebody with the big tits. Joyce somebody, who was playing beloved Cassie's nurse, was about nineteen years old, couldn't act, and resembled a cow. "You dirty old man," Alix said to the screen when the credits were rolled and Robert's name appeared. "You dirty old goat. You can't even write anymore."

Instead of the strawberries, she fixed herself another double Scotch for dessert and went into her father's study. She lay down on the brown plaid sofa and counted the Scott stamp albums that were in the bookcase above the desk and wondered if her father had fooled around with other women behind her mother's back. Fooled around. It sounded like playing doctor or something.

Robert had fooled around with BK once, but neither Robert nor BK knew that she had found out. Robert, who wrote notes about everything, who never let a minute pass without recording its effect on him, had never dreamed that Alix read every word of his notes, would spend whole days sometimes reading everything in his files. Including every word of what it was like to fuck BK Morrison in the guest room on August 14, summer before last, while she was enduring the heat in Phoenix with his children and his parents. From his extensive notes on the incident, Alix had gathered that BK was as innocent as one could possibly be under the circumstances. Robert was lonely, BK dropped off contracts for Robert to sign at Sidney's request, and Robert, charming, direct, authoritative Robert, had insisted that BK try one of his Manhattans. What puzzled Alix most was why Robert, who only drank wine, was fixing such a heavy, sticky drink as a

Manhattan in the middle of August. She sometimes suspected that he lied in his notes about details; part of his need to make order out of chaos, significance out of the mundane. In any event, he had taken BK to bed after she had consumed six Manhattans. Another puzzle for Alix: had Robert also had six Manhattans? And if so, how had he taken anyone to bed? Alix sometimes wondered at herself for catching on to such odd details and dwelling on them.

When she had read Robert's notes, months later, she had the entire house repainted, gave the guest room bed to Goodwill, bought a replacement the same day, and then burned the green striped sheets that were always on the guest bed.

She counted the Scott albums on the shelf above her father's desk. There were twenty-two. Eight were marked *International Postage Stamp Album,* each with a different numeral, and the remaining albums were stamped *Specialty Series* and began with British Asia.

She closed her eyes and wondered why she was still friends with BK. Originally the reason had been that she didn't want to make a scene, she didn't want them to know she had found out. To let them know she had found out was such an irreversible act that she could not even imagine the consequences. Everything would have changed; not one part, one neat section of their life, but the entire fabric. Nothing would have ever been the same again. She had fantasies of coming up with a devastating coded message for BK, some remark that would allow that she knew what had happened, but that she was so sophisticated, in such control of herself and her life, that BK was beneath her contempt. Instead she simply drank a great deal when they were with BK and Sidney, and became numb. And now she continued to see BK because none of it made any difference anymore.

"I really don't mind the ring on your grandmother's table, Alix. What I mind is my daughter in such a state that she drinks herself into a stupor and then passes out on the couch with her clothes on. You didn't even touch the chicken, and if I hadn't

43

covered you with an afghan when I came in last night, you would have caught your death of cold."

The ring from her glass of Scotch looked white and gummy, obscene on the oiled oak surface of the table. Early-morning sun, the first sun she had seen in weeks, came through the shutters and formed neat patterns on the worn Oriental rug.

"Mother, I'm sorry about the ring." Her head ached.

Her mother was wearing a blue quilted robe and bedroom slippers the children had given her for Christmas. The slippers were pink and looked like small fuzzy boats; Mark and Cindy had picked them out themselves.

"Your grandmother bought that table in London on her honeymoon." Her mother picked up the glass and went into the kitchen to fix breakfast.

6

"Do you want to sell this house? Please call me immediately," read the message from Betty Lee in the mailbox.

There were also bills from I. Magnin, the children's dentist, the pool-cleaning service and the gas company. There was an announcement of an antiques sale for preferred customers (Preferred to what? wondered Alix. And why?), plus a letter in a pink envelope from the Literary Guild warning her that if she did not pay her past-due bill of $8.24 immediately it would be turned over to a collection agency. She stuffed everything back into the mailbox and went into the house.

Music blared from a radio and she could hear the whine of the vacuum cleaner upstairs, accompanied by the angry thumping sound Juanita made as she vacuumed, wielding the vacuum cleaner like an armored tank, pushing small pieces of furniture out of the way as if engaged in a miniature war.

The house looked dreary in the gray afternoon light. Did she want to sell the house? Of course she did. It was just that she didn't know what would happen when she sold it. The house, as

45

much as she hated it, was the last refuge. She didn't know where to go. She had never thought that she would live on her own. She didn't have an image in her mind of herself in her new life. The house was still home.

Juanita was carrying the vacuum cleaner into Cindy's room. A transistor radio was attached to the belt of her jeans. "Yeah, yeah, yeah," a voice sang.

"Hello, Juanita. Have you finished in my bedroom?"

"Yes, Mrs. Kirkwood." Juanita balanced the vacuum cleaner hose on her shoulder. "The little ones are gone?"

"Yes. They're in Arizona."

"How long for?"

"A month. Would you mind turning down your radio just a little bit?"

Juanita reached down and clicked off the music.

"You don't have to turn it off, Juanita. Just lower it a little."

"That's okay, Mrs. Kirkwood." Juanita looked at her and chewed her gum thoughtfully. "I found dirty laundry under the bed."

"Yes; well, the hampers were full."

Juanita nodded and chewed her gum.

Her mother's maid wore a white uniform and sensible shoes and never chewed gum. Juanita wore jeans and rubber shower shoes and chewed what appeared to be three sticks of gum at the same time. She didn't know what to do about Juanita any more than she knew what to do about her house or her life.

She went into her bedroom and unpacked her bag. She'd do something about Juanita soon. Either fire her or get her to shape up. The telephone rang.

"Mrs. Kirkwood, this is Betty Lee."

"Yes. I'm sorry; I meant to call you. I just got your note."

"Well, I'm afraid we lost the Cardiffs. They found another home this morning."

"I'm sorry," said Alix.

"Well, no more sorry than I am." Betty Lee gave a little laugh. "Mrs. Kirkwood, the reason I'm calling is to try and get you to reconsider having a lockbox."

"A lockbox?" Alix couldn't remember what it was she was talking about. What was a lockbox? "I'm sorry; I seem to have forgotten . . ."

"You said you didn't want a lockbox."

"I mean, I can't remember what one is. I know I didn't want one, but you see, now I can't remember what it was I didn't want."

There was silence at the other end of the line. Then Betty Lee said slowly, "A lockbox is a small box that would be attached to your front door and inside the box would be the key to your home. All the realtors have a key that would open the box, therefore, since your home is on multiple listing, all the realtors on the peninsula would have access to your home when you were out."

"But what if I *were* at home?"

"The realtors always call first to make an appointment in the event you are home."

"But what if they didn't? What if they just showed up and I was in the bathtub or something and couldn't answer the door? What then? You do understand what I'm saying? There's a certain lack of privacy that I don't think I could handle."

Another silence. It grew. Finally Alix said, "I don't want to be unreasonable. Really. I just think it's best if I don't have a lockbox."

"Certainly," said Betty Lee.

"I mean, I do want to sell the house. I want to be cooperative about all of this. It's just that I can't handle a lockbox. If a realtor wants to show the house and can get in touch with me ahead of time and I'm going to be out, I can just leave the key under the pot of fuchsias next to the front door."

"Of course," said Betty Lee. "I'll be in touch, Mrs. Kirkwood."

Alix hung up the phone and went into Cindy's room. "Juanita, I'm very tired. I think I'll take a bath and then lie down for a while. Let me write your check out now."

"Okay." Juanita was dusting Cindy's glass animal collection. "Don't you miss them?" she said.

"Who?"

"The little ones. It's so quiet without them."

47

"Yes, I miss them very much," said Alix, dating the check.
"Such a big house."

"Yes." Alix wrote in Juanita's name and the amount and signed
the check. One of these days she would tell Juanita to stop chew-
ing gum and suggest that Juanita wear a uniform. She would tell
Juanita to scrub the grouting between the kitchen and bathroom
tiles with a toothbrush instead of wiping it with a sponge. She
would tell Juanita to stop pushing and banging small pieces of
furniture when she vacuumed. She handed the check silently to
Juanita.

"I found newspapers in the drier," said Juanita.

"Oh?"

"Yes."

"Well, I'm going to take my bath now."

"They could catch on fire."

"What?"

"The newspapers," said Juanita. "They could catch on fire in
the drier."

Alix went into her bathroom and filled the tub with steaming
water. When was she going to do something about Juanita? Why
did she feel that something must be done about Juanita? Did she
want to sell the house? Why was a house she hated so important,
the fact of moving out so terrifying? Someone had once told her
that everything in Los Angeles happens in cars or houses. Or had
she thought that up herself? She couldn't remember.

She soaked in the hot water and tried to imagine what she'd do
when the house sold.

What would a woman whose neck was beginning to show signs
of age, a woman without a job or training for a job, a woman who
couldn't remember to pay her book club bills or decide when to
turn on the sprinklers—what would this woman do with the rest
of her life? Alix turned on more hot water with her foot and
thought about this question as if she were thinking about another
person, a friend whose idiosyncrasies were familiar yet rather
puzzling.

She soaped her arms, her mind going from the house to the

children. Why had she let them go for such a long time? How would she fill her days without them? Of course she missed them. Why had Juanita asked her that question? Why did she have no control over the way other people affected her?

She finished washing, tucked a large bath towel around herself, found Virginia and Judson's phone number by the telephone next to her bed, and dialed the number.

Virginia answered the phone with her usual drawn-out "Ye-es?" managing to make two syllables out of three letters. Robert always said his mother sounded like a psychiatrist with all those lingering, questioning yeses.

"Virginia, this is Alix."

"Alix, ye-es. How good to hear your voice. How are you?"

"Fine," said Alix. "And you?"

"Oh, I'm fine." Virginia's voice trailed off in a way that left a certain doubt.

"And Judson?"

"As well as can be expected, I suppose. His stomach's been acting up again."

"I'm sorry to hear that."

"The doctor gave him pills, but he says they make him sleepy so he won't take them. He drinks Gelusil as if it were water."

"Virginia, how are the children? Are they around?"

"Oh, the children are right here. They're being angels, Alix. Little *angels*. Just a minute, here's Cindy."

"Hi, Mommy. You know what happened?" said Cindy, her voice so far away and grown up that Alix felt a stab of unreasonable anger. How could Cindy be so independent and happy-sounding without her?

"What happened, darling?"

"Mark can swim across the pool under water. But his eyes are turning red so Grandpa says he's not to put his head under water for twenty-four hours because the chlorine is so strong. And my hair is turning green again."

"Be sure and rinse it every time you go swimming."

"And you know what else happened? Mark peed in the pool

49

and Grandma told him he was disgusting and that he couldn't ever go in her pool again if he didn't start using the bathroom like nice people do."

In the background Alix could hear Virginia making hushing sounds to Cindy.

"And, Mommy, we're going out to dinner tonight and we can order the most expensive thing on the menu, Grandpa told us. We don't have to order from the middle of the menu."

"Oh, Cindy babykins, I miss you so much."

"I miss you, too. I think my tooth is going to fall out. Grandma said to be sure and put it under my pillow when it does." And then Cindy lowered her voice and whispered into the phone, "I bet the tooth fairy in this house leaves a dollar. At least."

"Cindy—"

"Do you want to talk to Mark?"

"Okay. Hey, first, did you ever find your new bathing suit with the ducks on it?"

"Yes. You didn't forget to pack it after all."

"Look, be a good girl. Help around the house. And write to me? Or call collect if you feel like it."

"Okay, Mommy. Here's Mark."

Muffled sounds and then Mark's high-pitched little-boy's voice. "Hi, Mom."

"Hi, darling. I miss you. The house is awfully empty without you two."

"Yeah?"

"Yeah. Are you having fun?"

"It's okay. You know what?"

"What?"

"Cindy wants holes in her ears."

"Holes?"

"Yeah. So she can wear earrings. She goes around acting like you ever since we got here and she thinks she can boss me around. What a butt."

"Mark, please watch your language around your grandparents, okay?"

"Okay."

"And let me speak to Cindy again. I love you."

"Bye, Mom."

Cindy got back on the line and said, "Mark used the *f* word the other day."

"Did your grandparents hear him?"

"No."

"Thank God. Listen, Cindy, you can't pierce your ears. Nine is too young. Wait until you're twelve."

"Don't worry, Mommy. Grandma said that only Gypsies pierce their ears at my age and she won't let me do it."

"I love you. Be good."

"I will, Mommy. I love you, too."

Alix hung up and then felt like immediately calling Virginia back and telling her that the children could not stay until the end of July. It was out of the question to have them gone for such a long time.

But it was out of the question to have them return early. To change plans now would involve discussions with Robert, explanations to Virginia and Judson, to the children. Robert would say she was being selfish. Virginia and Judson would be hurt. The children would be confused. And she would be put on the defensive.

She pulled an afghan from the foot of the bed and put it around her bare shoulders. Without the children to root her in time and situation, she would drift into a strange structureless way of life. She was in danger of losing track of the ordinary checkpoints of daily life. Without the dozens of small obligations that the children imposed on her, she felt she was floating into a void. The same void she had touched sitting in her old pink bedroom at her mother's house. Now her days were defined only by sunrise and sunset; and the fact that on Saturdays Juanita cleaned, Thursdays the pool was cleaned, and the gardener came on Friday. House. Pool. Yard. Her life.

7

SHE FELT VULNERABLE and conspicuous crossing the lawn to the Drews' house the next evening. She had never gone to a dinner party without a man before. She felt exposed; somehow larger than usual. As if there were more sides to her, angles, parts of her that could be seen. As if for years and years she had been safe, hidden in Robert's shadow.

The Drews' house, like her own, resembled a motel. The entire front consisted of sliding glass doors, as if the inhabitants were geared for an impending evacuation. When, in fact, the earthquake did come, the shattering of all the glass doors could decapitate an entire household. Alix had brooded over this possibility occurring in her own house.

Inside the Drews' house were soft lights and just-vacuumed carpets, the smell of perfume and furniture polish, and space that flowed—square footage ad infinitum. A hallway became a living room, which flowed into the dining room, and with a slide of a glass door the dining room flowed into the patio. Alix longed for snug, neat rooms. Defined space.

Milly kissed her cheek and said she looked wonderful, as if Alix were recuperating from an illness. Jim Drew, tall, skinny and intense, kissed her and asked her how she was doing, and then Sidney Morrison asked her how it was going, and she said fine, just fine, and stared at Sidney's stomach, which was straining against his tweed jacket, and wondered why he thought BK had fat thighs. She wondered if Robert thought BK had fat thighs.

Milly took her by the hand and led her into the living room, where BK sat on the sofa talking to a man wearing a blue-and-maroon-checked sports jacket. The man Milly had captured for her. Warren Sullivan. Milly introduced them and they shook hands; Alix said hello at the same instant he did and there was an abrupt pocket of silence which caught everyone unaware. Alix wondered what it was that made a man so obviously just divorced. And was it that obvious with her? Had she that same taut aura of sudden singleness? The blend of availability and panic? Half a couple. Incomplete.

Jim poured her a glass of wine and Milly passed pâté and crackers. The living room was not for living but for company, and Alix never felt comfortable in it. She sipped her wine and curled up in one of the Windsor chairs by the fireplace. Even the chair, a family heirloom, made her feel depressed and uncomfortable; she wondered what her mother had done about removing the water stain from her grandmother's oak table. She could imagine her mother using soft little cleaning rags and a bottle of lemon oil, working intently at the round white ring.

"Look at that," said Warren Sullivan, sitting on a hassock at her feet.

"At what?" she asked.

"A fire in June," he said, indicating the fireplace. "Back East you can't use your fireplace in June. It's too hot."

"Do you come from the East?"

"Yes. I'm from New Jersey."

"Oh."

He opened a new pack of cigarettes, tapped one out and lit it, inhaling deeply.

Alix watched the fire and sipped her wine.

"Why so pensive?" he asked.

She thought of boys in high school promising a penny for her thoughts.

"Pensive? What does pensive look like?" she asked.

He frowned. "Thoughtful, sad." His hair was cut badly and the color blond often turns to: a flat brown without benefit of highlights or sheen.

"Well, actually I was thinking about a table," said Alix.

"A table?"

"A mark, a stain on a table."

"Oh," he said. He spread pâté on a cracker, offered it to Alix, who shook her head, then ate it himself. "What kind of a stain?"

"A water stain. From a glass of Scotch."

He had a tan and she wondered how he had gotten it. Living at the Marina this time of year, there were only two ways to acquire a suntan—spending weekends in Palm Springs or from a sun lamp. The thought of a grown man standing in a bathroom under a sun lamp in order to look younger and more attractive made her feel so depressed she was afraid she might cry.

"Well," he said, frowning again, "why are you thinking about this stain?"

"No reason, really. I mean, it's rather involved."

"Oh."

She felt sorry for him. She was sounding ridiculous and he was so insecure, so anxious to be cool and fit in, that he was taking her seriously. "Are you in Los Angeles for good?" she asked.

"Or for bad," he said, and started to laugh. When he saw that she was not laughing, he cleared his throat and said, "What I'm trying to do is find a condo at the Marina."

"Condo?"

"A condominium."

"Yes, of course." She had never heard anyone call a condominium a condo. She had once heard someone refer to Madison Avenue as Mad Ave, but she had never actually heard someone say condo out loud.

54

Jim Drew refilled their wineglasses and Warren said, "Housing is so expensive out here."

"That's an understatement," said Jim. "Our last house right here on the peninsula is up for sale again and the asking price is two fifty. And we bought it—when, Milly? sixty-eight?—we bought it for fifty-one thousand dollars in sixty-eight."

Alix could remember a time when discussing the cost of one's house in public was tantamount to divulging the details of one's sex life.

"I have this theory," said BK, "about why we all move and change houses so much in California. People back East don't move all the time the way we do."

"That's true," said Warren.

"So what's your theory, BK?" asked Sidney.

"My theory is that we change houses so often because we don't have seasons, real seasons like back East, so we get bored with our houses. When you have real winters with snow and everything, your house seems different, it gets very cozy inside. But here it's always the same—grass, flowers, leaves stay on the trees. Your house never changes so you change houses."

"That makes sense," said Milly.

"But it rains here, doesn't it?" asked Warren.

More people arrived. Greta and Paul Hecht, who were both doctors, and the young couple who had just moved into the neighborhood, whose names Alix didn't catch. He was handsome in the bland and overeager way some men are before they reach thirty and she had her hair in two long braids and wore the kind of tinted glasses that grew lighter indoors and then darker outside in the sunlight. Alix wondered if they were prescription glasses and realized she didn't like people in their twenties anymore.

"How old are you?" she asked Warren.

"Forty-one last November."

"November what?"

"November ninth," he said. "You don't believe in that stuff, do you?"

55

"What stuff?"

"All that astrology stuff."

"No. I was just wondering when your birthday was. My ex-husband's birthday is in November also."

"Jim said he was a writer."

"My ex-husband? Yes." Alix wished she had not mentioned Robert, hoped that Warren would not pursue the subject of Robert's writing. "What do you do?" she asked.

"Insurance," he said.

"Oh?"

"I sell insurance policies."

"I see."

"What sort of stuff does your husband write?"

"My ex-husband."

"Your ex-husband. What does he write?"

"Oh, stuff for television." Alix felt her words floating out into the air as if encased in balloons like cartoon conversation.

"Anything I might have seen?" Warren asked.

"I have no idea."

"I mean, I watch everything; I've probably seen some of his stuff. Tell me something he's written."

Was she always to remain an extension of Robert? Was Robert always going to be her most interesting feature? "He wrote *The Brewsters,*" she said.

"*The Brewsters?* That's some show. I mean, that's really the big time."

"Do you think so?" Alix said. The room was growing blue with cigarette smoke and individual conversations whirred and buzzed like the chatter of insects. "I think it's a terrible show," she said. "I think it's the worst thing on television."

Warren gave a knowing smile, and she realized anything she said against *The Brewsters* sounded bitchy. Sour grapes.

"You must know a lot of fascinating people," he said.

"No, not really," said Alix. "Television people aren't any more fascinating than other people."

"Now, why do you say that? I don't know anything about show biz, but—"

She excused herself and went to the john. How could Milly Drew, with her perfect house and her gourmet dinners and her good-looking husband who wore John Denver granny glasses and turtleneck sweaters have gotten her involved with such a creep as Warren Sullivan for an entire evening? She could hear the television on upstairs and children's voices, and suddenly she wanted, more than anything else, to simply have life the way it used to be. She wanted to give dinner parties and worry over the food and how the house looked and have Robert take the children to McDonald's before the guests came. She wanted to fill up all the space in her house with friends and talk and at the end of the evening she wanted to go upstairs to bed with Robert. She sat on the john and cried. Then carefully dabbed at the streaked mascara under her eyes with a tissue and combed her hair. She washed her hands with Milly's fancy guest soap which smelled of strawberries and dried her hands on the embroidered guest towels and imagined Milly telling her children all day not to step foot in the downstairs bathroom because it was cleaned for company.

Before going back into the living room, she went upstairs and looked into the bedroom where the television noise was coming from. Tracy and Kristen Drew were sprawled on the bed and Jimmy Drew sat cross-legged on the floor.

"Hi, gang," said Alix.

"Hi, Mrs. Kirkwood," they said in a polite chorus.

"I talked to Cindy and Mark on the phone yesterday."

"Are they having fun?" asked Kristen.

"They're having a wonderful time. It's hot there and they swim all the time."

"That sounds neat," said Tracy.

"Next time you talk to them," said Jimmy, "tell Mark his mother guppy had her babies this morning. I put them in a jar like he told me to, but I only got five. She ate the rest."

"Can we have their address so we can write to them?" asked Kristen.

"Sure," said Alix. They found her a piece of paper and a pencil and she wrote down the address for them. "They'd love to hear from you."

5

She wished she could stay upstairs in this bedroom with the children and watch television for the rest of the evening. She envied them the comfort of their clean pajamas and their easy evening together.

Downstairs, Greta Hecht caught her arm. "How are you, dear?" said Greta. "I think of you, but there's never enough time for anything these days. So I don't call, never see the people I care about. I hardly even see Paul." Greta had blue-black hair twisted into a bun at the back of her neck, strands escaping and giving her the look of always being in motion. Her hands, perfect and small and white, flashed as she talked. "Paul and I have been trying for two years to get away and have a real vacation." She smiled. "How are you doing?"

Alix shrugged.

"It must be a bad time for you. And Milly tells me the children left last week for the summer?"

"Just for a month," said Alix. "Five weeks, actually."

Greta nodded, her eyes narrowing the way they did when she considered a medical problem. "Do you have anything to take— something to just smooth over the edges?"

"I'm okay, Greta."

"Well, if you need anything let me know. Nothing strong. Maybe some Valium to help you relax."

The medicine cabinet was still stocked with Robert's tranquilizers and other remedies for his assorted nervous disorders. None of his problems were chronic; all were sudden, startling and brief. "Thanks, Greta. I think we have some Valium."

Warren had remained on the hassock, waiting for her return, smoking and talking to BK. BK had the polite glazed expression of someone who has been making small talk for too long. "Here, Alix, try some of the fondue." She stuck a piece of French bread on the tip of a long fork and dipped it into the fondue pot. "It's marvelous. Isn't it marvelous, Warren?"

"Yes, it is." Wine sloshed out of his full glass onto the carpet. He dabbed at it with his handkerchief.

Alix found herself feeling sorry for him again; it was always so

58

embarrassing to spill something. "It's good for the rug; keeps the moths out," she said in a friendly voice.

"Moths?" said BK. "Wine isn't good for getting rid of the moths. Ashes are supposed to be. Cigarette ashes. But do you know what I just read? That's a lie. Ashes are terrible for carpets and it's just a lie that has been told by polite hostesses since time began. Or since carpets began."

Warren carefully stubbed out his cigarette in an ashtray. "I didn't know that."

"Isn't the fondue great?" BK asked Alix, and then to Warren, "Are you a bachelor or divorced?"

'Divorced," said Warren.

"Isn't everyone these days?" BK put more bread on the end of her fork.

Alix studied BK's mouth and thought that one's inner life registered by fractions of an inch around one's mouth.

"And you know what they say," said BK, "how amazing it is that forty percent of all marriages end in divorce, but I personally think that the amazing part is that sixty percent of all marriages last."

"I never thought of it that way," said Warren.

Later, during dinner at the big round table in the dining room, Warren said to Alix, "It was like there was this point where we could have stopped it. I mean, we went beyond that point."

"What is that point?" asked Alix.

"You're divorced; you ought to know."

"I was divorced over a pair of green socks," she said. "I'm not positive about that, but it's as good a reason as any, I suppose." She had had a great deal of wine to drink, but was finally beginning to feel on top of the situation. To be interesting, one must be interested. Another of her mother's maxims. It crossed her mind that she had no original convictions, that her basic philosophy of life was composed of her mother's random clichés.

"But tell me, what was that point for you?" she asked, leaning on her elbows toward Warren. Interested.

He put a raw piece of beef on the end of a fork, then placed it in a fondue pot of boiling oil. "I guess you reach that point when you start saying things to each other that two people shouldn't tell each other. There are ground rules to a fight, you know? When two people have been together for a long time they know things about each other, things that hurt. Really hurt."

"Yes," said Alix, wondering if Robert was somewhere tonight discussing his new-found insights. "Tell me about your ex-wife," she said to Warren.

He took a long swallow of wine and abandoned his beef in the fondue pot. "My wife? My wife is about the last thing I want to talk about tonight. My wife is a thirty-eight-year-old schoolgirl. My wife is getting a master's degree in a subject no one has ever heard of and she's turned her kids into household slaves to get what she wants. But what does she want—really want? I don't know. What does she need her master's for? When I married her we were still in college and all she cared about was being a cheerleader and her hair and stuff like that. I spent half my time saying, 'Marjorie, your hair looks fine, stop worrying about it.' And now she's got to have a master's degree. There was never any, you know, middle ground."

"Well, I can see your point," said Alix.

"My point?"

"About not wanting to talk about her." She sipped her wine and smiled at him.

The new neighbor was seated on her right. "We're into fasting now," he said. "It's an incredible high. Just herbal tea, no juice or anything, and wow."

"Wow?" repeated Alix.

"Wow. Yes. It's better than meditating. Better than drugs. After forty-eight hours there's this nice mellow buzz and then— wow." He was wearing a sterling-silver chain with a tiny avocado, also sterling, attached to the chain.

"Don't you get hungry?" she said.

"That's the whole point. No! You get high."

"I see," said Alix, realizing that in all probability she would never sleep with a younger man.

She turned back to Warren.

"I call my kids every once in a while," he said. "It's tough, though, trying to keep in touch with your kids by long distance."

"My children are in Phoenix with their grandparents," she said.

"Why?"

"Why?" She drained her glass of wine. "That's a very good question. You see, my husband—my ex-husband, that is—thought it would be a good idea and his parents, whom the children are visiting, thought it would be a good idea, and I'm very influenced by people who appear to know their own minds. You see, I can never say no. I don't like to cause a disturbance." She heard her voice droning on as Warren's face began to blur.

Somewhere inside her head she thought, I am boring and I am bored. I am filled up with my mother's discarded clichés like an old wastepaper basket. And as silly as most of the clichés are, I can't even live up to them.

"I could have gotten my kids," Warren was saying, "and I should've, but I was . . . I don't know. Tired."

"Tired?"

"Yeah. I gave up. I was tired. Tired of her, tired of talking about who did what. I just gave up."

Alix accepted a cup of coffee from Milly and tried to concentrate on Warren. He had a high forehead and flat, heavy features, blurred slightly from all the wine she had.

"I could have gotten them if I had just fought a little bit. If I had dragged it through court I could have gotten the kids. But—" He lifted his shoulders and dropped them.

Dessert, chocolate fondue, was served in the family room. Everywhere one looked there was a photograph of a Drew celebrating something. Christmas, weddings, christenings, graduations, birthdays—they were there in perpetual celebration on the family room walls. Kissing, unwrapping presents, holding up trophies and babies and diplomas for all eternity. And in every corner was a project—baskets of knitting, needlepoint, macramé, looms, tanks of tropical fish, thriving plants, books. Tonight the room made Alix feel suicidal.

BK was sharing a joint with the new neighbors, and Milly and the Drs. Hecht were studying the tropical fish. Jim poured brandy while Sidney frowned at BK and explained to Jim why his tomato plants had not yet set blossoms.

"You want to know what she said to me?" asked Warren. "You want to know?" His forehead looked damp and Alix hoped he wouldn't start crying or pass out. She imagined his life: the apartment with the Abbey Rents furniture and new stereo equipment, the king-size bed and one-night stands, the TV dinners alone. The silence of living alone.

"Let me tell you what she said to me." He took a snifter of brandy from Jim.

"What did she say to you?" said Alix, wanting the evening to end.

"We were having this stupid fight about the house or money or something, nothing really important, and all of a sudden out of nowhere she drops this bombshell. She says, 'You've heard me mention Professor Eckert?' I don't know, I never really listened to her when she talked about school, but I said yes, and then she said she had been seeing a lot of him lately. As a matter of fact, all those nights when I thought she was at the library she was at the Holiday Inn screwing the professor. Just like that she tells me. In the middle of a nothing fight. Like she was proud of it or something."

"So you divorced her," said Alix.

"So I divorced her."

He had made the connection between being unfaithful and divorce. If A happens, proceed to B. Alix had never made that connection; it never occurred to her to divorce Robert because he had been unfaithful. Of course, with Robert she suspected it was a constant activity, a condition rather than an event. And what had occurred to her was retaliation. Do unto others as they do to you. But she did not lead the kind of life conducive to furtive affairs; the logistics were too complicated. There were car pools to consider. Cub Scouts, Girl Scouts, Little League. The scheduling would drive her crazy. Plus which, she was simply too lazy. She did not have the energy or the resourcefulness needed to become accustomed to another man's personal habits; to get used to how he looked in his underwear, when he brushed his teeth, or how he made love. She was convinced that there was a great deal more to lovemaking than could be put into short affairs. It was a question of time, of familiarity and knowledge, and she wondered what Professor Eckert had offered at the Holiday Inn.

Warren lit a cigarette. "I didn't mean to dump all my problems on you."

"That's all right," said Alix. "I don't mind."

His hand was on her thigh, nothing overtly aggressive, just a rather pale, heavy hand on her thigh. She stared at it as though it were a separate object, an ashtray or a book someone had misplaced, and wondered what would be the most graceful way to dispose of it. Finally she patted it and rose. "It's late. I've got to go home."

He smiled slowly. "All right. Let's make our goodbyes."

"Our goodbyes?" she repeated.

"I'll see you home."

"There's no need. Really. I live right next door."

He got to his feet unsteadily. They were the same height and she looked directly into his eyes, which were having trouble focusing.

"A gentleman always sees a lady home," he said.

After good nights and thank yous, they walked silently and unsteadily across the wide lawns that separated the two houses. The fog had rolled in like smoke and the ocean was invisible. Alix held up her long skirt to keep it from getting wet in the damp grass.

"Aren't you going to invite me in?" said Warren at the front door.

"It's late," she said.

"Don't be coy." His eyes looked dead, as if during the course

63

of the evening he'd had so much to drink that part of him had died and now there wasn't any light in his eyes.

She was shivering in the cold fog. "I'm not being coy. I'm tired." Her voice sounded tiny, like a little girl's. "Look, we've both had too much to drink."

"That's a goddamn lie," he said, steadying himself against the doorjamb. "But I would like a cup of coffee. You wouldn't want me to drive home in this condition, would you?" He smiled suddenly, but there still was no light in his eyes.

Alix sighed. "All right."

8

"Is instant okay?"

"Fine." Warren sat on a kitchen stool, the upper part of his body slumped over the counter. His high forehead shone in the unflattering light.

"Sugar? Milk?" Alix asked.

"Both."

"Please," she said.

"Please what?"

"Both, *please*. You didn't say please." She took a jar of instant coffee from the cupboard above the stove. "I'm sorry; I've been around children too much. It's a reflex."

"You're so uptight I didn't think you had any reflexes."

"Uptight," she repeated, and spooned coffee into two mugs. "You think I'm uptight?"

He didn't answer but smiled in a way that annoyed her. It was a smile that took things for granted, implied an intimacy which didn't exist. The kettle began to whistle and she poured boiling water into the mugs and added sugar and milk to his.

"Cheers," he said, taking a sip of the coffee and grimacing because it was too hot. He lit a cigarette with unusual concentration, as if there was some question as to whether the flame of the match would actually make contact with the tip of the cigarette. He inhaled deeply with a sigh of pleasure. "Any brandy for a chaser?"

"Wouldn't that defeat the whole purpose?"

"The purpose?"

"The purpose of the coffee," said Alix.

"There is no purpose," he said, and wandered out of the kitchen, leaving his coffee on the counter. "Now, where do you keep the brandy?"

He walked through the house, examining and touching objects with a proprietary air that annoyed Alix as much as his intimate smile.

"Some place," he said, standing in the middle of the living room. Certain aspects of Warren Sullivan's appearance made her unreasonably angry. It was absurd to be upset by the way a near stranger looked; to let something like the cut and color of his jacket bother her. Or his shirt unbuttoned to show a chest sprinkled with grayish hair. Or the way his forehead shone and looked damp. Or his pale, heavy hands, which didn't quite match the tan on his face and chest. Or the length of his hair.

Warren snapped his forefinger against a silver bowl on the coffee table. There was a short, flat *ping* and Alix said, "That's what you do to crystal, not silver."

"*Do* to?"

"To test. That's how you test glass."

"Is that what you think I was doing? Testing your silver?"

He was so serious that she laughed.

"What's so goddamn funny?"

"Nothing."

"Did you think I was checking out your things? Testing your silver?"

"Of course not. I don't know why I said that. I didn't mean anything." Alix held her coffee mug with both hands to keep the coffee from spilling and to keep her hands from making vague, fluttery gestures. She realized that she disliked this man most of all for his ability to put her on the defensive.

Warren stubbed out his cigarette in an ashtray. "I'm sure it's sterling."

"What?"

"The bowl I was *testing*. I said I was sure it was sterling."

"Oh."

He staggered slightly and then steadied himself. "Have you ever *wanted* anything in your whole life?"

He was paraphrasing Robert. Why were men always asking her what she wanted? *If* she wanted?

"Have you?" he repeated.

She was tired, she wanted him to leave. How to get him out of her house?

He had wandered into the hallway. "Nice-looking kids," he said, looking at a framed photograph of the children.

"Thank you."

"You said they're away for the summer?"

"For a month. In Phoenix with their grandparents."

"You miss them?"

"Yes; very much."

"What's down there?"

"The family room."

"Mind if I have a look?" he said, already going down the steps. She followed him.

"Aha," he said, spotting the bar. He held up the bottle of brandy triumphantly. "Now, where are the glasses?"

She blew the dust out of a wineglass and handed it to him.

"You're not having any?" he asked, pouring some into the glass.

"No."

They sat on stools, the bar between them. He rubbed his eyes.

"It's late," Alix said, thinking he must be as tired as she was.

"You want to get rid of me?" His eyes had a blank, slightly stunned look.

"I just said it was late. I didn't mean anything else," said Alix, defensive again. She hated the feeling.

"Have some brandy, then. You'll sleep better."

"I really don't want any," she said.

"Have some."

It was too silly to argue about. She poured herself brandy in another wineglass, forgetting to blow out the dust. Of course she wanted to get rid of him. She watched the small particles of dust floating on top of the brandy and considered the fact that he had said "You want to get rid of me," rather than "You want me to leave." One got rid of garbage and old clothes and things without value.

"Good girl," he said. "Isn't that better than coffee?"

She nodded.

"What are you thinking about?"

Alix wondered what the effect would be if she pointed out this linguistic clue to his personality. Robert had always found her odd observations interesting, even when uncomplimentary. But then Robert was an egotist; and also a writer. "Nothing is ever wasted in life for the creative individual," he used to tell her. Whenever she watched *The Brewsters* on television she would remember that statement with wonder.

Warren leaned toward her and put his hand on hers. "I said, what are you thinking about?"

She looked down at his hand and remembered the bones in Robert's hands and said, "Nothing. I'm not thinking about anything."

"Some more brandy?" he said, holding out his glass. *"Please."*

She looked at him.

"I said, some more brandy? May I have more brandy? Please."

"My mother says that one should never say 'some more,' " Alix said, and poured another inch of brandy into his glass. " 'Some more,' my mother claims, implies a certain piggishness. But that's

68

my mother for you." She said this pleasantly, casually even, and was startled to see the anger in his face. "I didn't mean anything by that," she said, trying to smile at him. "I say 'some more' all the time."

He took a hard swallow of brandy. "Your mother sounds like Marjorie."

"Marjorie?"

"My wife. My ex-wife."

"Oh."

He reached for her hand again and played with her fingers. "Marjorie was very proper. About certain things. About other things, well . . ."

"I don't sense any real similarities." She didn't want to hear any more about Marjorie. She moved her hand from his and he caught it and gripped it tightly.

"What's the matter?" he said.

"You're hurting my hand." He let go of her hand and she rubbed the white marks where he had pressed too hard.

"Don't tease," he said.

"Tease?" She tried to make sense of the word, relate it to something she had done or said or thought. Tease? She couldn't connect. What she wanted was for him to leave; to be rid of him. But she couldn't concentrate on how to accomplish this. It should be such a simple action, but somehow more emotion and commitment were required for getting him to leave than just letting him sit here and drink her brandy.

Her brandy. Was it her brandy? Or was it actually Robert's brandy? This seemed a much safer train of thought. Something to focus on until he realized it was time to leave. She inhaled the sweet harsh smell of the brandy in her glass and wondered how community property applied to one's supply of liquor.

Warren lit another cigarette. He flicked the match toward an ashtray and it missed. Alix picked it up and put it in the ashtray.

"Sorry," he said.

"That's okay," said Alix. Her eyes felt grainy and she was beginning to feel desperate for sleep.

"My mother used to say that Marjorie had the balls in the family."

Alix looked at him. "Your mother said that?"

"Yes. That's *my* mother for you. And Marjorie."

"I see."

"Do you?"

She finished her brandy. "Look. I'm just too tired to see anything."

"Come here," he said.

"What?"

"Come here," he repeated, and patted the stool next to him.

Alix sighed. He had poured another inch of brandy into her glass and she walked around to his side of the bar and sat down on the stool next to him. She sat very straight. "I wonder if it's true," she said, "what they say about your brain cells."

"What do they say?" His arm went around her waist.

"That a few are killed off every time you have a drink. How, exactly, does that work? I mean, do they die in clumps, certain sections, or do they die off evenly?" She never had a drink without thinking about this. Just as she could not look at a sliding glass door without wondering what destruction it could cause during an earthquake.

"You talk too much," he said as he tried to pull her toward him. His face looked heavy and slack, as though it were made of clay. As if she could reshape it with her hands. "Stop talking," he said, slurring the words.

He leaned toward her and she could smell the stale odor of tobacco, and then could taste it as he pulled her to him and kissed her. She gritted her teeth together and tried to push him away. Abruptly he let her go, still holding her by her upper arms.

"What kind of a game are you playing?" he said.

His fingers were pressing into her arms and she tried not to react to the pain. "I'm not playing a game," she said. "Look, I think there's been some sort of mistake. You'd better go."

He slapped her. She was so stunned that she didn't make a sound, just stared at him with her mouth forming an O. The surprise of the slap was crueler than the pain; the unfairness of it. She had never been hit before. Ever. Robert had called her a lot of names, had once or twice threatened violence, but he had never actually hit her, and she found herself so shocked at being hit that she had no other reaction, not anger or pain or humiliation. She was suspended.

Then he kissed her again and she didn't struggle, didn't react, didn't even think. She could feel his tongue trying to get into her mouth and she thought she might be sick. She clenched her teeth together and wished she would be sick.

His body, hard and soft, was pressing against her. "Cock-teaser," he said. "Cock-teasing cunt." The words sounded even more vulgar than they were. She had never been shocked by words before. Cock-teasing cunt. She had heard those words, read them, but they had never been *meant.* In some distant part of her mind she thought her reaction to this was all wrong. Off center. Odd. Like wondering why Robert had fixed Manhattans in the middle of August. To be shocked by words indicated a certain leisure; space. She had no space. This man had invaded her space and would not let her breathe. His hands were fumbling with the top of her skirt. She pushed his hands away and twisted her head to one side, which made him even angrier. What had she done to make him so angry? Get out, get out—she thought she had screamed it out loud, but her teeth were still clenched and her hands were tight fists, her own nails digging into her palms. He pulled her away from the bar toward the couch and she tried to struggle, but he was holding her in such a way that every move of her body caused contact with his. His grip on her arms was so strong she thought his hands would tear through her flesh. He pushed her down on the couch and she began to scream. Out loud. She could hear herself and the sound of her own screams compounded the terror. His hand came down over her mouth and she thought she would gag on fear and the smell of his skin and cigarettes. She felt material straining and then ripping, and her legs exposed to air. A sense of modesty overwhelmed her and she could feel her tears running down the sides

71

of her face. She tried to press her knees together. The lower part of his left arm was held up against her throat and she thought that she might die. If he pressed hard enough against her throat she would die. This was something that happened in back alleys. In parking lots. By strangers creeping into darkened houses. Strangers did it. She was powerless. She could feel his thing. Not a penis, but a thing. Obscene. A weapon, something that hurt. She tried to shrink inside herself. Tried to avoid its touching her skin. She wanted to die. She wanted to turn off her mind. But it wasn't her mind, it was her senses she couldn't turn off. Touch and taste and smell and sounds of what was happening. That was what was being beaten into her. As much as the thing, the weapon, he had between her legs. That was what she couldn't turn off. The way he smelled. The way his skin felt rubbery and damp against her skin. The sounds he was making.

Let me die, thought Alix.

He groaned suddenly and became dead weight on her.

She kept her eyes closed. She didn't move.

After a moment she heard him say, "Oh, God," and he got off her. Her eyes still shut, she reached down and pulled at what was left of her skirt and tried to cover herself.

He was at the bar, looking for his cigarettes. He lit one. Then, finally, she heard his footsteps going across the room and up into the hallway. The front door opened and slammed shut. A few minutes later a car engine started, hummed a second, and then died away into the quiet night.

Alix opened her eyes. Two empty glasses stood on the bar. An ashtray. A cushion from the couch had been knocked to the floor. That was all.

She felt a warm stickiness between her legs and ran to the bathroom in time to be sick in the sink.

9

"WHAT'S GOING ON, Alix?" Robert's voice.

She held the telephone receiver with both hands and put her head back on the pillow.

"Alix? Do you hear me?"

"Yes, Robert." It was light out. Morning? Afternoon? Gray light behind draperies; the room blurred by the Valium she had taken. Images, sounds and smells from her nightmares floated into the gray light of her room. But the nightmare had been real this time. It had happened. The man under the bed, lurking in the closet, behind the door. It had happened.

"The realtor—Betty What's-her-name—just called me and said that she's having a terrible time getting in touch with you. She said that most of the time she calls you, the phone is either off the hook or you don't answer."

"Oh."

"Is that all you can say, Alix? 'Oh'?"

"I just answered."

"What?"

6

"The phone. I just answered it."

Robert didn't say anything for a moment and she could imagine his face, muscles tightening as he took a deep breath. Glancing at his watch. "Well, she's given up trying. She tried to get you all last evening and all morning. And the point is this. It makes no sense for you to stay in that house. You don't even like the house, and for what it costs me each month you might as well check into the Beverly Wilshire and live on room service. You've got to pull yourself together."

"Pull myself together?" said Alix. A vision of her arms, legs, fingers—rolling away, unraveling like a spool of thread. She gripped the telephone, as if by holding on to it as tightly as possible she could keep herself from unraveling. As long as Robert kept talking she wouldn't have to think. Wouldn't have to remember.

"That's the whole point," said Robert.

The point was she could never remember the point.

"The house . . ." Robert was saying.

The house was the point. Of course.

It was like a giant child or pet that had to be cared for. It had problems. It had a history, a future. Concentrate on the house. The house, not unlike herself, was beginning a physical decline. The ceilings were becoming dingy and the pipes were acquiring thin coats of rust. The paint was fading. The house was becoming more and more vulnerable to outside forces.

"Alix, call her and set up a time for these people of hers to come look at the house." Robert paused. "Is that so difficult?"

It was like a nervous tic, his habit of saying, "Is that so difficult?" It occurred to Alix that she had never heard him say that to anyone but her.

"Is it?" he asked.

It also occurred to her that she no longer liked Robert and perhaps she had not liked him for a very long time.

"I don't know, Robert. I can't talk about this right now. I just can't talk about it any longer." She hung up before he could say anything else.

Her body hurt. She pulled the covers up to her chin. Taut. Uptight.

Concentrate. Do not allow yourself to unravel. The Valium was wearing off.

She stared at the acoustic ceiling and thought hard about the problems involved with painting it. Could it be repainted? Or would more of that bumpy, popcornlike material have to be sprayed on? And how exactly was this done? With a machine? Would it smell, make a loud noise, spill? The complications and disruptions involved in this procedure made her feel desperate. To focus on the ceiling was a matter of discipline; like thinking about Robert's brandy or her father's stamp collection. A matter of finding a subject she could handle and then concentrating on it. If she concentrated hard enough she wouldn't scream.

She pulled back the covers and looked at her arms. On her right upper arm, on the pale inside part, there was one bruise the shape of a thumb. Four smaller bruises were on the outside. Slowly, as if she might discover something unexpected or shocking, she pulled up her nightgown and stared at herself. Pale, smelling of soap, her body was as separate as something that could float away from her. Her pubic bone ached. The Caesarean scar looked old and gnarled; the skin puckered like a badly sewn zipper.

She was shaking. Her teeth were chattering. She felt like ice. If she continued to shake like this she would shatter, break. If she could just stop shaking, maybe things would be all right. Maybe she could get out of bed then. Pull herself together. She began to cry.

She was dreaming. She knew this in the dream, yet there was a question as to what was more real—this dream she was in or being awake. She was with her father in the hospital and though he was extremely ill he was explaining to her how houses worked, how they were built and properly maintained. As he talked, he kept shrinking, becoming thinner and thinner until she was weeping and begging him to stop fading like that because if he didn't stop fading he would soon disappear. Odd shapes, lumps and

75

swellings appeared on his frail body, blooming like sudden exotic plants. Long trails of tubes appeared from nowhere. She was calling for doctors—someone to help—but no one came. There was no one to help her. The tubes were snakelike. Her father was so terribly thin now, so fleshless, that she couldn't understand how all the tubes and needles fit into his body. There was not enough flesh to contain them. She would not allow this to happen. She could not bear it. The tubes were devouring her father.

She awoke. She wanted to help her father. He was waiting there, in her dream, needing her. That fact was as real as the fact of her father's being reduced to an urn of ashes. The line between dreams and reality was as fine, as fragile, as a breath or shaft of light. She wanted to get back into her dream. She looked at her room. Oak dressers, yellow rug, the painting of the coastline that Robert had given her on their fifth wedding anniversary, lamps, draperies with the gray light filtering through. She thought of all the tubes that were connected to her father, the cancer growing and flourishing like tropical plants. Reality, like time, seemed to have movable parts; aspects that were not as simple and orderly as most people assumed.

She had always thought of life as vertical, unreeling like a film; the past drifting down and away, disappearing. And the future was up there someplace, hidden and blank, tight as unreeled film. But now her life appeared horizontal. Past, present, future stretched out in front of her like an incredibly long stage, or landscape; all action could be viewed simultaneously. As if definitions of time had been artificially imposed on her.

She wanted to scream. Howl. She had not screamed when her father died. Civilized people don't scream. All her life she had been taught to hold in the screams.

She got out of bed, carefully, shakily, as if she were navigating a tightrope. She went into the bathroom and swallowed another Valium. She brushed her teeth. And watched herself brushing her teeth as though she were watching a movie of someone brushing her teeth. She had never watched herself, seen herself, brush her teeth before. Had never really observed the fat white length of toothpaste. The grimace required to bare one's teeth. The ugliness of a mouth. Under her eyes were fine lavender shadows. The same color as the bruises on her arms. Her arm had been damaged. Damaged. It was a strange word, a word she never used. She took off her nightgown and turned on the shower, letting the water steam before getting in. How long had she stood in the shower last night? She had lost track of time. Time had become slippery again.

After her shower she dressed and went downstairs. In the kitchen she filled a pail with scalding water and a cup of Pine-Sol and carried it down to the family room. She yanked the slipcovers off the couch, for an instant wanting to shred them, tear them to pieces, instead carrying them into the laundry room and putting them in the washing machine.

She began to scrub the family room floor, inch by inch, concentrating on the design in the tiles, memorizing it, trying to fill her mind with the green geometric design. She had the vague, not completely formed idea that if she used up her energy, if she did physical work, she might conquer the feeling of wanting to scream, to shred her slipcovers. The feeling that something undefined and animal was expanding inside her.

She switched the slipcovers from the washer to the drier. The phone rang but she ignored it. The gray light was fading and she turned on a lamp. The family room smelled impersonal, like a public institution. The two wineglasses were still on the bar, sticky with brandy. Holding her breath, Alix carried them out to the garage and hurled them into a garbage can. The splintering glass and the sound of her own breathing filled the garage. One small window, facing the trees on the side of the house, let in a thin stream of gray light. The garage looked murky, as if under water, and the Mercedes appeared lost, adrift in the three-car garage.

Against the back wall of the garage, clung to like bad habits, were all the things they couldn't live with and couldn't live without. Bicycles whose brakes had failed or whose tires had gone flat, kitchen chairs that didn't match and she could not remember where they had come from or why they were being saved, only that they must be saved for some unforeseen development in the future. The rusted barbecue equipment. The exerciser Robert had used every morning until he took up jogging. The moving boxes that were labeled FRAGILE WINEGLASSES! or CHILDREN'S BEDDING: WINTER. How serious, how organized and optimistic they were whenever they moved. All the care that had gone into the sorting and labeling of their belongings, such faith that the cry FRAGILE! would be heard and heeded. Years ago the fragile wineglasses and the winter bedding for the children had been unpacked and absorbed into the household. Now the boxes held old magazines, clothes she had always planned on mending or lengthening or altering or giving away, but she could never decide which to do, and now they were outgrown or out of fashion. And the boxes held baby shoes—Mark's first pair of sneakers, which were so incredibly small she could not look at them without weeping. Cindy's smocked baby dresses. Copies of the literary magazine Robert edited in college. Yearbooks. Old letters. Christmas lights and tree decorations. Boxes and boxes of little pieces of their lives.

"Garbage," she said aloud.

This garbage is only a means to an end.

Something to get rid of, to throw out. Warren Sullivan was garbage.

Pull yourself together. If you look good you feel good.

Cock-teasing cunt.

Oh, God, what was she going to do? She had to erase it. *Get rid of it.* She felt as though she'd explode with it. Break into pieces. She'd seen a crazy lady at the airport once. The woman had stood screaming in the middle of the terminal: "I cannot take any more." But it had been more than a scream. She had been wailing. Keening. Her voice full of grief. *I cannot take any more.* People pretended not to see her or hear her, averted their eyes as if she had taken off her clothes or had approached them each personally with a demand. What would happen if she started to scream in her garage? If only she *could* scream.

Inside the house, she crouched on the stairs. She had been so carefully taught not to get rid of it. Lower your voice. Don't make a scene. Don't cry in public. Don't scream. Don't.

She had to think calmly. She had to concentrate. But there was nothing to focus on—just *this,* the feeling of shattering, of falling apart. Concentrate on remaining whole.

Pull yourself together.

Cock-teasing cunt.

She had to *do* something. To do meant power, offered choices, promised control. To be made powerless was to have sudden and clear knowledge of power.

She could not go to her mother. Nor Robert. Nor any of her friends.

The police. She closed her eyes and imagined getting dressed (carefully, in something conservative, something sensible and not sexy), then getting into the Mercedes and driving three miles to the police station. (Her hair—she'd have to do something about her hair. Pull it back or pin it up so it wouldn't look so wild.) The police station had a red tile roof, wrought-iron railings, authentic Mexican tiles. It was a charming building and the police were charming. (She felt her heart pounding as it would pound when she walked up the steps, holding on to the wrought-iron railing, going in the door, smelling the sudden office smell of paper and people and cigarettes and machines.) The police crossed the children on the main streets as they walked to school. The police checked houses when residents went on vacations. They were prompt and courteous and efficient when a robbery occurred. Alix imagined herself walking into the police station, being offered a chair, a cup of coffee. She would tell them she had been raped. The policemen would ask questions.

Did she see his face?

(Of course. She had dinner with him earlier that evening next door.)

How had he gotten into her house?

(She let him in. He had walked her home.)

Walked her home? Didn't she live just next door?

79

(True. But he said that a gentleman always walks a lady home.)

Did he force his way in, then?

(Not exactly. He said he wanted a cup of coffee.)

And did you give him a cup of coffee?

(Yes.)

And then he attacked you?

(No. First he had brandy.)

And did you have brandy also?

(Yes.)

How late did he stay?

(Very late.)

Why didn't you tell him to leave?

(It was easier to let him stay.)

And the charm would melt away and they would think: Whore. Vindictive bitch.

She felt very clear about the position of culprit and victim, and sensed that this knowledge was crucial to survival. She would not permit anyone to blur this clarity. She could not go to the police. She would not be judged. She had spent her whole life being judged.

She knew exactly what she had to do. The simplicity of it, the fairness of it, the *inevitability*, startled her. As if her mind itself had been locked in fog (for how long? a day? months? years?) and now everything was clear. Focused. There were no choices, no alternatives.

She was going to kill Warren Sullivan.

10

SHE SAT ON THE STAIRS in the almost dark of her house. It was still there, she could still feel it, but it was cooler now. She had a way to handle it. The incredible clarity of her vision made her high. The satisfaction of just thinking about it. Imagining the look on Warren Sullivan's face. She understood violence suddenly, the kind of bloody, face-smashing, killing violence she had always considered masculine, unfathomable. The purity of revenge.

She climbed the stairs to her room, aware of the space surrounding her. Sensitive to the fact that she had spent her life in rooms. Confined. Connected to the outside world by telephone wires and television antennas and newspapers.

She dialed 411.

"Information. For what city, please?"

"Marina del Rey," said Alix. "A listing for Warren Sullivan."

The operator gave her the number and Alix wrote it down on a copy of *Vogue* lying on the bedside table, the numbers marching across the pale cheek of a fashion model.

She stared at the number for a long time. She remembered a

joke she had heard once, ages ago, at a party. The joke was about a woman who had been raped. The woman had gone to the police station to identify her rapist in a line-up. She pointed to the man and said, "That's him. That's the man who raped me. But just to make sure, maybe he'd better do it again."

Robert had laughed at the joke.

And later criticized her for not laughing, because the man who had told the joke was a very important producer.

She thought of all the rape scenes she had read, seen in films. The steamy sex. The excitement.

She dialed the number.

After the third ring, "Hello?"

Her hands began to shake at the sound of his voice.

"Warren, this is Alix Kirkwood."

He didn't say anything for a long moment. "Look," he finally said, and then his voice died. Alix could imagine him suddenly sitting down. Looking confused. Worried. His forehead shining with nervous sweat. Then lighting a cigarette with fast, jerky motions.

She kept her voice smooth and impersonal, like a nurse or a stewardess. ". . . just an hour or so. A quick drink. Would tomorrow night be convenient?"

"I have to go to San Diego tomorrow . . ." he said, not ending the sentence.

"Wednesday night, then?" said Alix in her calm, professional voice. "Will you be back Wednesday, Warren?"

"Yes."

"Could you drop by Wednesday night?"

"I guess so. What time?"

She shut her eyes and concentrated. The Drews were sure to be in bed by ten-thirty or so.

"How about eleven?"

She heard the sharp intake of breath as he inhaled a cigarette. She tried not to think of the smell.

"Look," he said. He sounded less hostile. "I don't know what to say."

"Say you'll be here."

"Eleven o'clock, you said?" The hostility was gone. In its place was a horrible sort of insinuation, an audible leer.

"Yes," said Alix steadily, "if that suits you."

A pause and then, "I'll be there."

He thinks he has found himself one very kinky lady, thought Alix, hanging up the phone.

Her hands had stopped shaking.

She sat at the kitchen counter the next morning and looked out at the gray garden. Everything appeared wet, as though it had rained the night before. The canvas furniture around the pool was pearly with moisture from the fog, and a snail inched across the patio. She had two days in which to work out all the details.

She was going to shoot him. That would be the most direct, most infallible method. Poisons were tricky and took too long to work; stabbing or a killing blow would require too much physical strength. So. She would shoot him and she would use the gun that Robert had bought when they had moved into the house.

Robert had made a great point of leaving the gun when he had walked out on her, overdramatizing the situation as he overdramatized everything.

"I don't need it," she had said. "I hate guns. More people shoot themselves or their family than intruders do."

Robert distrusted facts. "That makes no sense. It'll make me feel better to know that you and the children are protected."

It had not occurred to her at the time to question why she should give a damn about his feeling good, when he was the one walking out on her.

The gun was in the top drawer of his dresser, hidden under a stack of old shirts he had left behind. She finished her breakfast, dry toast and an apple she had found in the back of the refrigerator, and went upstairs to look at the gun. Robert had called it a detective's special and she had always wondered why. It was one of those things she had meant to ask him but never remembered when she was with him. Yet it stuck in her mind. Was it the sort

83

of gun that detectives used? Or on some sort of special sale, in hope detectives would buy it? She never did find out. All she knew about the gun was that it had cost Robert ninety-eight dollars and was a Colt .38, though she didn't know what that meant either, and it had a two-inch barrel.

She held it in both hands and thought that there was something loathsome about the gun beyond what it was actually capable of doing. The design and construction were basically ugly and obscene. The ice-cold feel to the stubby handle, the concentrated weight of it. Weren't there smaller guns, lighter guns? she had asked Robert. But Robert had carefully researched guns; he knew about guns, he knew what was best. Men took guns so seriously.

She looked at the gun in her hands and found herself smiling. It was a steel phallic symbol, that's what it was. A mechanical penis, and that was what she was going to kill Warren Sullivan with. Sometimes, not often but sometimes, things connected, made sense. She was in charge now, she had power, and it was shaped like a penis.

But was it in working order? She stopped smiling. Firing order was probably the proper term. Robert had bought the gun seven years ago and it had never been fired. Perhaps it needed to be oiled? Checked? Cleaned? Surely guns, like houses and cars and everything else, required maintenance and care. Besides, she had no idea how to shoot the thing. Did one simply pull the trigger or did something have to be done to the gun first? It seemed that in books and on television and in films there was always a click before the shot was actually fired.

She had to be clever about this and not make any mistakes. She had to be sure about the gun. The sensible course of action would be to take the gun to a gunshop and simply say that she was alone and needed the gun for protection and could it please be checked out.

She wrapped the gun carefully in one of her scarves, placed it in her handbag and dressed in what she hoped were the kind of clothes that would leave no impression. She wanted her visit to the gunshop to be as inconspicuous as possible. Gray slacks, a loose beige sweater, flat sandals, and dark glasses that hid her eyes.

In the kitchen she spread out a map of Los Angeles on the counter and then took the Yellow Pages out of a drawer and looked up gunshops. Between "Gums" and "Gutters," under "Guns & Gunsmiths," she read: "We Pay More for Old Guns." "GUNS—BUY—SELL—TRADE. We Buy & Trade Used Guns & Buck Knives." "ANTIQUE & MODERN WEAPONS." "Authorized Police Suppliers." A whole new world. What were buck knives and who were these people who sold and bought and traded guns all over town?

She copied down the addresses of four gunshops nearest her and then tried to locate the addresses on the map. She loved maps. She could study and enjoy them the way other people loved art. Maps told you where you came from, where you were going, possibly who you were. The fact that she had been born and reared next to that gray expanse on the map called Santa Monica Bay, with the mountains and desert to the east, and the freeways, marked in red, twisting and tangling like snakes through Los Angeles, curling up and down the coast, stretching out to the mountains and desert, the entire incredible Southern California geography of mountains and beaches and desert, had shaped her life, influenced who she was and where she was going.

As she marked the addresses of the shops on the map, the telephone rang.

"Mrs. Kirkwood?" Alix recognized the voice immediately.

"Betty Lee, hello. I'm so sorry I missed some of your calls. Mr. Kirkwood called yesterday and said you were trying to get in touch with me again."

"Yes," said Betty Lee, and hesitated.

"Mrs. Lee, I promise to be very cooperative about the house—"

"Ms."

"I beg your pardon?"

"It's not Mrs. It's Ms."

"Oh."

"I am married, but I prefer Ms."

"Oh. All right."

"You were saying?"

"Well, what I was saying is that I am truly sorry about the difficulties you've encountered in trying to reach me. A number of complications occurred during the past week which made my schedule rather difficult to predict."

"I understand, Mrs. Kirkwood. It is a strain to have your home on the market," said Betty Lee. "The reason I'm calling you now is that I have a family here in the office who just arrived in town and they're looking for a home that offers everything your home has—five bedrooms, an ocean view and a pool—and I was wondering if I might show them your home tomorrow."

"Tomorrow? What time?"

"Let's see. We've set up some early-afternoon appointments on the other side of the peninsula. Would five o'clock be too late?"

"Five?" said Alix, trying to think, trying to plan. Five o'clock. Plenty of time. "Five would be fine," Alix said.

She finished marking the location of the gunshops on her map, noted the cross streets for each shop, put the Yellow Pages back in the kitchen drawer.

Aware of the added heaviness in her purse, she pressed the button that automatically swung open the garage door, and got into the Mercedes. She was feeling good, she realized. Calm, organized. There was a sense of direction and purpose to the day.

She backed out of the long driveway, humming and breathing in the soothing impersonal leather smell of the Mercedes. As she waited at the foot of the driveway for a car to pass, she consulted her map again. First stop was Torrance Boulevard.

The sun broke through the fog as she drove inland. Her sweater felt scratchy and uncomfortable and she wished she had worn something lighter. There was a strange, unreal quality to the morning. Strange simply to be out and driving again, as if she had been inside her house for months. And there was an unreal feeling to so much sudden sunshine. She felt like a visitor from another country, as if she had traveled hundreds of miles to arrive at this place where the sun was burning down and bouncing off cars and making colors so bright and vivid that her eyes hurt.

The gunshop on Torrance Boulevard was closed. She felt let down, as though she had known the person who should have been there waiting for her with the shop open, and he hadn't shown up. She looked at the map, spread out on the seat next to her. The next address was Pacific Coast Highway in Lomita, cross street Western Avenue.

It took longer than she had expected. She hated not knowing exactly where she was going, hated having to drive slowly, trying to read street signs and numbers, causing the drivers of cars behind her to become angry and impatient. She rarely drove anywhere that was unfamiliar and new. She had just been in downtown Torrance, seven miles from her house, for the first time in her life. She imagined a map of her familiar routes in Los Angeles. There would be a direct line from her house to the airport, another up the San Diego Freeway with two offshoots— one to Brentwood to her mother's house, and another into Beverly Hills for serious shopping—and fainter lines to various local shopping centers and restaurants. The perimeters of the area. The perimeters of her life.

The gunshop on Pacific Coast Highway was open. A man wearing a denim jacket sat behind the counter on a stool, smoking a cigarette and staring out the window. The first man she had seen since Sunday. The first person she had seen or talked to face-to-face in nearly two days. Again the feeling of having traveled a great distance to arrive at this place.

Silver rings flashed on his fingers in the dim light and through the glass counter filled with guns she could see the boots he was wearing, the leather carved into designs.

Alix cleared her throat. "I've got a problem. . . ." Her voice sounded loud and intrusive in the quiet shop.

"So what else is new?" he said.

For some reason—the guns, the denim and boots and silver Indian jewelry—she had expected a Western accent, Texas or

Oklahoma. This was nasal New York—Brooklyn. What was this man with a Brooklyn accent doing in a gunshop in Lomita, California, surrounded by guns and literature from the American Rifle Association? She felt transfixed by this question. He stared at her; fiftyish, but a hard fifty years. The lines of his face looked etched in.

"What's your problem, lady?" he said.

"I've got this gun . . ."

"Yeah?"

"Yes, and I don't know how to work it. Not that I want to work it, you understand . . ."

"Wait a minute. For openers, you don't *work* a gun. You *fire* a gun."

"Of course. Yes. *Fire* the gun."

"And it's probably not a gun you're talking about, it's probably a revolver."

"Yes. A revolver. Well, my husband is out of town and we have this revolver but I don't know how to use it and I'm scared to death alone and would feel much better if you could just look at the gun, I mean the revolver, and tell me if it's in firing condition."

"Sure."

"Thank you so much." Alix unwrapped the gun from her Hermès scarf, ignoring the way he was looking at her, or the way she thought he was looking at her, and handed it to him.

He opened it and chuckled. "Your husband's weapon?" he asked.

"Yes." What was so damn funny?

"And he left this with you for protection while he's out of town?"

"Yes. That's right. Is there something unusual about it?"

"It's not loaded, lady. No bullets in it. Not too much protection without the bullets."

Goddamn Robert, thought Alix. If it wasn't just like that prick to make a big deal about a fucking gun in the house and then not have the goddamn thing loaded. She could not remember ever

88

being as angry at Robert as she was at that moment.

"Well," she said, "in that case I suppose I'd better buy some bullets." She was so angry and embarrassed she had tears in her eyes.

"If you want to defend yourself you better." He started to laugh and then looked at her and didn't. "I've got a special here," he said, taking a box from the shelf behind the counter. "Eleven ninety-five. That's for fifty."

"*Fifty?*" she said. "Fifty bullets?"

"That's the way they come."

"You mean I can't just buy . . . however many fit into the gun?"

"The *revolver.* Six bullets fit in."

"Well, can't I just buy six?"

He looked as though he were in pain. "Look, lady. I don't make up the rules. These aren't cookies. You don't buy half a dozen. This is the way bullets are sold."

"All right. I'll pay you for the box and just take six."

"But you'll be paying for all the rest. You don't want to throw away forty-four bullets, do you?"

"I'm not throwing them away. I'm giving them back to you."

He made a steeple out of his fingers and stared at it for a few moments, and finally said, "Okay, lady. You're the customer and the customer is always right. I'll sell you six bullets for eleven ninety-five."

"Thank you very much," said Alix. She started to take out her checkbook and then took out her wallet instead. She was blowing this. She didn't want this man to remember her. What an incredibly dumb thing it would be to pay for the bullets with a check; complete with her name, address and telephone number.

He was whistling a tune she couldn't place. She opened her wallet and then noticed the pen and pad of forms he was holding out to her.

"What's that?" she asked.

"You have to sign for them."

"Sign for them?"

"I can't sell you the bullets, lady, until you sign for them. Your

John Hancock right there on the dotted line." He pointed to the line, the silver rings on his fingers shining. "And also I need some ID."

"ID?" repeated Alix.

"Right."

She had to sign for the bullets? She had to show this man her identification? She had never seen this happen on television, had never read about this in a book. People who were going to commit a murder did not show identification when they purchased the bullets for the murder. She felt as though she had been fooled all these years by fictional murderers. All the facts had not been presented.

"Lady, I don't make up these rules." His voice had a distinct pleading note. "I am required by law to have some proof of age or a driver's license. I need your name and address. And I've got to write down the date, the quantity, the manufacturer and the caliber. This is nothing personal. These are just the rules."

"Of course. I understand," said Alix. She gripped the pen tightly and signed her name, then wrote her address on the form and handed him her driver's license.

He copied down her license number and then paused and frowned.

"What's wrong?" she asked.

"Don't know what to put down for quantity. Can't put down six bullets."

"Well, just write fifty or whatever it is I'm paying you for."

"I guess so," he mumbled. "Hate to, though. Feels like I'm lying." He filled in the blank after "Quantity." "Sure you don't want the rest of your bullets?"

"Quite sure, thank you."

He lit another cigarette. "Smoke bother you?"

"No, really. I'm fine."

"My wife wheezes if I light up around her. I have a chair and this rug set up out in the garage. I go out there and smoke. She just can't take it in the house. Keep trying to give it up, but I can't make it any longer than three days. I start getting dizzy. So I figure, what the hell."

"You just sit out there and smoke?" Alix asked.

"Yeah. Sometimes I read the newspaper while I'm smoking. Or a magazine, and drink some beer."

"Don't you get lonely?"

"No. Cold sometimes, but not lonely."

She handed him a twenty-dollar bill to pay for the bullets. He handed her back the change, picked up the gun and said, "I'll take this out in back and check it out for you. Check the operation. See if it needs oil and if the cylinder's clean."

"Thank you," said Alix. She leaned on her elbows and rested on the counter. Stay cool, stay cool, she kept repeating to herself like a little chant.

She was startled by a shot from the back of the shop. That was what the gun would sound like when she shot Warren Sullivan tomorrow night.

A few minutes later the man returned with her gun. "Fires fine," he said. "And I loaded it for you."

"Thank you," said Alix.

"If, God forbid, you ever do fire this thing, be prepared for a recoil."

"Recoil?"

"Yeah. A kick. It'll kick back when you fire it."

"I see." She wrapped up the gun in her scarf again, and then asked suddenly, "It won't go off or anything in my purse, will it?"

"No. No, lady. It won't go off in your purse."

She slung her purse over her shoulder, feeling comfortable with the added weight, as casual as if she were carrying a bag of groceries.

"Oh, one more thing," she said. "If, for instance, an intruder did get into my house and I felt as though my life were in danger, what exactly would I do? I mean, would I just aim and pull the trigger?"

"I hope no one picks your house to rob, lady. Here." He took a gun similar to hers from the glass counter. "You'd be shooting from a distance, right? I mean, the burglar isn't going to be nice and cooperative and stand a foot away so you can get a good shot at him. Most likely he's going to be off in the distance, so if he's off in the distance you're going to have to cock it like this."

"I have to what?"

"You'd have to cock it." He showed her.

"I would have to *cock* it. I see."

She thanked him and walked out of the shop into the sunshine of Lomita. She had to *cock* the gun if she shot at a distance. She was afraid that if she started to laugh about that she might never stop. Cock. She was smiling as she crossed the street to her car.

11

HER MOTHER'S NAVY-BLUE BUICK was parked in the driveway and she could see her mother sitting patiently behind the wheel.

Oh, hell, thought Alix. Not right now. Of all people, not her mother. And sitting there in the car like that, as if she were waiting for Alix to get out of school or something. And why? She never came to visit without calling first.

The children. The children had drowned in Virginia and Judson's pool and her mother had been elected to break the news to her. Or they'd been in an automobile accident. Bitten by rattlesnakes. Kidnaped. Poisoned. Molested. A gas leak had caused Virginia and Judson's house to explode and the children had been burned beyond recognition.

"Hello, dear," her mother said, getting out of the car slowly.

"The children—" said Alix.

"What about the children?" Her mother frowned.

"Are they all right?"

"How on earth would I know? Why wouldn't they be all right?" She was wearing a navy-blue suit and for an instant Alix focused on the fact that her mother matched her Buick.

"Alix, are you watering your lawn enough? See those brown patches? It looks to me like it needs to be fed. Tell your gardener that, or perhaps you ought to look for a new gardener. The fellow you have doesn't appear to have his heart in his work. There's really no excuse for a lawn looking like this when it's being cared for by a professional. Do you still have that odd fellow with the ponytail who looks like a hippie?"

"You didn't hear anything about the children?"

"No, I have not heard anything about the children. Not that I ever do hear anything from them when they're in Phoenix. You'd think that Virginia would have them drop me a postcard. What is wrong with you today?"

"I'm just surprised to see you, that's all," said Alix, as they walked up the steps into the house together.

"I tried to phone you but there was no answer, and I know you get peculiar about the telephone sometimes and won't answer for days, so I thought I'd just go ahead and drive down and see you."

"Were you waiting long?"

"About ten minutes. I read the paper. It was quite pleasant. Were you out shopping?"

"Yes."

"Clothes?"

"Yes," said Alix. "I didn't find anything." She realized this was the second lie she had told today. And she also realized that she had never knowingly told a lie in all her adult life. She was probably, besides her mother, the most honest, law-abiding person she knew.

"Would you like some coffee or tea or anything?" she asked.

"Actually I came down to take you out to lunch—if you don't have other plans." She followed Alix into the kitchen. "You could be friendlier, Alix. You've been so sulky lately. I've left my warm, sunny house to come down here to take you out for a decent meal and you act as though I'm intruding."

"Oh, Mother, I'm sorry. I didn't mean for you to feel that way. Really. I'm glad you came down." Alix slid her purse over her arm and placed it carefully on the kitchen table.

"Good lord," said her mother, staring out at the patio and pool.

"What?"

"It's so dreary and damp here. When did the sun last shine?"

"I don't know. I really don't remember, it's been such a long time," said Alix. She picked up her breakfast dishes, which she had left on the counter, and put them in the dishwasher. "Are you sure you wouldn't like a cup of coffee?"

"Quite sure. Maybe some juice, though." Her mother went to the refrigerator and examined its contents. "I'm worried about you," she said.

"Why?"

"Look at this," said her mother. "One jar of olives, half a bottle of taco sauce, hot dog relish and—what's this?"

Alix looked at the bag her mother was pointing at. "I think it was a hamburger bun." She rinsed out some glasses that were standing in the sink.

"And how old is this?" Her mother carried an opened can of V-8 juice to the sink as though there was the possibility of an explosion and turned it upside down to drain. "You can smell the tin corroding. People can die from old cans, didn't you know that?"

"Not anymore," said Alix. "They've done something to the cans so they can't poison you."

"What?"

"I don't know. Something."

Her mother went back to the refrigerator. "I really can't believe that a daughter of mine would have a vegetable crisper in this condition."

"A what?"

"Your vegetable crisper—"

Alix put the glasses in the dishwasher. "I never heard anybody actually call it that before."

"Just tell me one thing. How long have these cucumbers been in here?"

"I don't know."

"Well, they're oozing. They're all slimy and they're oozing."
Her mother stood up and closed the door to the refrigerator.
"You still have that maid, don't you?"

"Yes."

"Then have her scrub this out next time she comes if you can't
do it yourself. Be sure she uses baking soda."

"Yes, Mother."

"Of course, if it were *my* vegetable crisper, I'd do it myself. I
couldn't bear to think what those cucumbers were doing while I
waited for the maid."

Alix dried her hands on a kitchen towel and picked up her
purse, surprised for an instant at the weight of it. She had a
loaded gun in her purse and her mother was worried about oozing cucumbers. "I'm going up to change for lunch," she said.

"I must say that is an odd outfit you're wearing. I hope you
didn't go to any smart shops looking like that. You look like
you're going bowling."

"No, Mother, I didn't go to any smart shops this morning."

"Why don't you put on that lovely pants suit Lucy sent you last
year? You never wear it and it's so becoming. The color did
wonders for you."

"I gave it away."

"You what?"

"I said I gave Lucy's pants suit away. I gave it to the maid, as
a matter of fact. Mother, it was a hideous shade of blue. Lucy
hated it, too; that's why she sent it to me. She couldn't return it
to Saks because she bought it on sale."

"Waste not, want not," said her mother. "Lucy was only trying
to do you a favor."

"I didn't waste it; I gave it to the maid. And the last time Lucy
did me a favor was about thirty years ago."

"I don't know." Her mother sighed and sat down on a kitchen
stool. "I'm sure it isn't my business, but I don't understand why
everything has to be so difficult between the two of you—so full
of hidden motives and innuendos."

"I don't understand either, but that's the way it is," said Alix. "I'll only be a couple of minutes. Are you comfortable in here or do you want to sit in the living room?"

"I'm fine in here." Her mother studied the row of cookbooks at the end of the counter. "I'm looking for a good recipe for filet of sole. Do you have any?"

"In my recipe file. It's in the cupboard down there."

Upstairs in her bedroom with the door shut, Alix took the revolver from her purse and hid it again in the dresser drawer beneath Robert's old shirts. There was so much to do. She had to get rid of her mother after lunch so there'd be time to get it all done. She needed space and quiet to think everything out. Every detail, every minute of what would happen when Warren Sullivan arrived at eleven o'clock tomorrow night.

She tied a scarf around her head, tucking the ends in turban style, slipped heavy gold hoops into her ears, and dressed in a silk blouse and light wool skirt. When she went downstairs her mother said, "That certainly looks better."

"Thank you. Did you find a recipe?"

"Yes." Her mother put her glasses back on and studied a recipe card. "This one uses tarragon and lime juice. Have you ever tried it?"

"Yes. It's delicious."

"It calls for a quarter of a pound of butter. It isn't too rich, is it?"

"I don't think so."

"May I borrow the recipe card?"

"Of course." Alix looked at the kitchen clock; almost one. Lunch would take at least an hour, probably closer to two hours, which meant it would be after three o'clock before she could start getting organized. Just what exactly had to be organized was still vague in her mind. "Where shall we have lunch?"

Her mother put the recipe card in her purse. "I was thinking of that place right across from the beach with those funny dark windows that you can see out of but can't see in from the street. . . ."

"Frankie's?"

"That's the place. They have marvelous shrimp marinara. They seem to respect the powers of garlic." She straightened her suit jacket. "When did you say your maid comes again?"

"I didn't, but she comes on Saturdays."

"Do you still have the same one? What was her name? The one who chews gum all the time."

"Juanita."

"Yes, that's the one. How do you find these people? Your gardener is the most peculiar fellow I've ever seen. A ponytail on a grown man, for heaven's sake. You seem to have a talent for collecting odd people to work for you."

"As you would say, Mother, you can't tell a book by its cover."

"I've never said that."

"I know."

Her mother frowned. "Sometimes I don't understand you."

"Well," said Alix. "Are you ready to go?"

"Yes. But what I was about to say is be sure and have the maid do this floor on Saturday. I don't mean to give unsolicited advice, but there's nothing like really clean floors when you're trying to sell a house. It's the same with shiny faucets. Be sure and wipe off the faucets with a towel just before people come to look at the house. There's a certain psychological effect to shiny faucets and clean floors."

"Yes, Mother."

In the car, her mother said, "I would never mention any of this if the house weren't up for sale. You know that, don't you? It's none of my business how you run the house, but I realize how important it is for you to sell it."

"Yes." Alix drove along the cliffs toward Redondo Beach. The fog had cleared but gray clouds hung low over the coast.

"Yes, what?" said her mother.

"Yes, I do understand the importance of selling the house."

"Well, I'm glad you finally realize that."

In the restaurant, her mother unwrapped a little cellophane bag and took out a saltine cracker. "It's time for you to move back

98

into town. Start to have fun again. Become involved in things."

"What sort of things exactly?" asked Alix.

"People, Alix, for one. Your own kind of people."

"But who are these people? Why are they my own kind of people?"

Her mother shook her head and sighed.

"Really, Mother. I'm curious."

"You find this amusing, don't you? I don't know what's come over you, but you're behaving very strangely today." Her mother turned her head to study the view. The gray June beach, water, sand, sky; gray all the way north to Malibu. She sat erect with her chin tilted slightly upward. Her hands—the only part of her that had not become padded with extra flesh as she grew older—were beautifully groomed, manicured. Her heavy rings made her fingers look thin and fragile. "I tried. I really did try," she said finally, still looking out at the gray, bleak beach.

"You tried?" said Alix. "Tried what? What are you saying?" She had to start keeping track of what other people said, what they were trying to say under the words. For years she had let other people's words, opinions, implications and conclusions wash over her like water, not paying attention.

"I tried to make you happy," said her mother. "Tried to make things go right for you."

"I know."

"Your father and I only wanted the best for you and Lucy." The heaviness of her mother's face looked soft, quivery, as if she might begin to cry. Alix could see the faint dusting of face powder. No one seemed to use face powder anymore except her mother; just as no one seemed to go to the hairdresser once a week or wear a girdle anymore except her mother.

"Mother, do you ever feel . . ." Alix searched for a way to phrase what she wanted to ask without hurting her mother.

"Feel what?"

A waitress set down a carafe of wine and two glasses on their table. "Are you ready to order now?" she asked.

"Not quite yet," said Alix. When the waitress had cleared the

99

opened cellophane cracker bags, poured the wine and left, Alix said, "Do you ever feel cheated? I mean, your whole life was devoted to Daddy. And now Daddy's gone and . . ." Alix sipped her wine and thought this wasn't coming out the way she had intended. Or maybe it was and she should never have brought it up. "What I'm trying to say is I had this feeling when Daddy died that, well, I had always said yes to Daddy, tried so hard to please him, even shaped my life to please him, but I'm the one who was left with this life. I'm the one who has to live it. And the same thing happened with Robert. I lived to please Robert. I lived where Robert wanted to live, in the house Robert wanted to live in. I did everything for Robert and now he's gone, too, and I'm left with this life that is set up around Robert. I've never had my own life."

Her mother was quiet for a moment, and then said, "I don't see how you can mention your father and Robert in the same breath. There is absolutely no way to compare them."

Alix wanted to say, "You missed the point," but didn't.

"Your father was a good man."

"I know."

"He only wanted the very best in life for you. God only knows what Robert's motives were. But I can tell you this: they were purely selfish. He didn't care what happened to you; your father did. He cared very much."

"I know, Mother," said Alix.

They drank their wine silently and looked out at the beach. How much safer it was to discuss the contents of refrigerators and the condition of floors, thought Alix.

"Mother, do you remember that day when you took Lucy and me out of school and pretended there was a family emergency, but you thought we should play hooky because it was such a beautiful warm February morning and we went to the beach for the whole day?"

"Vaguely."

"Oh, remember, you made us cream cheese sandwiches and you cut off the crusts the same way you did for your own parties, and you had a thermos of lemonade and sugar cookies from the bakery—"

"Chocolate chip."

"What?"

"The cookies were chocolate chip. I remember distinctly. But what is the point?"

"I don't know. I was just thinking about it the other day."

"Well, instead of thinking about what you did in the first grade try thinking about what you're going to do when your house sells. I do think you should come home for a while until you're back on your feet."

"I am on my feet, Mother. You know that? I really am."

"Seeing is believing," she replied.

The waitress returned for their order and her mother ordered shrimp marinara for both of them.

Later that afternoon, after her mother had left, Alix got her period. As she rummaged in the cupboard under the bathroom sink for the box of Tampax, she realized that she had not even considered the possibility of Warren Sullivan's getting her pregnant. What he had done to her had nothing to do with the act that made babies. That was important for her to remember. Whether it was true or not. She tried to think of other acts for which the basic mechanics were identical but the motives were as different, literally, as love and hate. Life and death. She couldn't think of any.

The Tampax hurt as it went in. She made herself think about the gun hidden under the shirts in the dresser. What he had done to her would heal.

No wonder men loved guns so much; if you had a gun you were in control. She had never thought in terms of being in control before, just as she had never thought about power before. It was as if she were learning and thinking in a foreign language. All her life she had had things done to her, said to her, ordered and planned for her. Had she ever planned anything in her whole life?

She changed into jeans and thought about that. Dinner parties.

She had planned dinner parties and children's birthday parties. She could plan and organize magnificent children's parties, no easy feat. She could keep twenty children happy and under control for hours. She imported puppet acts, clown acts, magic shows; and once she had found a pony that gave rides to the children all afternoon. She could always plan exactly how much food would be consumed, and ordered fantastic birthday cakes from the local bakery, Mark or Cindy's name spelled out in frosting, and candy animals or gnomes or baseball players or whatever cavorting through the frosting. It was all a question of paying attention to details and being organized.

She untied her scarf and brushed out her hair in front of the dresser mirror. Murdering Warren Sullivan, and not getting caught, would take paying attention to details and being organized. She began to pace the room. She would shoot him in his car.

To shoot him inside her house would be out of the question. She would have a difficult, if not impossible, time dragging his body out of the house and back into his car. Plus there'd be blood. And clues. What kind of clues were left behind after murders? Fingerprints. She'd have to be careful and consider fingerprints. Though if one didn't have a police record and fingerprints on file, how could the prints be traced? No matter; she must pay attention to fingerprints.

But what was she going to do with his body and his car? If she drove it to some remote area (that was an expression the newspapers always used: "The body was discovered in a remote area of . . ."), how would she get back? How did the murderers of the bodies discovered in remote areas get back into town? She had read about so many murders, both factual and fictional. What had been done with all those bodies? How were they carried around? How do you get rid of a body?

The car was complicating the situation. If she had only his body to worry about it would be much simpler, but on the other hand, if she didn't have his car, how could she move his body? She couldn't have him bleeding all over the Mercedes. He had to be shot in his own car at close range; she couldn't take the chance of missing. But then what?

She paced her bedroom and thought about tomorrow night, Warren Sullivan dead, and herself driving around in his car with his body, wondering what to do. She had to work this out now and not leave anything to chance tomorrow night. She could not afford to panic at the last minute. Where the car would be when she shot him in it seemed less complicated. It would be dark; she could be flexible about the place. But she couldn't be flexible about how to get rid of his body and his car. She paused at her window and looked out. A lone jogger, two teen-age boys riding their bikes, a few cars parked along the road, the occupants out looking at the foggy view from the cliffs.

The cliffs.

Why not the cliffs? And right there in her front yard. It was perfect. The accessibility of the cliffs, which dropped two hundred feet to the rocky narrow strip of beach below, was a subject of public debate. Only fields separated the cliffs from the road. No guardrails, no warning signs; just a field and then a two-hundred-foot drop down to rocks. Suicides went over the cliffs regularly, and teen-agers high on drugs or showing off. So many people went over the cliffs that there was now a charge for the helicopter rescue, if one made it back up alive.

She could drive the car to the edge of the cliffs late tomorrow night. And then what? Could she push it over? If she could get the car within a few feet of the edge of the cliffs, or find a place with a slight downward slope . . .

Her palms were wet. She hated heights. So much so that she could not sit in balconies at theaters, she could not look out of windows in tall buildings or drive over bridges. She could see herself, feel herself, hurtling downward. Could feel the falling in her stomach, imagine the air rushing against her skin, her face tightened, drawn back like a mask, ready to shatter.

Organization and logistics. Details. That was what she had to concentrate on. She took a deep breath.

The most important detail was: could she push a car over the cliffs? She wouldn't have to push it far—just enough to get it rolling. There was only one way to find out.

She backed the Mercedes out of the garage, put it in neutral, left the brake off, got out and walked around behind it. And began to push.

Nothing. There was not the remotest possibility that she could push a car as much as one inch on flat ground.

"You need some help?" She looked up and saw Jim Drew crossing his lawn toward her, wearing a coat and tie. "What's wrong?"

"Well," said Alix, catching her breath from the exertion of pushing, and trying to think of some reason to be out here pushing her car. Jim looked at her, attractive, open, wanting to help in any way he could.

"Jim, it was the strangest thing," said Alix. "I was going to the market and backed the car out of the garage and it just stopped. I mean, it's running but it won't go anywhere, so I thought I'd try and get it back into the garage and wait until morning, then call the service station and have them come tow it."

Jim's eyes narrowed behind his round granny glasses as she explained the problem. She was relieved that alternatives did not occur to him, or if they did, that he was too polite to point them out. He stood with his arms folded across his chest, nodding and studying the car. "Let me give it a try," he said.

He got into the car, glanced at the dashboard and gear shift, and then leaned out and said, "The reason it won't move, Alix, is because you've got it in neutral."

"Well, I know that. I put it in neutral because it wouldn't go anywhere in drive. And then it got stuck."

He shifted to drive, stepped gently on the gas, and the car moved forward. "Hey, it's fine. I've got it going."

"A man's touch," said Alix. "I'm just no good at all with cars. Thanks so much, Jim. I really appreciate it."

He smiled and held the door open for her. "Now you can get to the market," he said.

For an instant she didn't know what he was talking about.

"Yes," she said. She didn't have her purse, though; she couldn't get into the car and drive away without her license. But if she told Jim she didn't have her purse he'd think it was very peculiar that someone was planning to go shopping without her purse. And if she didn't get into the car and drive off he might start to wonder and think about it and realize she had been lying. It would be so like her to botch this all up because Jim Drew wondered why she was trying to push her Mercedes.

"Oh, damn," she said.

"What is it?"

"I forgot my shopping list. I swear, if my head wasn't attached to my body I'd forget it half the time. Listen, Jim, thanks so much for getting the car going again."

"No problem. Want the engine left on while you get your list?"

"I'm not sure where I left the list. Maybe you better turn it off. It might take me a while to find it."

He reached into the car and switched off the ignition. "If you have any more problems with it, just give me a call." He gave the car a pat, as if it were a large animal. "It really is a good car."

She wondered what it was about cars that excited men so much. They seemed able to form emotional attachments to certain cars.

Jim paused, his hand on the rear fender. "Alix, I want to apologize for the other night."

"Apologize? For what?"

"My old college buddy. I don't think he's all that bad, maybe a little pathetic, but Milly was mad and told me I had stuck you with—to quote Milly—a real jerk for the evening."

"Oh, well." Alix smiled at him. "It was just for an evening. Please tell Milly I've been meaning to phone. Her fondue was great."

"I'll tell her," said Jim. "See you soon. And I mean it—if you have any trouble with the car just give me a call."

"I will. Thank you."

Jim headed home across the lawn, home to Milly and his children and his dinner. She always thought of the Drews grouped around their fireplace in an orangy-glowy light, looking just as

8

they did in the photograph on their Christmas cards; never exchanging cruel words, happy and loving, day after day. There had been a time, right after Robert left, when she couldn't bear to drive through her neighborhood and imagine all the happy families inside the houses, loving each other the way people loved each other in the movies.

Alix turned and walked into her motel-like house, thinking she had to be more careful and not risk any more mistakes like the one she had almost made with Jim. Which she had in fact made, but he hadn't realized. She would have to come out again and drive off so if Jim was still outside he wouldn't wonder why she hadn't gone to the market. And she might as well go to the market anyway, because there wasn't any food in the house. She found her purse and went out to the car again.

Jim was turning on the sprinklers and waved to her, then watched as she started up the car. Life goes on, she thought. Laundry, groceries . . . life goes on. More of her mother's philosophy. But in a curious way, life was doing more than going on; it was beginning. Or at least a new phase of it was beginning.

She did not usually enjoy grocery shopping. The decisions, the temperature of the store, the smells, the sounds, the sudden, unprepared encounters with neighbors and friends—all of it upset her. She could never understand how people could make casual small talk in the face of so many decisions. How could one smile and discuss tennis while confronted with the bloody slabs of meat in their neat plastic jackets, all labeled and weighed like so many bright-red corpses, or talk about children and gardens when all those thousands of boxes presented labels to be read, compared, the weights and prices analyzed?

Today, however, it seemed easier. Even fun. She guided the cart up and down the aisles, shopping at random, not caring what she bought as long as it might be useful. She stored up on essentials: coffee, tea, paper napkins and towels, toothpaste, toilet paper, sugar, flour, cans of vegetables. Fresh fruit. She bought chicken breasts and small packages of ground meat. Cheese. A dozen eggs. Cans of frozen orange juice. She would no longer neglect her health and live on Twinkies and old pizzas. No more junk food. She would run a proper house and eat healthful food.

She stopped suddenly in the middle of detergents and paper products. The car. The damn car. She still had to figure out how to get it over the cliff. She moved her cart to the side of the aisle so a woman with three small children could pass her. She took a box of laundry detergent off the shelf. Maybe she could manage it if she could find a spot that sloped down. An incline. She could park the car on the incline, very, very carefully, then put the brake on while she got out. . . . She realized she'd have to go inspect the cliff.

She continued down the aisle, picking up furniture polish, Clorox, a new bottle of Pine-Sol, spray starch and an economy box of Brillo. The more she bought, the safer she felt, the more organized and in control of things.

Her cart was stacked high when she had finished. Waiting in the check-out line, she picked up a magazine and learned how a famous rock star had changed his life with meditation and bean sprouts. How a famous movie star went camping with his wife, six children and three dogs. How a television personality had her breasts lifted after the birth of her last child. She put the magazine back in the rack and watched the checker ring up her groceries.

The total came to $74.96. "Good lord," said Alix, writing out a check.

"Yeah, prices are going up again," said the checker. The checker was wearing a brown wig and a name tag that said, "Hi, I'm Daisy. Have a nice day." She handed Alix a little green card.

"What's this?" Alix asked.

"Bingo," said Daisy.

"Bingo?" $500,000 BINGO, read the card, and then in red letters, HALF MILLION $$.

"The store just started sponsoring a bingo game. Every time you buy something you get a bingo card." She handed Alix a larger card. "Now, this here is the collector card. You see the two little boxes on the bottom of your green card?"

"Yes," said Alix.

"Okay, you tear those off and see if they fit on your collector card. You've got to collect numbers to complete any straight row of four numbers. Okay?"

"Okay," said Alix, confused.

"Now, they're covered with silver stuff, right?"

"Right."

"Well, scratch it off."

"With what?"

"With your *nails*," said Daisy.

A man standing in line behind Alix moved to a different check-out counter. Alix scratched at the silver. Little pieces of it gummed under her nail.

"Very good," said Daisy. "Now, you see the nine squares up above? Scratch the silver off of those, too. Those are your Instant Win squares."

"Look," said Alix, struggling to scratch off the silver. "Is it me or is this a very confusing game?"

"You get the hang of it after a while. A lady won two dollars right here at my check-out counter this morning."

"Can I take it home and do it?"

"Well, of course you can. That's smarter. You can use a spoon or a knife to scrape off the silver stuff," said Daisy.

Alix pushed her cart out to the car and began to load the groceries. All she needed was to find a slope to park his car on at the edge of the cliffs. She'd walk over there this evening before it got dark. Everything was falling into place, working out.

The gun. The car. The cliffs.

Bingo.

12

It was half-past six. There was plenty of time to get to the cliffs before dark. She filled the kitchen cupboards with the groceries she had bought. Ordinarily she hated putting groceries away; it was tedious, boring work. But this evening she felt soothed by the repeated, mechanical motions—reaching into a brown paper bag and taking out a can or a carton and putting it in its proper place.

If she could find a slope far enough from the edge, there was a very good chance she could get the car over.

She threw out an empty cornflakes box, a box of hard, dried-out raisins and a potato that was in the process of changing its appearance with long, white tuberlike strands. She put the slimy cucumbers down the garbage disposal and placed the eggs in the egg basket in the door of the refrigerator. She filled the freezer with orange juice cans and the packages of meat and chicken, made neat stacks of packages of cheese, and then filled cupboards in the laundry room with her new cleaning supplies.

And if she could get the car over the cliff, there would be no way for her to ever be connected with the strange death of Warren Sullivan.

When the kitchen was in order she left the house. It was odd to make direct contact with the roads and fields along the cliffs after years of driving past them. When she was in her car, places seemed to exist on her terms. But outside, they existed on their own terms, became real in a physical way that could not happen when she was safe in the Mercedes. People returning home from work, the evening joggers, a few children on bikes, passed her. There was a different rhythm outdoors.

The field across the street from her house was filled with brown, harsh, pointy weeds, and the ground was hard and cracked from lack of rain. She walked along the street side of the field to a path that led from the street to the cliffs. It was a wide path, wide enough for a car, bare of weeds, yet there was no access from the street unless one drove over the six-inch curb. She studied the curb, trying to be casual. How difficult would it be to drive a car over it? She had occasionally seen cars parked right along the edge of the cliffs, so it couldn't be impossible.

She could hear the familiar, yet at the same time startling, sound of the ocean, the waves beating against the foot of the cliffs. The air smelled green and briny. She walked along the path slowly, noting cracks wide enough to be felt in a car, making them familiar so there would be nothing to surprise her tomorrow night. She kicked a large stone off the path. When the path neared the edge of the cliffs it fanned out, and at one point began a gentle slope downward, dropping sharply after five or six feet. She walked over to the point where the land began to drop and tried to memorize its location. If she could park the car on the slope, get out of the car and release the brake, the car would either begin to roll on its own or would roll with a very slight push.

Hesitantly, she looked over the edge. Two hundred feet below, the surf broke against the rocky shoreline. Her hands were wet. She would not think about the drop; she'd just think step by step what she had to do. She'd keep her mind focused on the moment.

From the time Warren arrived tomorrow night until his car went over the cliff, she would concentrate on what she was doing and not think of what had happened before or what might happen in the future.

She studied the path again, thinking how much simpler this would be if all she had to do was push him over the cliff, not bother with the gun and the car. If this were reversed, if he were going to kill her, he could do it that way. It wasn't fair. But that was what this was all about, wasn't it?

The good guys were going to get the bad guys. It was that simple, that *fair*. She had seen it done a million times. When John Wayne shot some bad guy who had messed around with his woman, the audience cheered. But what if John Wayne wasn't around at the right time; what if his woman shot the bad guy herself? Would that make any difference? She poked around in her mind, searching for holes in the logic of this.

The logic held, made sense. She did not have any choices. It had to be done.

She nudged a stone with her foot. It rolled slowly down the slope, gathering momentum, and then disappeared. The fog sat offshore, gray, heavy and solid, blotting out mountains and lights and sunsets; all the familiar signposts of geography and season.

She could do this. And it was going to work. She realized that the anger had solidified into something as hard and unyielding as a stone. An object, not an emotion. An object that she was in control of.

She put eggs on to boil for supper, took a can of orange juice from the freezer and tried to open it, but the pronged wheel of the can opener jammed and then spun without cutting the top of the can. "Oh, hell," said Alix, and opened the can with a bottle opener. She cut her finger as she pried back the jagged edges of the can, and held her finger under cold water. How easily and unexpectedly things could get screwed up. Marriages, orange juice cans. She didn't want anything to get screwed up tomorrow. As she looked at her finger and the tiny trickle of blood, a new problem occurred to her. One that she didn't like to think about.

What exactly was going to happen to Warren Sullivan when she shot him? She wanted to be prepared. Would the bullet go in neatly or would there be—she closed her eyes for a moment— would there be a mess? Would there be more than just blood? Would she be shooting him at such close range that he might splatter? Dear God, she thought. She had to find out. She had to know exactly what was going to happen so she'd be prepared. So nothing would rattle her suddenly.

She forgot about her cut finger and the orange juice and tried to think of a way to find out what a Colt .38 revolver would do at close range to Warren Sullivan. (And *where* to shoot him? What exact spot on his body? His chest? Neck? Head? Oh, God, could she do that?) There would be no gunshops open at this hour. She couldn't call anyone she knew. Could she call the police? Not give her name, simply say that she had a Colt .38 for protection and she'd appreciate information on its use? Ask what would happen to an intruder if she shot him at close range? And then two days later have the police discover a body at the foot of the cliffs shot by a Colt .38? No. She could not ask the police. She would have to wait until tomorrow morning and call a gunshop. Preferably one in another area. She certainly couldn't call the shop in Lomita. But how would she get the name and a number for gunshops outside Los Angeles?

She felt overwhelmed by details. There was still so much to do.

A solution for finding the number of a faraway gunshop suddenly came to her. The library had telephone books for all California, for major cities all over the world, as a matter of fact.

It was almost eight o'clock. The library stayed open until nine. She could go to the library right now, look up the phone numbers, and then call first thing in the morning. To be absolutely safe, she would call from a pay phone so the call would not appear on her telephone bill.

Driving to the library a few minutes later, she thought of another problem she had not yet solved. How was she going to get Warren into his car with her along? Perhaps she could simply say she wanted to go for a drive, and then get him to park somewhere. Before she shot him she would have to get him to kiss her. The thought of it made her feel ill for a moment.

And where were they going to park? This seemed less urgent, more open to improvisation. The gun would make a noise, but how loud a noise? People were always mistaking gunfire for cars backfiring and vice versa. It was mentioned all the time in the newspaper.

Terraced steps led up to the library; at one level a fountain full of goldfish splashed in the still night air. Alix parked and locked the car at the foot of the steps. This was one of her favorite places to go with the children. They'd buy ice cream cones at the plaza just down the hill and then sit by the fountain eating the cones and watching the fish. The children. She didn't want to think about the children until this was over. The children were part of another world. She would do what Robert had such a talent for doing: she'd compartmentalize her life. She'd juggle.

She smiled at the librarian and went to the shelves of out-of-town telephone books. San Francisco sounded far enough away yet wouldn't require too much change to call from a phone booth. She copied down the numbers of six gunshops, wanting to make sure there would be at least one open tomorrow morning.

The card catalogue stood next to the phone books. Why not look up guns here? she thought.

"May I help you with something?" the librarian said from her desk.

"No, thank you. I can find it," she said, and turned so that her back was between the librarian and the drawer she pulled out of the card catalogue.

R for revolver, found between "Revolutionists, Russian" and "Rewards (Prizes, etc.)." She wrote down the number—623.443 —replaced the catalogue drawer, smiled at the librarian, who said, "Let me know if I can help you," and casually and slowly wandered through the aisles of books until she reached the 600 section.

A man wearing a blue blazer with gold buttons was kneeling down by the bottom row of books, his head tilted to the right as he read titles off the book jackets.

"Excuse me," said Alix.

He stood up and rubbed his neck. "They should print the titles straight across," he said.

"I beg your pardon?" said Alix.

"You get a crink in your neck reading the titles," he said.

"Oh," said Alix. "Yes."

"You wouldn't happen to know where cookbooks are?" he asked. "I need a wok cookbook."

"No, I'm sorry. There's a card catalogue to the left of the librarian's desk, though. You can look it up there."

"Of course," he said. "Thank you. Thank you so much."

"You're welcome," said Alix.

623.443.

The Story of Colt's Revolver. She took it down from the shelf and carried it to a table. There was everything about a Colt revolver except how to shoot it and what happened when you did shoot it. Sketches of old guns, patent notices. She put it back on the shelf. *The World's Great Guns, Antique Weapons for Pleasure and Profit, The Gun That Won the West.* Nothing. She went back to the card catalogue. *Guns & How to Use Them—Safely, Legally, Responsibly:* 799.31.

"If you're having any problems let me know and perhaps I can be of help," said the librarian. A slow Tuesday night at the library.

"Thank you," said Alix. She excused herself past the man looking for wok cookbooks and hurried down the aisle to the 700 section. *Guns & How to Use Them* and various other books on big-game hunting were found nestled between *Trout Magic* and *Chinese Theories of Literature.* She took the book back to the table.

Pistols, revolvers, derringers. Dear God, she had not had any idea how confusing all this would be. She studied sketches of basic positions for handgun shooters. Two-hand standing, standing, seated and kneeling. She'd be sitting; she'd use two hands.

Sections on loading the pistol. It was already loaded; she didn't have to worry about that. On the Pistol Range. Selecting a Pistol. Rifles. Sketches of deer and tigers with dots for proper targets. "Browning Arms shows where to hit 'em if you want to down 'em." She was developing a thorough dislike of gun lovers. Personal Safety. "There are things that you can do to keep you a healthy, happy shooter." *But what happens afterward?*

She put the book back, smiled at the librarian and left. She'd have to call a gunshop in San Francisco in the morning.

13

THE NEXT MORNING the fog was so thick that she could not see the road from the house. It misted in from the ocean, cold and white as smoke off dry ice. The foghorn was bleating out over the water like something that was lost and looking for home. It was as if the other houses in the neighborhood had disappeared during the night and the ocean had been misplaced.

Alix went downstairs in her robe, put a kettle of water on to boil for instant coffee, and turned on the heat to take off the morning chill and to keep the dampness from turning to mildew. Everything she touched was limp and cold from the fog. Towels hadn't dried completely on the towel racks; everything was turning old and musty. Even her robe felt damp this morning.

While the water heated for coffee, she collected the morning paper from the foot of the driveway, struggled with the string it was tied with, finally slipped it off, and in the kitchen spread the paper on the counter. She fixed her mug of coffee and sat on a stool and began to read. She had two hours before any gunshops might open in San Francisco. And two hours before the bank would open. She would have to go to the bank to get enough change to make the call from a pay booth.

She ignored the headlines, as she always did. World events were becoming more and more incomprehensible to her. Since she was no longer looking for ideas for Robert to use, she read the paper for messages from outside her perimeters. How were people managing? How were they coping with life? She read between the lines for survival tactics.

She always paid attention to "Dear Abby." Sometimes she would become so involved with the column that when Abby wrote back to a reader, "Let me know what happens, dear. I care," tears would come to Alix's eyes. She also read "Newsmakers" on the second page, letters to the editor, op ed essays, personals in the classified ad section and the weather map.

She finished her coffee, fixed herself a second cup and ate a hard-boiled egg. A headline stood out on the third page. HANGED MAN SLOWS FREEWAY RUSH. She read carefully. The man had hanged himself next to the Santa Ana Freeway with a brand-new rope, and slowed rush-hour traffic practically to a standstill, resulting in one of the largest traffic jams of recent memory. Why was the brand-new rope mentioned? Was it important in some way that was not immediately obvious? Perhaps a reporter was trying to fill out a story that had nothing more to say than that a hanged man created a traffic jam. Or was the new rope some sort of clue as to why the man had committed suicide in this public fashion? Perhaps he had simply used a new rope because he didn't have any old rope to use. She thought of people all over Los Angeles who had sold rope recently and how they would feel reading about the man found by the side of the freeway.

On page five: A woman in Texas was sitting in her bedroom, talking on the telephone to her relatives in Sweden, when a twin-engine private plane crashed into one corner of her two-story house, the corner in which her bedroom was located, and burst into flame, killing her. The house was filled with friends and relatives celebrating the woman's newly acquired American citizenship; all of whom escaped injury. A sister told police that when she entered the bedroom her sister's hair was on fire and she was trying to say something.

Alix read the article over and over, trying to imagine the series of events, a series of split seconds, that had placed the woman at that telephone at the exact moment of the crash. If her relatives' line had been busy, perhaps she would have returned to the living room. If a clerk somewhere had made a small clerical error and her citizenship papers had not come through . . . Or did the series of split seconds start earlier, years and years earlier? And what of the split seconds that caused the pilot of the plane to be flying at that moment, crash at that spot?

And what was she trying to say as her hair burned?

Alix turned to the weather map. Unlike life, there were certain conditions for weather. Disasters could be predicted, determined by geography and season. The weather map always had a very soothing effect on her. The temperature in Richmond, Virginia, was 78. It was 67 in Buffalo, New York. She read the temperatures and precipitation for every major city in the United States. For foreign cities. For Pan American stations (Mazatlán, high 90, low 77, no precipitation). Her bones ached for sun. If only the sun would come out soon.

The foghorn cried.

Cars in the distance made muffled whooshing sounds, as if driving through snow.

It was almost nine o'clock. One hour until the bank and the gunshops in San Francisco opened. She remembered that Betty Lee was bringing people to look at the house later that afternoon and began to tidy the kitchen. Then went upstairs and did the same to her bedroom and bath, and got dressed in a pair of old jeans and a sweat shirt.

It was a quarter to ten. She decided to walk to the bank, which was located in a small group of stores about half a mile from her house. There were no sidewalks and she was careful to stay clear to the side of the road. The visibility was equal to that of a snowstorm.

At the bank she cashed a check for twenty-five dollars and asked for five dollars in change.

The teller yawned. "Are you Xeroxing?" she asked.

"What?"

"I asked you if you're Xeroxing something, because if you're Xeroxing you'll want dimes and I'll give you a roll of dimes."

"No, I'm not Xeroxing."

The teller counted out two ten-dollar bills. "How do you want your change, then?"

"Oh, some quarters and dimes."

"How many?"

"Five dollars' worth."

"No, I mean how many quarters do you want and how many dimes do you want?"

"Oh, about six quarters and . . ." Alix tried to think. "The rest in dimes would be fine."

She filled an inside pouch in her purse with the dimes and quarters, and crossed the street to the gas station, which had a pay phone. She closed the door of the glass booth and dialed the first number on her list.

"Please deposit one dollar and sixty cents for the first three minutes," said the operator. Alix dropped the dimes and quarters into the telephone.

After five rings someone answered. "Hal's Corral. Hal here."

"Hello. My name is Mrs. Brown and I was wondering if you might answer some questions for me."

"Sure. Shoot." Hal started to laugh. "Get it?"

"Get what?" said Alix.

"Nothing. Just a joke. What are your questions?"

"I've recently acquired a Colt .38 and I was wondering if you could tell me, in the event I ever had to use it for self-protection, exactly what to aim for."

"Aim for whatever you're shooting at." Hal laughed again. A hundred gunshops in San Francisco and she had to call the one run by a comedian.

"I mean, if an intruder were within close distance, say for instance I woke up and he was right there in my bedroom, really close, and I only had one chance to shoot him, where should I aim?"

"At his heart if he's facing you. If he's turned to the side, about six inches below his armpit. Get him in that area close up with a .38 and you won't have to worry."

"One more thing," said Alix. "I know it's silly and I don't mean to be squeamish, but could you tell me what would happen. Would there be a lot of blood or . . ." She let the "or" hang in the air.

"Blood. You can't blow him into bits with a .38, if that's what you're worried about."

"Thank you, Hal," said Alix. "Thank you very much."

She got back home before eleven, feeling as though she had accomplished a great deal that morning. She could relax for the rest of the day and have time to go over every inch of her plan in her mind.

She felt such restless energy, though, that she was unable to sit still. She dusted the downstairs, the living room and the dining room. She changed the towels in all the bathrooms. She scrubbed the kitchen counters and arranged the spices in alphabetical order.

Just before noon the telephone rang.

"Alix?" His voice was uncertain, hesitant. "This is Warren."

"Yes."

"Something's come up for tonight. I have to work."

A pause. She could hear the humming of the telephone wires.

"But I'm down your way now—about ten minutes from you— and . . ."

"Yes?"

"How about if I drop over right now? Instead of tonight."

"Now?"

"Yes."

Now. She had to think. To clear everything from her mind and concentrate on this. *Now.* There was no reason it couldn't be now. The only change in plans would be not getting rid of his body and the car immediately after she shot him. She would bring his body home and hide the car in the garage until late tonight, when she could drive it to the cliffs. The heavy fog right now would act as darkness. She would have to think of a secluded spot. She felt her mind racing, alive and confident.

"Now would be fine, Warren," she said. "Perhaps we could go out to lunch?"

"Sure. I don't have much time, but . . ."

She noticed he was having trouble finishing his sentences. She waited.

"Half an hour?" he said finally. "Could you be ready in half an hour?"

"I'll be ready," she said, and hung up. Lunch. It was perfect. She would be in his car with him. If she stayed calm she could improvise. The trick was staying calm, open to chance and improvisation. She knew the gun and what it would do. She knew the cliffs, and had paid attention to detail. Everything would be fine. From now on play it by ear.

She changed her clothes quickly. Good jeans and a jersey turtleneck sweater. Her hair loose and the heavy gold earrings. She put on eye shadow and mascara. She went to the john, washed her hands and straightened the towels. She put the gun in her purse and went downstairs.

He was a few minutes early. The fog was still so thick that she didn't see his car until it was halfway up the driveway. He was driving a red Toyota.

She was smiling when she opened the front door; a distant smile, in control.

He was trying to keep his face expressionless, trying to be cool, not knowing what was expected of him, which gave an edge of rudeness to his voice. "I don't have much time . . ." he said, another of his open-ended sentences.

"You don't have much time?" Alix repeated, closing the front door behind her and walking down the steps, which were glossy with moisture. "You do have time for lunch, don't you? I mean, you do eat lunch?"

"Yes," he said. His confusion made him sullen. Like someone who didn't know the rules very well and refused to play. He

9

hesitated by the front of the car. Alix walked briskly past him and opened the car door herself. He hurried to the driver's side, his indecision about opening her door settled for him.

As he started the engine, Alix wondered over the fact that he was hung up on token acts of chivalry. Wasn't he aware of the joke?

He was wearing a beige leisure suit. The back seat was filled with folders and papers, the paraphernalia of an insurance salesman. A traveling salesman. The car smelled of constant smoking with the windows shut.

"Wait a minute," said Alix. "I forgot something." She got out and opened the garage door with a key on her key chain.

"What did you do that for?" Warren asked when she got back into the car.

"My gardener comes today. I have to leave the door open so he can get to the gardening tools."

"Your gardener," repeated Warren, with the built-in smirk to his voice.

Alix slipped her hand into her purse and ran her finger along the ice-cold barrel of the gun. "That's right. My gardener."

He lit a cigarette and flicked on the radio to a rock station. "Where to?"

She was staring at his profile. What she was about to do was so easy. The line so thin. Like the line between being sane and keening in public at airline terminals. How fragile life was. She would simply lift a small object from her purse, make a motion with her index finger, and he would be dead. Ended. Gone.

"Well?" He turned and looked at her.

"Well, what?"

"You said you wanted to go to lunch," he said.

She liked this moment. She liked the feeling of control, of power. Power was peaceful, quiet, even tranquil. A kind of high.

"Yes," she said. "I wanted to go to lunch."

He backed the car down the driveway, cautiously, with the car lights bouncing flat against the fog. "Where?" he asked at the foot of the driveway.

Where? The houses on either side of her own were hidden by fog. Milly was at work, her children at day camp. The couple who owned the house on the other side had moved in just a few months ago and she didn't know them or their schedule.

The thickness and silence of the fog made her feel that she and Warren Sullivan were the only two people left on earth. There was the same hushed, wrapped-up feeling one had in heavy snow. Anything that happened wouldn't be quite real.

Where?

"Before we go to lunch . . ." Alix began to say slowly.

"Yes?"

"Can we talk?" She smiled. "Alone?"

"Where?" He looked uneasy, not quite comprehending. And then his face changed. "Yeah," he said.

She looked out the window, unable to look at him. His face revolted her: heavy, self-indulgent. Slack.

"What's wrong with right here? Your house?" he said.

"The gardener. Neighbors. Phone rings all the time." She thought hard. "Listen, let's drive down to the beach. There's a cove about five miles from here. No one goes there when the weather is bad."

"The beach?" he said.

"It's very private, Warren. No one will be there."

"Anything you say." He pulled out of the driveway onto the road and proceeded cautiously through the fog. Twenty miles an hour.

"Good thing there aren't any traffic lights," he said.

"Why?"

"You couldn't see them in this fog."

"That's true."

What if there was someone at the beach? Then what? She could hear her mother: Don't cross your bridges until you come to them.

"You'll have to let me know where the stop signs are," said Warren.

Alix thought of the Swedish woman in Texas sitting on her

bed, talking to her family in Sweden, not knowing that in minutes her hair would be on fire. Just sitting there chatting, telling them good news, happy little details of her new life in Texas—maybe what her house looked like or the view from her kitchen window, what the children were doing. Maybe she was just telling them that she loved and missed them. And all the while that airplane was zeroing in on her house, about to set her hair on fire.

"Don't worry about the stop signs," she said.

The cove had once been a private beach club. A narrow dirt road, precarious even in good weather, treacherous in the fog, curved down to the little beach. He parked in the empty parking lot. Occasionally the deserted clubhouse could be seen through the fog. Empty life guard stations. Picnic benches. And above the parking lot, handball courts. Everything empty, deserted.

"About the other night," Warren started to say. The radio was playing something tinny by Elton John. The foghorn made its lonely lost sound, keening out over the ocean. The surf washed against the narrow beach. The clock on the dashboard ticked.

"Yes?" said Alix, looking at him.

He lowered his eyes and drummed his fingers on the steering wheel. "Well . . ."

"What about the other night?" she said.

Something in her voice startled him, put him on the defensive. He shrugged. "Nothing. Just that . . ."

"Just that *what?*"

He smiled. "You wanted it."

Fury flooded her body with adrenaline. And at the same time something cool and sane inside her head told her that if she gave in to temper she would ruin everything. All the careful planning and paying attention to detail would have been for nothing; she would lose control. She could not let him know about the gun. He would get it away from her, maybe even shoot her. The fact was he was physically stronger than she was.

"Yes," she said, letting the word out with difficulty.

He relaxed. He pulled her toward him. "That's what you want, isn't it?" He pushed her hand down to his lap. His voice was thick.

"That's what you want." He was swelling down there like a toad. She kept that image in her mind. A toad. She didn't want to be sick. She pretended to feel around for the zipper of his fly. With her other hand, her right hand, she reached into her purse. His breathing was heavy. She let him kiss her. His eyes were closed.

The shot was so loud she thought her ears would burst; the recoil threw her back against the car door.

For an instant everything was obliterated by the ringing in her ears and then she saw all the blood. Warren's eyes were still open, staring speechless and disbelieving at her. He slumped forward against her; the stain seeping through his jacket grew larger. There was blood on the car door behind him. She could not take her eyes off all the blood. It was real, not television blood. Warren Sullivan was gone. Over. Yet all this blood was spilling, pouring out, making a mess. And he was still so warm. She tried to move backward and felt behind her for the door handle. She had to get away from the blood. There was so much of it. And it was warm and thick, darker than she had expected. But of course, she hadn't expected all this blood. Maybe she could just leave him here. She could walk home. That's what she would do. It would make everything so much easier, less complicated. Then she looked down at herself. Blood was splashed across the front of her jersey sweater and blood was staining her jeans. She couldn't walk home, all those miles, covered with blood. How could she explain such a large amount of blood? Blood was smeared on her hands like red paint. Her ears were still ringing. She had to get the car and Warren's body out of here. Didn't she leave the garage door open so that she could drive the car in quickly and not be seen in case any of the neighbors were home? That was part of the plan, part of her ability to plan and to be in control of details. Everything would be fine if she just didn't get rattled by all the blood. If she could stay calm. She pushed the door handle down and felt the door open and as she moved backward the upper portion of Warren's body sprawled across the seat. She went around to the other side of the car and tried to push his body across the seat. Dead weight. Her hands slipped in the blood covering his back. Half pushing, half rolling him, she got his legs into a partial jackknife position, his shoes dragging on the floor. His face was turning a horrible shade of white and his eyes were open and staring at the dashboard. She realized the radio was still on and turned it off. If only his eyes weren't open. She could manage all the blood but she wasn't sure she could get home with Warren staring at the dashboard like that. A thin stream of watery blood drooled out of one side of his mouth. She tried to push him down lower in the seat so that he wouldn't be seen if a car pulled up next to them on the way home. Blood was dripping everywhere. She hadn't counted on there being so much blood, so much noise.

She stared at his feet. His pant legs had been shoved up, to expose very thin brown socks and tan oxfords. He was lying almost face down now, as if he were crouching in an awkward way, hiding from someone. The red stain, like something with a life of its own, spread out around him, looking black on the upholstery of the car.

The gun was on the floor. She hadn't considered the gun. What was she going to do with the damn gun? Leave it in the car? Throw it in the ocean? It would be found in the car. And it might be found if she threw it in the ocean. The safest place to hide it was in its original hiding place. Under Robert's old shirts in the dresser drawer. She picked up the gun and put it back in her purse.

Start the car. Get out of here. Then suddenly panic so strong that for a moment she couldn't see: the dashboard, the steering wheel, melting like a Dali painting. She reached out her hands, forced her eyes to focus.

Thank God. Yes.

The car was an automatic shift.

14

IN THE GARAGE, she opened the trunk of the Mercedes and took out a plaid beach blanket which smelled faintly of mildew and was still gritty with last summer's sand. She then carefully tucked the blanket over and around Warren Sullivan. He looked like a large, lumpy package.

She pressed the button next to the door leading into the house, which automatically closed and locked the garage door. In the laundry room, she stripped down to her underwear. She put her jeans and sweater into the washing machine, added detergent, and turned both wash and rinse temperature dials to cold. (Somewhere in the back of her mind her mother saying: Soak bloodstains immediately in cold water. That was her mother's reaction to her first period. Her coming of age reduced to a laundry problem.) She wrapped her sandals in the morning paper, placed the package in paper bags and put it in the trash container under the sink in the kitchen.

Upstairs, she removed the gun from her purse and returned it to the dresser drawer. She took a shower and washed her hair, watching the water run pale pink and then clear. She had to move, had to keep busy, couldn't sit and think now. This morning she'd had all that nervous energy to get rid of, but now doing something, keeping in motion, was vital. Crucial. There were at least ten hours before she could get his body out of the garage. Ten hours. She had to move. Do something. Not think.

She combed out her wet hair and pinned it into a knot on top of her head. From her bottom drawer, lost under summer shorts and halters, she found her ballet slippers and leotard. She put on the slippers and the leotard and went downstairs and turned on the stereo.

Coppelia. The music filled the spaces of the house. The valse, the mazurka—cymbals reminding Alix of thousands of little bells jangling, ringing, celebrating. Disconnected by the music, she swayed and dipped and stretched and jumped; lighter than air, she danced the downstairs of her house, her energy limitless, feeling as though she could (if she wished, if she really needed to) fly. Nothing was impossible when music filled her head like this and her body responded without need of thought. A direct link from the music to her body. Ordinary processes and routes of everyday life were skimmed over, flown over—unnecessary. Rendered meaningless by so much joy. Direct, undiluted by words. Drum rolls. Cymbals. Horns. And then, delicate as crystal, her bones precious and light and sure, following flutes, violins, small tunes tucked away like secrets. A long, sweet stretch of sound.

The telephone shrilled into the music.

The Gypsy swirls of mad music now.

The phone rang again and again. Flat, insistent.

She lowered the volume on the stereo and went to answer the telephone. She was beginning to hate the telephone. Hated the incredible rudeness of the thing. Its insistence and intrusiveness. Maybe she'd have it removed. Where was it written that one must have a telephone?

But it was here and ringing. She picked up the receiver.

"I'm going bananas." BK's voice, calm and hysterical all at

once. "Alix, this weather. Everywhere I look it's gray. Even Sidney looked gray at breakfast this morning. Why are you so out of breath?"

"I've been dancing."

"Dancing? What do you mean, you've been dancing?"

"To *Coppelia.*"

A pause, and then BK said, "Oh."

Another pause, which lingered into silence. There was nothing to fill it with. Alix had nothing to say. What was there to say? Hey, BK, there's a body in my garage. The body seemed as unreal to her as BK's voice traveling through air and somehow coming out of the receiver she held in her hand. *Coppelia* played on in the background.

"Alix?" said BK.

"Yes. I'm here."

"You're over there all alone and dancing?"

"Yes."

"Dancing?"

"I'm thinking of taking ballet lessons again. You know, for exercise."

"Well, I'm thinking of going back to my shrink. I met a lady at macramé class this morning who said she had put her house up for sale yesterday because of the fog. Didn't even tell her husband what she was going to do. She said she had three children home with sore throats and the dog had ear mites and had to have drops put in his ears twice a day and she thought that maybe a complete change would help her avoid a nervous breakdown. But I suppose dancing is as good a solution as any. What are you up to later?"

"Later?"

"This evening. How about having supper together? Sidney just left on a trip."

Ten hours. How long had she been dancing? Thirty minutes? Nine and a half hours left. Nine and a half hours to fill.

"We could go to the Red Onion," BK was saying. "Margaritas and tostadas. Early. I'm starving."

"Some people are coming to look at the house at five—"

"Well, you don't have to be there, do you?"

"There's no lockbox. I've got to let them in," said Alix. And not let them out of her sight. Not for a minute. Find a way to keep them out of the garage. "How about six-thirty? Would six-thirty be too late?"

"Fine. I'll drive."

Betty Lee's polyester pants suit was pale yellow today. She wore a complete pair of earrings (had she ever found the missing pearl earring?), tiny gold balls suspended from thin wire; they moved and bobbed even when she was still. Just breathing must make them bob like that, thought Alix.

The people she was showing the house to were in their early or mid fifties and looked anxious. And there were children. Huge, sullen children who looked as if they would rather be somewhere else.

"Mrs. Kirkwood, I'd like you to meet the Shoemakers, and their children, Ron and . . ."

"Jennifer," said Mrs. Shoemaker in an absent sort of way, her eyes already darting ahead as if mentally positioning tables and chairs and sofa.

Alix was surprised there were only two children. They were so large it seemed as though there were more of them. Mr. Shoemaker kept frowning and nodding no matter what was being said, jangling the change in his pocket.

Betty Lee was discussing the view that no one could see. Mrs. Shoemaker said, "Schools!" in a high and sudden voice.

They all looked at her.

"Schools," she repeated, more softly this time. "Are they good? Are they far?"

"The high school is a few blocks away," said Betty Lee.

"And it's a good school?"

"Excellent. One of the very best. Scholastically it ranks with Beverly Hills High, plus which it has a spectacular view of the coastline."

"Oh, we've looked at so many houses," said Mrs. Shoemaker,

"so many, many houses. I'm exhausted." Even her clothes seemed to droop, and her hair had gone lank and thin in the damp air.

"We're from Ohio," said Mr. Shoemaker, frowning.

"Oh?" said Alix.

"Cleveland," he said.

"Shaker Heights," said Mrs. Shoemaker.

"Can Jenny and me wait in the car?" asked their son, looking at his feet.

"We are b-o-r-e-d," said his sister, for some reason spelling out the word.

"I," said Mrs. Shoemaker. "*May* Jenny and *I* wait in the car?"

"May we?"

"Ask your father."

Mr. Shoemaker cleared his throat. "I thought you wanted to make sure that there would be a place for your workshop." And then to Alix: "He makes ship models."

"You know the kind that come in tiny pieces in kits? That take about a year to glue together?" said Mrs. Shoemaker. "Well, Ron makes them in weeks. Literally weeks. He just built the— What was it, Ron? The one with all the sails and itty-bitty ropes?"

"The *Cutty Sark*," said Ron, backing out the front door with his sister.

"But that's all he does," said Mr. Shoemaker. "Just works on his ship models. No homework or anything; just ship models."

"I've never figured out how to dust them," said Mrs. Shoemaker.

"Well!" said Betty Lee. "Since we're right here in the hallway, why don't I show you this closet, which is huge, all kinds of possibilities. Perhaps it would do for Ron's workshop. There's an overhead light, shelves, loads of space."

Mrs. Shoemaker peered into the closet. "Oh, I don't know. Phil?" she said, looking back at her husband. "Would you want him right here, right in the middle of the house?"

"Well," said Mr. Shoemaker, "if he had his radio on in there I don't think we could stand it."

"Oh, there are so many places for a workshop in this house!

So many possibilities. Isn't that right, Mrs. Kirkwood?"

"Yes." The word sounded odd. As if someone else had said it. "Please don't let us keep you."

"That's all right," said Alix, concentrating on each word, trying to make each word clear and logical. Damn it, what she should have done was postponed having the Shoemakers look at the house; not allowed Betty Lee to show the house at this time. It was awkward. She settled on the word "awkward" with a certain satisfaction. This was not a dangerous situation, she decided; it was merely awkward.

"Well, then. Let's go into the living room." Betty Lee had perfect posture and the habit of walking directly to the center of each room she was showing, like a general conquering a miniature country. Alix trailed after them. Her home was immaculate. Her carpets plush and spotless. The motel-like aching emptiness was, in fact, spaciousness. The wallpaper showed taste. She had to keep them out of the garage. She had to improvise. This was an awkward situation.

"And when you have teen-agers there's nothing like having your own pool." Betty Lee flicked on the pool lights from the kitchen and led the Shoemakers outside. Alix tagged along behind. "And a Jacuzzi!"

"And a Jacuzzi?" said Mr. Shoemaker. He looked startled. "What is a Jacuzzi?"

"A Jacuzzi is your very own spa, Mr. Shoemaker. Here, let me show you. Six jets circulate the water for you and you can heat the temperature to over one hundred degrees and all you have to do is just sit there and let the water do the swimming for you. You and Mrs. Shoemaker can have cocktails right out here sitting in your Jacuzzi."

The Shoemakers stared at her.

"I don't think anyone in Shaker Heights has a Jacuzzi," said Mrs. Shoemaker after a moment. "Phil, have you heard of anyone back home who has a Jacuzzi?"

"No. Not in their backyard. Maybe at their club. But not in their backyard."

They both stood staring down at the swirling water, the lights glowing the water blue. There was a slight trace of a smile around the corners of Mrs. Shoemaker's mouth.

"And trees?" asked Mr. Shoemaker. "The trees over there. May I ask what they are?"

"There are two lemon trees, a nectarine tree and an apricot tree, which only produced seven apricots last summer," said Alix.

"All it needs is a little fertilizer," said Betty Lee.

"And the hedge on the other side of the pool," said Alix, "is called mock orange. It has a lovely smell."

Mr. Shoemaker nodded and smiled. "Thank you."

They went back to the house. "Everything is so different out here," Mrs. Shoemaker was saying to Alix. "It's really quite exotic. I mean, a Jacuzzi. Imagine! It sounds like something that Playboy bunny fellow would have in his house. When Phil told me he was going to have to come out here and run the L.A. office I just about fainted. Us in California? We never dreamed we'd leave Shaker Heights, but now that Daddy's gone . . ." She straightened her shoulders and tucked a strand of hair behind one ear. "And Mother's been gone ten years next September, so there really wasn't that much to keep us in Shaker Heights. Just friends and the house." Her voice faltered.

In the kitchen Betty Lee was showing Mr. Shoemaker the double ovens.

"It's going to be so hard to leave my house," said Mrs. Shoemaker, lingering on the patio with Alix. "We moved in when we were married and since then we built on a little den out back and an extra bedroom and bath for Phil's mother when she comes up from Florida to spend the summers with us. I've lived in just two houses all my life. First Daddy's and then the one Phil bought right after we were married, the one we're in now. I just never dreamed we'd move. And to California of all places."

"You'll like California," said Alix. "You'll get used to it and it won't seem so exotic after a while."

Mrs. Shoemaker smiled. "I'm sure you're right. And I'm sorry; didn't mean to talk your ear off."

They walked through the open sliding glass door into the kitchen, and Betty Lee suddenly snapped her fingers and said, "How many cars do you have, Mr. Shoemaker?"

"Two."

"Well, there's your workshop!" she said. "There's a three-car garage, so the extra garage space would be ideal for your son's workshop. You wouldn't even hear his radio if he worked out there." She beamed at the Shoemakers. "Right this way!"

"I've done the dumbest thing, I'm afraid," Alix said, her voice loud and unnatural.

The Shoemakers and Betty Lee looked at her.

"It's so stupid, but I locked the garage doors and then proceeded to lose my keys. I mean, they're right around here someplace, probably right under my nose, but I can't seem to find them. All my keys—car keys and everything." Her heart was pounding so hard she thought if she spoke loudly enough perhaps the Shoemakers and Betty Lee wouldn't hear it.

"But the door from the house into the garage—isn't that locked from this side, the house side?" asked Betty Lee, looking confused and her earrings bobbing.

"Yes," said Alix, "but there is an extra lock on the door which is locked from the inside of the house with a key. I know it sounds peculiar, but my husband is—was—" What tense to use? She was panicked over the proper grammar. As if they would discover she was lying about losing the keys if she used the wrong tense. Robert was not dead, she thought wildly. Therefore he *is*. "The fact is that my husband is extremely thorough. Meticulous. And he installed a rather elaborate lock system for fear of burglars." This was true. Robert had installed extra locks everywhere, and the lock on the door to the garage did require an extra key. The locksmith had tried to point out that such locks were usually used only on glass doors, but Robert went overboard on everything he did. The extra lock was installed and after the first week no one remembered to lock it. The key was eventually lost. It was just like the unloaded gun.

There was a long space of silence. Alix concentrated on her

breathing; six counts in and then slowly exhale six counts.

"We don't have to see it," said Mrs. Shoemaker. "I can visualize how much space there is if you say it's a three-car garage. But is there any light in there? I mean, natural light?"

"Yes," Alix replied. "There's a small window on the far side of the garage."

"That's important. Don't you think so, Phil?"

"What, dear?" He stood with his arms folded across his chest, studying a framed map of the UCLA campus which hung in the downstairs hallway. "What's important?"

"There's a window in the garage. It's so gloomy and depressing to work in a place during the day that doesn't have natural light."

Mr. Shoemaker nodded. "Is the freeway far?"

"Twenty-four minutes during non-rush-hour periods," said Alix.

Betty Lee said quickly, "It depends on which freeway you take, Mr. Shoemaker. If your office is downtown you would use the Harbor Freeway. However, if your office is in Beverly Hills or the Wilshire district, you would use the San Diego Freeway."

"The office is downtown," said Mr. Shoemaker.

"Well, then, you would use the Harbor Freeway."

"Which is eighteen minutes away during non-rush-hour periods," said Alix.

"And what does your husband do?" asked Mrs. Shoemaker as they followed Betty Lee into the family room.

"My husband?" said Alix. "He—" Why did she keep wanting to say *was?* "He's a screenwriter. We're divorced."

For a moment Mrs. Shoemaker's face was suspended between two reactions. Finally she said, "I'm sorry."

"Don't be. I'm not." The words came out hard and rude, which Alix had not intended. She had read or heard someone say that once and she had always wanted to try it out. Maybe she had heard it on *The Brewsters.* It sounded like one of Robert's lines, now that she heard herself say it out loud. The thought of Robert's lines somehow getting stuck in her head, like a recorded

135

message in a Mattel toy, made her feel desperate and she pressed her fingers to her mouth as if that would stop any more of Robert's words from popping out.

She looked at Mrs. Shoemaker, thinking that the last thing in the world she wanted to do was hurt this gentle frazzled lady from Ohio. "What I meant was—I've adjusted."

Mrs. Shoemaker nodded and smiled.

"A wet bar," Betty Lee was saying. Her heels tapped across the tiles as she went behind the bar and turned on the faucet in the little sink to illustrate her point. "And the glass doors open on the lower level of the patio, which is really an ideal arrangement when you have teen-agers."

Alix felt her nerves stretching and snapping like thin little rubber bands. Be cool, be cool, she tried telling herself, but this was too *close*. If only Warren had stuck to the original schedule. If only the Shoemakers and Betty Lee would go upstairs. Get away from the door that led into the garage. They were less than forty feet away from Warren's body.

She stared at Betty Lee and forced herself to think about Betty Lee. Would she have to go home and cook dinner for Mr. Lee when she finished showing houses to the Shoemakers? Maybe Mr. Lee had fixed their dinner himself and had it waiting in the oven. Maybe he had stopped off at Kentucky Fried Chicken on the way home and had little cartons of mashed potatoes and gravy keeping warm on top of the stove.

"On clear days," Betty Lee was saying, "there is a lovely view of the ocean from this room."

She sounded tired. Perhaps she had cooked dinner this morning and all Mr. Lee had to do was put it in the oven to heat it. Would he fix the salad? Or maybe Betty Lee had a crock pot and the meat and vegetables had been cooking all day. Or perhaps they would have dinner at a restaurant.

It was twenty-five past five. To be safe, she'd wait until midnight to drive his car to the cliffs. Six hours and thirty-five minutes.

"Mother's mahogany bookcase would look nice down here,"

said Mrs. Shoemaker. "Don't you think so, Phil?"

He frowned and considered this for a moment. "The hallway by the front door might be better," he said.

She nodded in agreement. "Or maybe the extra bedroom. You could use it as a study and it would be nice to have a place for your books."

"That's a thought, dear."

"Now for the upstairs!" said Betty Lee. She gave Alix a long look. "Are you sure, Mrs. Kirkwood, that we're not keeping you from something?"

"Positive," said Alix.

They went upstairs. Alix explained the idiosyncrasies of certain windows and faucets. The shower dial in the children's bathroom, which had been installed backward so that it was necessary to point the dial to Cold if one wanted hot water. The creaky floorboard at the top of the stairs. The closet door that stuck in hot weather.

Betty Lee's mouth grew tight around the corners.

"Wouldn't a fireplace just make this room perfect?" said Mrs. Shoemaker in the master bedroom. "Oh, wouldn't that be cozy?"

"One could very easily be installed," said Betty Lee. "It would have to be in an outside wall, but since this is a corner room it could be done quite easily."

"A fireplace," repeated Mr. Shoemaker.

"You do get good use out of fireplaces in California, don't you?" Mrs. Shoemaker asked Alix.

"Oh, yes," said Alix.

"I mean, it isn't too hot to use it at least half the year, is it?"

"Not at all," said Betty Lee. "You can use a fireplace here practically year round."

"Then it would be worth the investment. Don't you think so, Phil?"

"If that's what you want, dear, yes, a fireplace would be splendid."

"I wonder if it could be brick. Do you think brick would be too heavy?"

10

"I think a small brick fireplace could be done nicely," said Mr. Shoemaker.

"Not that your house isn't perfect just as it is," Mrs. Shoemaker said to Alix, a look on her face as if she had just realized she had been intolerably rude.

Alix tried to give her a reassuring smile. It was almost a quarter to six. Her nerves had that rubber-band feeling again. BK was due in forty-five minutes. At least with BK she'd be out of the house, in a restaurant. And then after dinner? Maybe she'd take a nap. Or maybe she wouldn't have to wait until midnight. If it was still foggy she might be able to go to the cliffs at eleven.

The Shoemakers and Betty Lee were all looking at her. She realized they had just asked her a question and now were waiting for an answer—Betty Lee with the tired, tight lines around her mouth and her little earrings which bobbed and bounced continuously; Mrs. Shoemaker with her sad hair and sweet eyes; Mr. Shoemaker in his neat vest, frowning and not realizing he was frowning. Would they never leave? What did they want from her?

"The stereo equipment," said Betty Lee.

"I'm so sorry. I didn't hear the question. I was thinking of something else."

Mr. Shoemaker cleared his throat. "We were wondering if you would consider leaving—selling—the stereo equipment."

"We have so many, many records," said Mrs. Shoemaker as though their question was somehow peculiar and required further explanation.

"Classical mostly," said Mr. Shoemaker.

"He plays the violin," said Mrs. Shoemaker.

"You do?" said Alix.

"I'm a member of a string quartet. We meet every Thursday at seven-thirty," said Mr. Shoemaker.

"I see."

"The stereo, Mrs. Kirkwood?" said Betty Lee.

"Of course I'll leave it; yes."

Like the lock system and so many other projects that Robert got carried away with, the stereo was elaborate, complicated,

138

expensive, and never quite worked properly. Speakers in certain rooms had never once uttered a sound. But by the time this was discovered, Robert had lost interest in the stereo system and moved on to another project.

They went downstairs. "Such a nice house. Don't you think so, Phil?"

"Yes, dear. It's a lovely house."

"And I love this wallpaper."

Mr. Shoemaker nodded.

"It is the last house today, isn't it?"

"There are a few more," said Betty Lee, "but if you want we can see them tomorrow."

"Tomorrow. Oh, yes, tomorrow," said Mrs. Shoemaker. She straightened the collar of her blouse; her charm bracelet jingled.

They stood at the front door, lingering as if they had been to a party.

"Goodbye," said Alix.

"Thank you so much," said Mr. Shoemaker.

"Oh, one more question," said Mrs. Shoemaker. "The weather. Is it this foggy here very often?"

"Well," said Alix, and looked at Betty Lee.

"There is a rather unusual weather pattern on the peninsula during the month of June," said Betty Lee, "but by early July the weather should be perfect. The average temperature for this area of the peninsula is about seventy-three degrees during the summer."

"Seventy-three degrees. Did you hear that, Phil? Seventy-three degrees. That's just about perfect, isn't it? Last summer was so hot back home that Phil's mother said it was just as bad as Florida and she wondered why she had bothered to make the trip. And it was really the humidity that just about did her in. I've never seen the humidity as bad as it was last summer."

"Well, there's very little humidity here," said Betty Lee.

"No humidity," said Mrs. Shoemaker, shaking her head back and forth. "Can you imagine that, Phil?"

"Usually the weather is very nice," said Alix.

"Thank you so much," said Mr. Shoemaker again.

"My goodness, yes," said Mrs. Shoemaker.

"Goodbye," said Alix.

"Goodbye," said Betty Lee.

"Goodbye," said the Shoemakers.

The door shut and Alix leaned against it. She breathed in six counts and then breathed out six counts.

15

"THIS FRIGGING LIZARD running around my house was the last straw. Give me a drink before I faint." BK had fled her house without putting on makeup. She looked oddly unfinished. Alix had never seen her without mascara before; her eyelashes were very pale and fine, almost nonexistent.

"I know. I look like hell. Give me a drink and I'll put on my face."

"You look fine, BK," said Alix.

"My mother-in-law once asked me what I used to take off my eye makeup when I went to bed at night. Take it off? Hell, I put it *on* before I go to bed with Sidney. I mean, I don't want to scare him away. I don't think. We had that conversation a number of years ago. Alix, if I don't have a drink immediately I'm going to start screaming or crying or something. You have no idea what I've just been through."

"What would you like?"

"Oh, I don't know. It doesn't matter. As long as it's alcoholic."

"A Manhattan?" said Alix.

"Too much bother," said BK. "Just something simple like straight Scotch."

Too much bother?

"On the rocks? Water?" asked Alix, still standing in the hallway.

"Straight on the rocks," said BK. "I'll put my makeup on in the john while you fix the drinks."

"Wouldn't you rather put it on upstairs?" said Alix. "You can use my dressing table."

"No problem. The downstairs john has a mirror, doesn't it? That's all I need." BK went down the short flight of steps and into the guest bathroom. Ten feet away from the door to the garage.

Alix took ice cubes from the small refrigerator behind the bar, filled two glasses with them and poured a jigger of Scotch in each. It had been years since she returned from the beach in the red Toyota. There was only so much that one could plan, foresee that might go wrong. Getting out of the house to have dinner with BK had seemed a fine idea at the time. She could have thought about it for a thousand years and never considered the possibility of a lizard entering BK's house and frightening her so badly that it was necessary for her to leave home without her makeup on.

Alix carried the drinks into the bathroom. BK's makeup bag was open and she was smoothing pale-pink foundation cream over her face. "Thanks," she said, taking a sip of the drink. "Oh, God, that tastes good." Alix put down the toilet lid and sat on it, watching BK put on her face.

"Let me tell you about this damn lizard," said BK, applying half moons of blue shadow over her eyelids. "I was in the kitchen and this creature flicks across the floor—a *reptile,* for God's sake—and I started to scream. I screamed and screamed and climbed up on a chair. And then I thought, This is dumb. Right? When was the last time you heard of a lizard—a tiny little garden lizard—attacking a grown woman? So I got down off the chair and the closest thing at hand was the morning's paper, so I tried to sort of swish this lizard out of the kitchen door and Jesus Christ, Alix, do you know what happened?"

Alix stared at BK, thinking that if for any reason BK walked ten feet to the garage and opened the door and saw Warren's car, it would all be over.

"Alix, don't you want to know what happened?"

"What happened?"

"This goddamn lizard goes out but *leaves his tail behind.* The lizard is gone but the tail is lying there on my kitchen floor and Jesus God it's still *twitching.*"

"You're kidding."

"Why would I kid about something like that?" She stared at Alix, the alarming blue half moons of shadow not yet blended in, the stick of shadow still in her hand like a tiny wand. "Really, Alix. Why would I make up something like that?"

"It was a meaningless phrase, BK. Like saying 'Oh' or something."

BK turned back to the mirror and blended in the eye shadow with the tips of her fingers. "Somebody once told me that you should put on your eyes before the rest of your makeup, but you know, I have never once remembered to do that."

"What about the tail?" said Alix.

"What about it?"

"What did you do with it?"

"Put my soup pot over it. I couldn't handle getting rid of it. Not tonight. Maybe tomorrow. Or maybe I'll just wait until Sidney comes home. I looked up lizards in my encyclopedia and learned that it was a foothill alligator lizard and he can just drop off his tail to confuse his enemy while he makes his escape. And this tail can keep on twitching for up to two hours to keep his enemy in a state of confusion. Or hysteria, as the case may be. You've got to admit that's clever. It's a pretty shitty trick to pull on somebody, but nevertheless clever." She widened her eyes and stroked mascara on her eyelashes. "I'd love to be able to do that. Have a fight with Sidney and leave part of me behind, twitching and scaring him to death."

"What happens to the lizard?" A second coat of mascara. Hurry up, BK.

"He laughs all the way back to the foothills. I don't know. What do you mean, what happens to the lizard?" BK drew two pinky-orange slashes of blusher across her cheeks, then fanned the color out over her cheekbones.

"He doesn't have a tail anymore," said Alix, standing up. "Doesn't he need one?"

"He grows a new tail, according to my encyclopedia." BK put on lipstick with a brush and then sprayed her wrists with perfume. "Now. A few margaritas, some supper, and I'll feel human again. I know I said I would, but how would you like to drive?"

"Drive?"

"To the Red Onion."

"No. I'm sorry, but the car has been sounding funny lately. As a matter of fact, Jim Drew had to start it for me yesterday. It got stuck in neutral." For an instant Alix thought that was the truth. And then she remembered she had lied to Jim also. The lies were becoming threads, all knotted and linked together. She had to keep track of them.

"It doesn't matter," said BK. "I'm low on gas but I'll get some on the way."

Macramé equipment and library books filled the back seat of BK's car. Collected poems of Roethke, a novel by Colette, a biography of Paul Klee. Alix could never connect BK with the books she read. It was as if BK absorbed the books in some secret part of her, and never gave evidence of reading anything heavier than *Cosmopolitan.* Alix didn't know anyone else who would have looked up lizards in the encyclopedia.

The fog was wispy this evening, drifting off the ocean in clouds. One minute clear and then the next minute thick as cotton. The windows of the car were opened a crack and the smell of the ocean and eucalyptus trees floated in, spicy and clean. BK pulled into the gas station at the top of the hill and filled the car with premium and had the oil and water checked.

The gas station attendant said, "You're a quart low on oil," and showed BK the stick.

"Well, do whatever is necessary," said BK, and handed him a

credit card. "I never know what that means," she said to Alix. "They never tell you how much is left. A quart low. But how much is left in there? A few ounces? Ten quarts?"

Alix was wondering how much gas was left in Warren's car. She was only going to drive it a fraction of a mile, but what if he had intended to buy gas before they had lunch? What if he had been one of those people who let their gas tanks get practically empty before refilling? The cove had been about a five-mile drive, then five miles back. She'd better check before she started it. The possibility of the red Toyota running out of gas in the middle of the street on the way to the cliff was no more absurd than a lizard scaring BK out of her house without her makeup.

The walls of the Red Onion were covered with endless photographs of men wearing mustaches and sombreros. The men stood close to one another—some had their arms around each other's shoulders—and they all carried guns in holsters. Or were they revolvers? Shelves on the walls held old books and china, and antique furniture filled every available corner in the restaurant.

BK and Alix sat facing one another in a booth.

"Did you have fun Sunday night?"

Alix shrugged.

The waitress brought corn chips and a bowl of hot sauce with their margaritas. BK dipped a corn chip into the sauce. "Well?" she said, the chip suspended over the bowl.

"Well, what?" said Alix.

"Well, what happened after— What was his name? Warren?"

Alix nodded.

"He took you home, didn't he? What happened?"

"Nothing."

BK bit into the corn chip. "My God, that sauce could take your tongue off."

The waitress came for their order and BK ordered a tostada, looked at Alix, who nodded, and said, "What kind of dressing?"

"Oil and vinegar," said Alix.

"Avocado for me," said BK, "and two glasses of water." She licked the salt off the rim of her margarita. "Well, frankly I thought he was rather schleppy. He was definitely a Rudolph."

"What's a Rudolph?"

"Rudolph was the fellow in fifth grade who wore funny corduroy pants, sort of knicker-type things, and his hair was cut like a soup bowl, and he still sucked his thumb when he didn't think anyone was looking."

"Oh." Alix drank her margarita in small, steady sips.

"Older Rudolphs are sometimes harder to spot. But they can usually be detected by their letters. They put certain phrases in quotes all the time. As in, I really had a terrific time this weekend, 'terrific' in quotes. They use exclamation points all the time instead of periods and they refer to women as gals."

"BK, has anyone ever told you you're a snob?" said Alix.

"Yes. Sidney tells me that constantly. I tell him it's a symptom of upward mobility. The insecurity of the nouveau upper middle class showing." BK turned her glass around and around by the stem. "So. Ciao, Warren, huh?"

"You might say that," said Alix. She stared at BK's fingers turning the glass, the clear glass smudging slightly from BK's fingers. *Fingerprints.* She had forgotten all about the fingerprints. How could she have been so stupid? So sloppy? The car and Warren's body would eventually be found at the foot of the cliffs. Maybe right away by one of the helicopters that patrolled the coastline. What if they had a way to check fingerprints with the thumbprint they took when you got your driver's license? Computers could do anything these days. Surely there was a computer somewhere that would tell the police that the thumbprints found on Warren Sullivan's car belonged to Alix S. Kirkwood. What was she going to do about the fingerprints?

"Did the people like the house?" asked BK.

Alix looked at her, not knowing what she was talking about.

"The people who looked at your house at five today," said BK. "Did they like it? Do you think they'll buy it?"

"Oh," said Alix. "They seemed to like it." And the damn beach

146

blanket. That wasn't so clever. Might it be recognized? Traced? And if she lifted it off Warren— No. She couldn't take it off, unwrap his body. She had to leave it covering his body.

"Do you think they're serious?" BK asked.

"I don't know. It's hard to tell." Was there a label on the beach blanket? She tried to remember. It was so old, surely any labels or tags had long ago fallen off.

"Were they there long? Didn't they say anything?" asked BK. "If people are interested, they kind of linger and check out the closet space and everything."

"They were there quite a while."

"Well, maybe they'll buy it."

"Maybe."

"And then what?"

"You mean for me?"

BK nodded.

"I don't know yet, exactly. But I will soon. I'm going to start making plans. . . ."

Their tostadas were served. Mountains of shredded lettuce, hot refried beans, cheese. BK ordered two more margaritas.

"Just one, BK," said Alix. "I'll have coffee."

"Bring two," said BK to the waitress. "I'll drink them both."

"When does Sidney get back?" Alix asked.

"Late tomorrow or early Friday if he can't get a late flight out of New York. Or is it Chicago? Jesus. Where is he? I forget." BK poured avocado dressing all over her tostada. "I'm going to look like a blimp tomorrow."

"Why?"

"Look at all this food."

"It's mostly lettuce."

"It's what's under the lettuce that concerns me. You know, every once in a while I think to myself, Well, okay, so what if I do turn into a blimp? I'll buy silk caftans and develop a whole new personality. I'll be majestic. Regal."

"How much do you weigh, BK?"

"I don't know."

"Of course you do. You weigh yourself at least twice a day."

"All right. This afternoon I weighed one hundred twenty-two pounds."

"And you are of medium height. BK, by no stretch of the imagination are you fat."

BK ate silently.

"Why is it so important to you to think that you're fat, to feel fat?"

BK set her fork down. "Do you know what Sidney's ex-wife weighs?"

"Is she fat?"

"No. She's thin. She's the thinnest person in Beverly Hills."

"Well, I don't follow you, then," said Alix.

"*Now* she's thin. She wasn't thin when he left her."

"But he left her for you."

"That was six years ago. I was still in my twenties."

"Oh, BK."

The two margaritas and the coffee came. "What a witch that woman is. Alix, I feel as though she's in a bunker up there in Beverly Hills planning day and night how to sabotage my life. Usually, just sending her daughters down for the weekend will do it."

Alix sipped her coffee.

"Now Shana wants a horse and Melody called me today to see if she could bring her boyfriend down this weekend when they visit their daddy. Last time she was down she asked me a lot of questions about the pill. The *pill,* Alix. The kid is fifteen years old. She has teddy bears on her bed and she's asking me about the pill, for God's sake. And her mother says she can no longer exist living on alimony checks that are barely above poverty-level income. Oh, God, if only that woman would remarry. Sidney said he'd give her away. March her down the aisle. Anything to get her off our backs. Eat, Alix; you're too skinny."

Alix picked at her food. "I'm not very hungry."

"Sidney has told the girls no horses, no boyfriends, no nothing until they get their grades up. And this of course gives him the

148

perfect lead into his old number of you-don't-want-to-go-through-this and I say, look, I won't fuck it up the way their mother did. I'd be a great mother. So then he goes into how free we are and would a baby be worth giving up all that freedom for?" BK was midway through the second margarita on the table in front of her. "And from there it's down to the bottom line, which is he's got enough family already and can't afford any more." BK's eyes were beginning to look blurry. "I mean, how much could a baby cost, for God's sake?"

Alix shook her head. "I don't know."

BK finished her tostada silently, placed her knife and fork neatly together, then pushed her plate away. "I'm sorry."

"For what?"

"You've got your own problems. You don't need mine."

My problems, thought Alix. Beach blankets, fingerprints. There must be a better way to handle all this. What was she doing having dinner with BK at the Red Onion tonight? "It's good for you to talk it out, BK. I don't mind. Really." You want to hear some real problems, BK?

They ordered sherbet for dessert.

Wouldn't the car explode when it went over the cliff? They always did in the movies. Sometimes they even exploded when they were just hit by another car. But always over cliffs. And when cars exploded they burst into flames. A fire would get rid of that damn beach blanket and the fingerprints.

"Nightcap?" asked BK.

"I've really got to be getting home."

BK looked at her watch. "It's so early. . . ."

"I know, but I'm exhausted."

BK shook her head. "It's probably all that dancing you were doing. You know, Alix, sometimes I think you're even weirder than I am."

16

ELEVEN-THIRTY. No cars had passed the house for an hour.

Something she had read in the paper: An interview with a famous dress designer who mentioned what his "mental set" was at a particular time in his life. Mental set. The term had stuck in her head. As if one could dial a mood or a thought, like the temperature for the washing machine or a prayer on the telephone. Or a poem. There was a telephone number in Los Angeles one could dial to hear a poem read. Once a week they changed the poem, like sheets. There was also a number to dial for Inspiration.

Mental set. She wished she could dial Cool.

She stood in the downstairs hallway of her house, facing the framed map of the UCLA campus. A small heart was drawn on the map, next to Royce Hall, which was where she had met Robert for the first time. She had given the map to Robert on their first wedding anniversary. She thought of all their anniversary presents to each other. She wondered what her mental set was.

Images and pieces of conversation clattered inside her head, catching at her nerves; as if buttons on a TV remote control were being punched and the channels were flicking past in fragments. The stories she had read in the morning paper seemed no less part of her life than driving through the fog with Warren Sullivan, or Betty Lee showing the house to the Shoemakers, or BK drinking margaritas at the Red Onion. It was all in the same frame of reference as the Swedish woman sitting on a bed in Texas with her hair on fire.

Had the woman hung up the phone? Or were there people somewhere in Sweden who had heard a plane slicing into a bedroom in Texas?

She didn't want to go into the garage. She listened for sounds —a car, footsteps—something that would give her an excuse not to go in there. She stared at the UCLA map in the dim light of the hallway. There were no cars, no footsteps. Only the sound of the foghorn and clocks ticking.

She had had the map framed in chrome for twenty-eight dollars at Aaron Brothers.

What kind of sound did a plane make as it sliced into a house? It would have been unrecognizable over the telephone. There was no precedent for recognizing such a sound.

Mental set: Fragmentation.

Was there such a word? Years ago, when Robert and she were first married, he would share words with her that he had mis-typed. In those days he worked at the kitchen table and he would call out the words to her from the kitchen and they'd laugh. Ridiculous words. Luzzle, when his finger slipped from the *P* down to *L*. Foman. Tamous. Grazzle. Sometimes he'd put them in sentences, which made her laugh even harder. Once when she was very pregnant with Cindy, he made her laugh so hard she wet her pants.

Such silence. The street, the house.

Finish this.

Sanity was having realistic goals and proceeding toward those goals with sureness of purpose. Had she read that or did she hear someone say it?

The children's faces floated in front of her. A child makes you a hostage to fate. Had she read that somewhere, too?

She moved down the short hallway. Past the guest room, the guest bathroom, the extra bedroom Robert had used as a study. To the door that led into the garage. Then leaned her forehead against the door, with her hand on the knob. How quiet everything was.

She was glad she had killed Warren Sullivan. People thought it was such a big deal to kill someone. At least the people she knew thought it was. But it wasn't. Not when you killed someone who deserved to be killed. When you had no other choice. The feeling she had right afterward, when it felt as though her own rage would smother her, annihilate her, had made it easy. She realized her lips were moving as though she were reciting prayers.

She opened the door into the garage. Snapped on the light switch next to the door. She was shaking.

The red Toyota looked ordinary, incapable of anything bizarre or extreme. A car that would be parked in front of the post office or Safeway. A car that might pick up children after school.

The bicycles, the moving boxes, gardening tools, the mismatched kitchen chairs hanging from nails on the wall. An ordinary garage.

Cold. Ten, fifteen degrees colder than the house. She thought of meat lockers at the butcher shop.

The cold of the cement floor felt through the rubber soles of her sneakers. Like standing on ice.

She stood in the dark, thinking. She would press the button to open the garage door and then get into the Toyota. She hadn't planned these moves, hadn't even thought about them. What if she was seen? She turned the lights off, pressed the garage door button. In the darkness she could hear the whir of the automatic opener and for a moment there was no difference between the darkness of the garage and the darkness of outdoors. Then gradually a change in texture. The dark framed by the garage door grew grainy, like the dark of a photograph.

She felt her way. The right front fender. A thin gritty layer of dirt on the car. The chrome was colder, icy under her fingers. Her fingers turning black in her mind from the layers of dirt. Past the headlights. Spaces of the grille. She could see the shape of the car now. She reached for the door handle, colder than anything she had touched. She listened to the sound of her own breathing. Concentrated on the frozen, cramped feeling in her feet. She ran her finger over a slight indentation on the door handle and envisioned two sections of metal being welded together. The heat involved, the assembly line, the predictability of such procedures.

She opened the door. As she did so, the car light went on and she saw the plaid beach blanket covering Warren Sullivan's body. Part of one hand stuck out from beneath the blanket, the fingers curled toward his palm like a paw. Puffy, no bones, the bottom part of his hand turning dark blue.

Blood had turned to black smears in the interior of the car. It had dried and in places was flaking like old paint. Some was splattered on the papers in the back seat. How could she have so misjudged the amount of blood there would be? Was her whole idea of death and murder and violence shaped by television, movies, novels? Perhaps cars only exploded on television. What if the car didn't explode when it crashed at the foot of the cliffs?

It came to her clearly and calmly that if a fire was started in the car there would be no chance of its not blowing up. She would have to get a fire going, then push the car over the cliffs. Impact, sparks, flames, and the gas tank explodes.

A fire. How the hell was she going to start a fire? She looked around the garage. Chairs, boxes, bicycles, barbecue equipment. Sitting on the shelf next to the barbecue equipment was a small can. Wizard Charcoal Lighter. *Yes.* "No muss, no fuss. Starts fires quickly without kindling." She took the can off the shelf, climbed into the car and closed the door.

In the sudden darkness the ticking of the dashboard clock was unexpectedly loud, and the odor of stale smoke was overwhelming. She opened a window carefully, holding her body rigid so that she would not brush against the beach blanket.

The engine started easily. She turned on the panel lights and saw that the gas tank was almost full. She let the car warm up for a few minutes, closing her mind to everything but the reassuring hum of the engine, ignoring a new and sharper smell now detected under the stale smell of cigarettes.

She backed slowly out of the garage. No headlights, marking her way down the driveway by bushes, the pepper tree, and then finally the mailbox at the end of the driveway. She switched on the headlights as she turned onto the road. She turned the car slowly and as evenly as she possibly could, aware that the blanket-covered bulk on the seat next to her could shift and fall against her.

She drove a few hundred careful, painful yards down the road. She could see no lights on in any of the houses. The early-evening wispiness had been replaced by thick billowing fog. It was impenetrable. Worse than it had been at noon.

She reached the path leading to the edge of the cliffs, and on the second attempt she eased the car over the curb. But as she did so, Warren's body jolted against her. With her right hand she pushed and the stiff mound beneath the blanket shifted back to the other side of the car. Nothing mattered but to keep his face covered. That was her only thought. If she saw those dead eyes staring she would not be able to continue. She would sit out here in the fog and begin to scream.

She inched the car forward, the fog so dense she could see only the cracked earth directly under the headlights. Finally, guessing the halfway point from the road to the cliffs, she stopped the car and got out. She had not really understood this problem of visibility, had not taken the fog into proper consideration. She could see only a couple of feet in front of her. The positioning of the car was crucial. She had to somehow mark off the remaining distance to the cliffs. Such a simple necessity. Why hadn't she thought of it yesterday when she was out here?

Off to the left of the car she found a clutter of empty beer bottles; damp, still beery-smelling. She picked up five of the bottles as if they were contaminated, thinking litterers should be arrested. She strained to see into the fog.

Stay cool. Finish this.

She slowly paced off the path toward the cliff, and when she felt the ground begin to slope she stopped. She could hear the ocean beating against the bottom of the cliff, and she sensed rather than saw the drop just a few feet beyond.

She placed one of the bottles at her feet. Then, moving back toward the faint beam of the headlights, she placed the other bottles at intervals along the path.

The car looked blurry, its edges not quite real. The tips of her fingers were numb again. She stretched her fingers and then made tight fists.

She shifted the car into drive, released the hand brake and stepped gingerly on the gas pedal. The car crept forward, inch by careful inch. She would not allow herself to think about the two-hundred-foot drop ahead of her. She concentrated on the pressure of her foot against the accelerator. The milky flat beam of the headlights against the fog. The carelessness of people who leave beer bottles behind. The first bottle appeared suddenly beneath the headlights, not visible until she was almost on top of it. Rocks, weeds. Why was this path here? The second beer bottle. Slowly, slowly, barely moving. Each revolution of the tires felt, counted. The third. The fog made this so difficult. Yet without the fog she might be seen from the road. The fog was like a curtain. The fourth. Tires turned, crunched over the stones and weeds. The foghorn cried. The dashboard clock ticked like a heartbeat. It was just past midnight. She felt as though she had been out here for hours. The fifth beer bottle. And beyond it the milky light darkened down two hundred feet.

The car moved inches beyond. She felt the edge of the incline and jammed her foot down on the brake pedal, then put the car in neutral and pulled on the parking brake, leaving the motor running. She waited for an instant, her foot just over the brake pedal, to see if the parking brake would hold the car. It did.

She opened the car door, tested her footing on the loose rocky surface of the incline, and got out slowly. The edge of the incline.

155

Five feet sloping gently down and then nothing. A rock could give way. The earth could shift. Her footing was firm and sure as a cat's. Nothing was going to give way or shift or do anything she didn't want to have happen. She had gotten this far.

She reached into the back seat of the car and crumpled papers and letters—anything she could find—then grabbed the charcoal lighter and squirted the papers.

Matches.

Oh, shit. *Matches.*

There had to be matches. All he ever did was smoke.

Attached to the dashboard was a little green plastic tray. Gum, change, a comb, matches. Scarcely breathing, she struck a match and held it to the edge of the crumpled paper in the back seat. The flames caught.

Quickly she reached down and released the parking brake. The fire in the back seat crackled, cheerful as a fire in a fireplace. Flames began to lick over the top of the seat. The blues and reds in the plaid beach blanket glowed. The awkward, hunched shape of Warren's body was visible now.

She slammed the door shut and ran to the rear of the car. The motor sounded like someone humming impatiently.

She pushed, aware of her balance, her feet planted on the loose earth, aware that she would have to fall backward as soon as the car began to roll so that she would not be caught in its forward thrust. The flames had caught onto the other papers and books and now filled the back seat.

The car was moving forward, slowly, then gathering speed. She crouched down on the path, digging her fingers into the scrubby mixture of dirt and stones. The car rolled forward on its own like a huge mechanical ghost. Rocks spurted from under the tires. The car creaked and made queer sounds as though it might fall apart before reaching the edge. Creaking, protesting, it disappeared from view—so silently that for a moment it seemed as though it must be floating down to the ocean. And then she heard the crash. A boom. Faraway. A sound that suddenly seemed to have nothing to do with her. An explosion. She crept closer to the edge and looked down. The car was burning, blazing down there in the dark like a bonfire.

Ciao, Warren.

17

SHE WAS BONE TIRED. Her muscles ached. She tried to concentrate on what Robert was saying. He emphasized his words with firm, precise steps in his polished loafers, back and forth across the living room. He was making a path in the thick plush carpeting.

"You've really done it this time. That poor woman was almost in tears when she called me last night," he was saying. "Said you crept around the house after them—"

"Crept?" said Alix.

"Yes."

"Did she say *crept*?"

"I think so. You know I'm not making this up."

"I know that, Robert."

"She wants to bring them back as soon as convenient and she's asked me to do something about you—"

"Do something about me?"

"Yes."

"Makes me sound like an unruly pet or something."

"Be serious."

"I am. Remember those signs we used to see in houses when we went house hunting? 'Dog is locked up in the garden. Please do not antagonize him.' Or, 'Cat is in the kitchen. Please do not let out because she will claw furniture.' "

"This isn't funny, Alix," said Robert, looking down at her.

"Yes, it is."

Alix was stretched out on the couch, still in her robe. "There are amusing aspects to most situations. You just never see them, Robert." She stood up. "Would you like some breakfast?"

"I'm not hungry. I want to settle this."

"At least coffee. It isn't even ten o'clock yet. I think you're overreacting." She walked out of the living room into the kitchen without waiting for him to reply. He followed. She put a kettle of water on to boil and took a pitcher of orange juice from the refrigerator. "Some juice?" she asked.

"All right."

She poured two glasses of juice and put bread in the toaster.

"I did try to call you last night. Twice, as a matter of fact," said Robert, sitting down on a stool and giving a slight tug at the knees of his slacks. "I called you around dinnertime and then very late. You were out."

"Yes." She handed him a glass of juice.

He took a sip and then said, "A date?"

"What?"

"A date. Were you out on a date?"

"Well, yes," she said. Was that why Robert had rushed down here this morning? Did he think there was a man upstairs in the master bedroom?

Robert was frowning. It had always alarmed her when he frowned. The lines of his face were so perfect, the planes so chiseled, that a sudden frown threw everything abruptly off balance. It was like watching a tiny earthquake take place on a tiny perfect landscape.

"The point is," he was saying slowly, "we are two rational adults who happen to be the parents of young children and—"

Whatever point he was about to make was spoiled by the kettle whistling and the toast popping up simultaneously. He waited silently while Alix fixed coffee and buttered the toast.

"Would you like a piece of toast, Robert?"

"I don't suppose you have any jam in the house, or marmalade?"

"No."

"You know I hate plain buttered toast."

"Well, I had no idea you were coming for breakfast," she said.

"But you never had jam or marmalade in the house when we were married. It was such a simple thing."

"You were making some sort of point about rational adults who are parents?" she said, sitting on a stool on the opposite side of the counter.

"Yes," he said. "If we're going to rear the children properly there must be cooperation between the two of us."

"Absolutely."

"There must be some form of communication without all this hostility. I think it was of great value to the children to have both of us see them off at the airport last week. Cooperation. We're no longer married but we still are parents. Do you understand what I'm trying to say?"

"Of course," she said, biting into her toast. "But what is this hostility you're talking about? I don't feel hostile; do you?"

"No, I don't feel hostile," he said. "But I have the definite impression that you're hostile as hell."

"Erroneous impression, Robert," she said softly.

He put both hands flat on the counter, palms down. "What's with you today?"

"Nothing."

"I've never seen you this mellow, except after—" He stopped and looked down at his hands.

"Except after what, Robert?"

"Except after you've been laid."

She smiled.

He got off the stool and walked around the kitchen. "My children," he said, "may be—" He stopped pacing for a moment and

160

looked at her. "They *are* the most important thing in my life and for their sakes I don't want our divorce to turn into two enemy camps trying to negotiate for the children. I want their happiness and well-being to be our common goal. And if we're to accomplish this, Alix, we must be able to communicate. Is that so difficult?"

"Well, it is and it isn't," she said.

"What is that supposed to mean?"

"Communication is one of those push-button words. Push the communication button for instant everything. Love forever after. Total happiness. The perfect divorce. Life is just so bloody complicated—" She looked at him. "But I think you're right about the kids and I'll do everything in my power to, as you say, cooperate and communicate."

"Good," said Robert with a long, tired sigh.

"We do owe them. And if it takes communication or standing on our heads or whatever, we'll do it."

"You make me nervous when you're reasonable."

She sipped her coffee. "I'm a reasonable lady."

"A new development."

"Yes." She felt clean and light, unburdened of all the angry baggage she had carted around, carefully guarding, for so long.

"Alix, I have never understood you, and now I understand you even less than I did before."

"But, Robert, I've pulled myself together. Isn't that what you always told me to do?"

He swallowed half his orange juice as if gathering sustenance for further debate and she watched the convulsive action of his throat with interest. He put down the glass and sat on the stool again. "All right. You've pulled yourself together, and I think that's great, Alix, I really do—and since you're in this laid-back mood—"

"It's not a mood."

"Okay, okay, it's not a mood. Since there has been this startling change in your personality, let me briefly explain my position about the house."

Robert always sounded as if he were in the midst of a war or a football game when he conducted a serious conversation. His position. She smiled again.

"This is important, Alix."

"I know. You have my full attention."

"What's so funny?"

"Nothing. I'm not laughing; I'm smiling."

"Alix, I'm not telling jokes. Carrying this house financially is a very serious matter. I drive down here for a serious conversation with you and you sit there laughing at me."

"Oh, Robert," she said, sensing what his life must be like deep under the surface. He was accustomed to writing his own dialogue. He must have imagined their talk while he drove down this morning, as if writing a scene. Confident that he knew and understood his main characters. His whole life must be this way, imagining reactions and words and plots that never turned out the way he expected in real life. How thin the line must be between reality and the words and scenes of his imagination.

She reached across the counter and touched his hand. "Go on. What about the house?"

"We've got to sell the house."

"Yes."

"You sit there and say 'Yes,' but you simply are not cooperating with the realtor. She says you refuse to have a lockbox put on the front door so the house can be seen more often."

"True."

"And then she said yesterday you had somehow managed to lock up the garage and then lost your keys."

"As a matter of fact, I had lost my keys to the garage." She picked up the coffee cups. "Would you like another cup of coffee?"

"You've got to help Betty Lee get this house sold," he said. "It just costs too much money."

Alix stood by the stove, waiting for the water to boil again.

"I mean, I can't afford this house," said Robert. "Do you understand that?"

"You can afford it, Robert. But I do understand."

He looked confused for a moment and then said, "Do you think money grows on trees?"

"For someone who has a series running on TV, yes. In television, for someone in your position, Robert, yes. Money does indeed grow on trees. It is neither fair nor justifiable, but the fact is you are overpaid." She handed him the cup of coffee.

"You have one of the great financial brains of the fifteenth century. You have absolutely no conception of money. This house is a goddamn drain. I keep pouring money down it. You and I used to live for a whole year—food, rent, clothes, the works —on what I have to pay for the taxes on this house. Just the fucking taxes, not mortgage payments, not maintenance, not utilities—*taxes.*"

"The taxes on this house are now forty-one hundred dollars a year," said Alix. "We have never in our lives, neither together nor separately, been able to live on forty-one hundred dollars a year. And let me point out one other fact. This house is an exceptionally lucrative drain. It has more than tripled in value since we bought it."

He inhaled deeply, as if he were going to hold his breath and needed as much air as possible. His face had changed color, which happened whenever he became truly angry or upset. It was such a subtle change that she doubted if anyone else would have noticed it. His face became pale, almost translucent, the way the children's faces looked just before they came down with fevers.

"But none of that makes any difference, Robert, because *yes,* I want to sell this house. It's much too large for just me and the children, and I don't even like it."

He studied her face and then said, "What are you going to do?"

"First of all, I'm going to find a smaller and more practical house to live in, and then I'm going to get a job."

"A job?" he said. "What kind of a job?"

"I don't know yet. Maybe I'll have to go back to school first. You know all my life I was trained *not* to have a job. My father made it very clear that if I followed the rules and looked feminine and pretty at all times I would attract the kind of man who would cherish me forever, the kind of man who would be appalled at the idea of his wife working."

"That's ridiculous."

"Of course it is."

"Your father didn't think that way. He was too smart."

"Deep down he did, Robert." She suddenly missed her father. The simplicity of the feeling made her realize that up to this moment, anger had been mixed in with her grief. She had felt that he had abandoned her, had somehow let her down, when he died.

"A pet," Robert was saying. "I really do think a cat or a dog might help."

"What are you talking about?"

"I worry about you being alone sometimes. Maybe it would help if you had a pet."

He was serious.

"Help *what?*" she said, trying not to laugh. "Oh, Robert, I'm in the process of simplifying my life. I don't want a pet."

"Well, maybe the kids would. Don't you think a dog might be nice for them? And have you ever considered the fact that a large dog would make it safer for you and the children? Do you lock all the doors at night? You're so careless about things that I can't help worrying about you. Do you check the doors at night and make sure the windows are locked on the ground floor?"

"Yes, I'm very careful."

"But don't you see—a dog would bark if anyone came into the yard and I would feel much easier about you and the kids. Is that so difficult to understand?"

"I understand, Robert."

He got up and opened the sliding glass door that looked out over the garden and pool. He stood on the patio for a few minutes, his hands in his pockets.

There was a faint breeze, and the pepper trees with their lacy branches dotted with red berries looked as though they were moving in time to music. Dancing. Maybe the breeze would blow away the fog and clouds, and summer would finally come. She thought of what it would be like to lie in the sun and switch off her mind, her thoughts; simply grow warm and brown in the sun.

Perhaps she'd take a trip while the children were gone. Go to a place that was sunny and hot right now. It was an exciting and extraordinary idea. Betty Lee could have her lockbox and people trooping through here night and day, and by the time she returned from her trip the house would be sold and she could start her new life.

"Why don't we call them?" said Robert from the patio.

"Who?" She walked outside and stood on the patio with him.

"The kids. Why don't we call them and see how they're doing?" Robert's face looked tight, as though if she said the wrong word it might fall apart in small pieces. "They're probably just about finishing breakfast now." He looked at his watch and ran a finger over his eyebrow. "Don't you think that would be a good idea?"

"No," she said.

"No? Why not?"

"Because it might get their hopes up. They might think we're getting back together."

"Yes. You're probably right." He stared at the pool.

When he had moved out of the house she kept seeing parts of him in the children. In Mark's ears, small and close to his head. In Cindy's cheekbones, showing through the round baby fat. Parts of Robert showing up in their bones and ears and sounds and silences. And now it seemed to be reversed. It was Mark she saw in Robert's small, well-shaped ears, and Cindy in the clean bones of his face.

"I spoke to them Saturday night," she said. "They seem to be having a marvelous time."

"Yes. I called them a few nights ago."

"Had Cindy's tooth fallen out yet?"

"Yes. Monday night."

She wanted to touch Robert, but knew if she did it would be misinterpreted. She wanted to touch him and tell him that somehow they'd manage and they'd start new lives and the children would continue to thrive. She realized that she no longer felt connected to Robert. And with this realization he was no longer a villain. He was an ordinary man. He loved his children and worried about his health and whether his clothes fit properly and what people thought of him. An ordinary man trying to get from day to day.

"Is the pool sweep working all right?" he asked.

"Yes." The breeze blew at her robe and she retied the sash.

"It's not tilting and getting water all over the deck the way it used to?"

"No; the service fixed it."

"Well," he said, "I guess I'd better be going."

"Yes."

"If you need anything . . ."

They walked through the house to the front door together. "Tell Betty Lee to just call when she wants to bring the Shoemakers back and I'll plan to be out and leave a key for her."

"All right," said Robert. "I'll stop off at her office."

He paused at the front door and looked at her. "Take care of yourself."

"I will. Don't worry." She smiled at him.

When he had left she went into the living room and stretched out on the sofa. She could hear a helicopter flying back and forth, over the roof of the house, along the cliffs.

18

THE GRINDING NOISE of the helicopter was at the edge of her consciousness, like a fly or mosquito that was annoying, but not annoying enough to acknowledge. To acknowledge the sound would require action, though what kind of action she had no idea. Involvement perhaps.

She was tired; the relaxed tired that comes after expending great physical and mental effort. The helicopter passed over the house again. She turned on her side and looked out the window. She could see it circling the cliffs, then hovering over one spot beyond the cliffs, the blades of the propeller almost level with land. She watched it curiously, wondering what was left to be seen of Warren Sullivan's car on the rocky beach below. The helicopter circled again.

Like a vulture.

She closed her eyes and thought about the trip she was going to take. And she was going to take it. There was no reason not to. Perhaps she'd go to Mexico, Mazatlán or Puerto Vallarta. Or Hawaii. Kauai, where she and Robert had honeymooned and the water was like silk, like going back to the womb and floating and rocking, and the sun was hot and white. She thought of the miles of empty beaches and the lazy sound of the surf rolling in over the beaches, the rustle of palm trees. How quiet and safe and easy it would be. She felt so sleepy and warm. Light and glowing as the images in her mind. She'd leave soon. Soon. She dreamed of the ocean. The beach. Sun. A long, placid dream that stretched out like a sunny landscape.

A siren. The curling wail broke into her dream like a whip. The sound grew louder, then suddenly faint as corners were turned, side streets navigated. Alix opened her eyes. Sirens used to make her cry. A lump in her throat, tears—an instant reaction to the sound. But now she didn't feel like crying. She went to the window and watched as a police car, red lights revolving and flashing on its roof, sped down the road in front of her house, squealed to a stop a few hundred yards beyond, then drove up over the curb and onto the path, toward the cliffs. A few seconds later it was followed by two fire trucks, the fire chief's car and the paramedic van. The trucks and the lights and the sirens seemed a paradox; so real, so solid, they were unreal. The efficiency and energy were out of context.

This was the same feeling she had had when her father died, the outside world abruptly, rudely, involved in a private matter. Schedules to follow, certain procedures. Rules and regulations.

And now Warren Sullivan had become a public problem, something the city would dispose of.

A second police car arrived. The fire trucks and paramedics were parked on the path now, a few feet from the cliffs. Everyone, ten or twelve men, stood by the edge and looked down. What did they see? She wondered how much of the car had burned. Was there anything left of the beach blanket? Of Warren Sullivan?

A man wearing a tan windbreaker and dark-brown slacks, walking an Irish setter, joined the police and firemen at the edge of the cliffs. The dog began to bark. The helicopter made one more circle and then flew away. Something was happening with ropes.

She wanted to follow exactly what was happening out there.

She tried to remember where the binoculars were. When had they been used last? By the time she had found them in Cindy's desk and returned to the living room window, a tow truck had joined the group of vehicles out on the cliffs.

She adjusted the binoculars and the distant toy figures turned into real people with distinct features and expressions on their faces. One policeman was talking to the man with the Irish setter and they were both smiling and laughing. The policeman had curly hair and she wondered if he had a permanent. It seemed a peculiar sort of thing for a policeman to do. Somehow frivolous.

The man with the dog looked vaguely familiar; someone she had met at parents' night at the school or seen at the market or hardware store. She wondered why he was out walking his dog at this hour. Cars were now pulling up along the road, people getting out to see what had happened. A Volkswagen with a young couple and their child. The child was about three years old and was wearing a green sweat suit with yellow stripes down the sides. A 1950s car, chrome tail fins gleaming, in perfect condition, drove up slowly and parked and an elderly couple got out.

The men near the edge of the cliff, including the man with the dog, were now moving away and standing in a loose circle, talking and making gestures. Apparently one of them had gone down the cliffs attached to ropes and now had returned.

She could hear snatches of the police radio, blaring what sounded like non sequiturs into the still, foggy morning air. It seemed to be coming from a device attached to a policeman's belt. It reminded her of Juanita's transistor radio.

There were even more spectators now; at least ten cars. They surged out toward the edge of the cliffs and after a few moments the police began to motion them to stay back. Teen-age boys on motorcycles arrived and there was a flurry of gestures and movement from the police when the boys tried to bring their motorcycles over the curb and out onto the cliffs. Another police car arrived, sirens wailing, red lights flashing, tires squealing. This was a true disaster, a true emergency. A happening. More cars slowed and stopped. Why did people flock to such scenes? A

12

policeman hopped out of the car that had just arrived and motioned people away from the edge. Then he erected a rope barricade with three tiny red flags attached to the rope. People began to walk a few hundred feet farther along, where there were no barricades and they could get to the edge of the cliff and watch the rescue operation.

Ghouls, thought Alix, adjusting the binoculars.

Two young girls in cut-offs stood on the curb, pretending not to notice the boys on motorcycles, doing snatches of dance steps, carefully looking in the opposite direction from the boys. A woman wearing a blazer and jeans, pushing a baby in a stroller, stopped and talked to the policeman who was keeping the immediate area clear. A phrase Alix had read in one of her newspaper articles came to mind. Crowd control. That was the officer in charge of crowd control. The phrase had an exciting ring to it. Suspenseful. It left open to speculation the alternative.

All of this, what she was watching, what she had caused, would become news. Tomorrow this would become a newspaper article. She could clip it out for the files. There was an element of power involved. Causing news to happen. Knowing that one had done something important enough, or at least bizarre enough, to be noticed by the media. It was a curious feeling.

The woman pushing the baby stroller reached into her purse, a large canvas shoulder bag, and pulled out a small box. Alix tried to focus the binoculars better so she could see what was in the box, but she was too far away. The woman handed something to the baby, who threw whatever it was to the ground and then began waving his hands up and down. Why would a woman bring her baby to such a scene? Alix wondered. Was ordinary life so boring, so uneventful, that even a disaster, requiring fire trucks and paramedics and police, was an improvement?

The sound of the helicopter again, and heads turned in the direction of the sound. The Irish setter began barking and ran in small, nervous circles around his master. The baby's mother rocked the stroller back and forth.

The helicopter hung over the ocean and then disappeared below the rim of the cliff. Police and firemen stood very close to the edge now. There was more tension and energy in the motionless figures than there had been when they were moving. Something dangerous was going on and it involved the helicopter. The thought of anyone coming to harm, being hurt, dying, while recovering Warren's body was so shocking to Alix that she realized she was holding her breath.

The line of cars parked along the road now reached the front of her house. Was there some sort of grapevine that spread the word of rescues and fires and accidents? Were there people who actually looked for this sort of thing? So many people out there. What *was* going on? She suddenly had an urge to be out there herself, to know exactly what was being discovered. Could there be any harm, with so many people? She wouldn't be noticed, and if she was, it wouldn't make a difference.

The telephone rang as she was getting dressed.

"Shall we meet the plane together?" It was her mother.

"What plane?"

"Lucy's. She called you last night."

"She did not call me last night."

"Oh." Her mother paused. "Well, she tried to."

"I was out." Alix could hear the helicopter overhead, flying away. She tried to see it from her bedroom window, but the gray stretch of sky was empty. She looked down at the cliffs. The distant figures were toy size again and anonymous.

"It seems that things are not working out with Peter." Her mother's tone was composed of layers—speculation, innuendo, reproach, hurt. Alix was always amazed at how her mother could pack so much comment into fairly simple statements.

"Mother, it might be best if you meet Lucy on your own. You know how she is when she gets off a plane."

"I'm not sure that I do. How is Lucy different from anyone else getting off a plane?"

For openers, she's usually stoned, thought Alix, but she didn't say it. "You yourself are always saying how high-strung Lucy is,

171

and she's just more so when she's been on a plane for six hours. She always gets into fights at the airport."

"Fights?" repeated her mother. "I don't recall Lucy ever getting into a fight at the airport."

"Last time I met Lucy's plane she accused TWA of losing that red maxi-coat she bought in London, and the whole time it was hanging in her closet on Seventy-third Street. And another time she left her cosmetic case under the seat and it went to San Francisco by mistake and she threatened bodily harm to an American Airlines stewardess."

"I take it you don't want to come to the airport, then."

"That's right."

"You're not coming."

"No, I am not coming. You meet Lucy and I'll drive up to see you both tomorrow. Is she planning to stay very long?"

"She didn't say."

"Now, Mother, don't be hurt or mad at me. I'm awfully busy today and really couldn't get to the airport even if I thought it would be best. I'll see you both tomorrow."

After she hung up, she finished dressing and left the house. The air outside was warmer than she had expected, softer. Dampness no longer cut to the bone. She felt the air meeting her skin as though she were entering a strange new element. She walked along the road toward the cliffs, her eyes on the crowd, thinking of different kinds of air. Air in houses, in cars, in airplanes. The oily metallic air in Los Angeles on smoggy days, the tropic gentle air in Kauai, which smelled of rain and hot sun, the two smells overlapping, sweet and incongruous. She would make plans for her trip soon. She'd call Milly's travel agency.

With an odd sense of recognition, as if seeing a television actor in person, Alix passed the woman with the stroller. She was feeding Sunshine Vanilla Wafers to the baby, who was now laughing, and every time he finished a cookie he'd bang his hands on the little tray in front of him until his mother gave him another.

"What happened?" Alix asked.

The woman pushed her hair off her face and said, "Oh, a car

went over. But I can't find out if anyone was in it or not. They won't let you go out there and see." The baby began to cry. She jiggled the stroller up and down. "Come on, Clark, stop it. You want another cookie?" The baby banged on the tray, then smiled at Alix.

Alix smiled back at the baby. "How old is he?"

"*She.* Clark's a girl." She offered a cookie to Alix, who declined it, and then gave one to the baby. "She'll be ten months next Wednesday."

Alix nodded, smiled, and began to move away.

"Hey, if you find out anything, let me know," called the woman.

"Yes," said Alix.

"That's what he said. That guy over there heard him say it. Something was in the car." The comment floated out, disembodied and androgynous. Others heard it also and a low buzz of speculation began.

Something was in the car, or someone? Was that what the helicopter had been doing? Removing Warren's body? What could have been left of it to remove? She thought of the pale, puffy hand, darkening on the underside, that had stuck out from beneath the beach blanket. And what of the blanket? It was odd to think of something as ordinary and familiar as their old beach blanket being at the center of all this activity.

A second tow truck had arrived and was now parked side by side with the first one. Their engines were running; cables had been lowered from reels in the back of the trucks down the side of the cliff. Garage mechanics stood talking to the small group of policemen and firemen. The firemen wore helmets and short-sleeved shirts, their bare arms looking pale and vulnerable. Did they fight fires in those outfits? An orange light on the back of one of the fire trucks kept flashing.

Through the binoculars the people out here had seemed whole, connected—a crowd. But standing in the midst of them, Alix realized that there was not really a crowd at all. There were dozens of individual persons, who happened to be in the same place at the same time, but they were not part of a whole. There were teen-agers playing Frisbee; a woman in a tennis dress leaning against her station wagon as she waited for something to happen; a family speaking excitedly in Spanish; a very elegant woman wearing an expensive gray skirt and alligator shoes, carefully picking her way along the rocky, dusty field, trying to get a better view. The owners of the old car with the shiny tail fins stood together by the curb, frowning and whispering to one another. There was a strange mixture of impatience and anxiety, of excitement and anticipation. What happened? Alix heard the question over and over. The colors and sounds and textures of this crowd that wasn't really a crowd caught at Alix, as though she hadn't seen other human beings for a long time. She studied them with curiosity, noticing details. Silver buttons on a sweater. The brightness of a pair of yellow slacks. The way some bodies curved comfortably toward each other, almost touching, and others arched away with a few subtle inches of rejection. She looked out at the ocean beyond, which made this little flurry of activity seem insignificant.

"There was one last month right down the road," said a male voice behind her. "A stolen van was pushed over. Nobody in it, though."

"I saw one last year. A little sports car went over with two guys in it. High on something. I think they found bottles of booze in the car. Took them hours to get the bodies up."

"Yeah; if they get caught in the rocks it can take forever."

"But they've got quite a system worked out. You've got to hand it to these guys. They know what they're doing."

The teen-age girls in cut-offs were still bobbing up and down, giggling, though the boys on the motorcycles paid no attention. The girls were about fourteen or fifteen and beautiful in the blond, healthy, bland way of California teen-agers. Alix felt her age as if it were a coat or a hat she was wearing, something that one should be able to remove at will.

Two surfers wearing wet suits, looking amphibian and awkward, wandered past Alix. "They've blocked everything off," said one.

"Shit," said the other.

A girl wearing a red-white-and-blue T-shirt that said ESPRIT stopped and asked Alix, "Somebody go over the side?"

"That's what I heard," said Alix.

A group of women riding bicycles pulled up along the curb and peered around expectantly, as if looking for a host or leader.

The action by the edge of the cliffs seemed suspended. One policeman whirled his sunglasses in his hand. Another smoked a cigarette and kept an eye on the spectators.

"They're waiting for the coroner," someone said.

A bearded jogger, wearing navy-blue shorts with white stripes down the sides, came up beside Alix. "What's happening?" he asked, panting slightly. His shirt clung to him with dark stains of sweat. He walked in place, flexing his leg muscles.

"I'm not sure," said Alix.

"Is there a car down there?"

"Yes, I think so."

"Anybody in it?"

"I don't know." Alix looked down at the path and saw a jagged piece of brown glass. It looked as if it came from a broken beer bottle.

"Suicide probably," he said.

"Oh?"

"They do it all the time here. The street should be called Suicide Alley. The county should put up signs or a fence, but then who wants a fence ruining their view? Or a sign. I don't want to look out of my house and see a big sign that says DANGER. Do you?"

Alix shook her head.

"They're either out here trying to kill themselves or out here looking at the ocean and accidentally killing themselves. Do you live around here?"

"Yes," said Alix, wishing she knew how to gracefully end chance conversations like this.

"Did you see that rescue at night a few weeks ago?" he asked.

"No," said Alix. "I'm afraid I missed it."

"You see, at night they have to use two helicopters. One provides the light, and the other does the actual rescue. Some kids had been smoking pot and started playing Chicken or something near the edge and they both went over."

"What happened to them?"

"I don't know. The helicopters got them up, but I never heard if they lived."

The woman wearing the gray skirt and elegant shoes joined them. "They found a body in the car," she said. "I talked to one of those policemen and he said they have to wait for the coroner to come and inspect the scene. Now they're trying to get the car hooked up to ropes, but it's wedged against a rock. It's badly burned."

"The body, too?" asked the jogger.

"I don't know. They said it takes an hour and a half for the coroner to get out here."

Neither of them noticed when Alix moved away and began to walk toward her house.

19

"WHAT'S GOING ON across the street?" asked Milly over the phone. "When I left for work this morning it looked like the whole fire department and police force were out there."

"I think a car went over the cliffs last night," said Alix, twisting the telephone cord around one finger.

"Anyone in it?"

"I don't know."

"I bet my ivy and gazanias are being trampled to death."

"I didn't notice." Alix straightened out the phone cord. "Listen, the reason I called is that I'm going on a trip and I'd like you to make the reservations for me. May I stop by the office this afternoon?"

"Of course. Let's see—would four be okay with you?"

"Yes."

"Where are you going?"

"Hawaii."

"Great. I'll have some brochures and stuff ready for you to look at when you come in."

"Thanks, Milly. See you at four."

She hung up feeling pleased that she was going through with her idea of a trip. Going away, getting away from things, had always been a constant idea, like a tune she was always humming. "I should go away for a week," she used to say to Robert. "I need a change." But she knew and Robert knew she never would. It was just something she repeated and wished she would do, but she couldn't break free of the inertia of her own life. And now she was finally going to do it. Get away.

Getaway.

She called Coast Realty and left a message for Betty Lee that she'd be out later that afternoon and would leave a key under the pot of fuchsias by the front door in case the Shoemakers wanted to see the house again.

Activity across the street was suspended, everyone still waiting for the coroner to arrive. She didn't want to watch that, didn't want to think about it. She filled the bathtub with water, added one of the capsules of bath oil, undressed, and picked up a copy of *Vogue* from her bedside table to read in the tub.

At first the phone number puzzled her; as if she ought to recognize it instantly but couldn't. It gave the model on the cover an injured look, an intricate scar. *Warren Sullivan's telephone number.* Dear God, how could she have been so careless?

She ripped out the number and tore it into tiny pieces, which she flushed down the toilet. A Bergdorf Goodman ad showed through the model's missing square of cheek. Alix climbed into the tub and thumbed through the magazine, trying to concentrate on moisture musts for the summer ahead, sixty-five ways to update her accessories, "Inner Tubes: A Bosom's Best Friend." Soon they'd all be gone across the street and then she'd be fine. Not so nervous and edgy. She knew this for a fact, but at the moment she was having difficulty concentrating on *Vogue.* When the coroner came and took the body away and all the ghouls went home and the red Toyota was hauled up and towed away, she'd be fine.

She dressed with care. Extra makeup to compensate for her June pallor. Hair brushed and tied at the nape of her neck with a ribbon. Earrings, gold bracelet. An embroidered cotton vest over her shirt. Nail polish. Using up time.

In the backyard, the man from the pool service was skimming leaves and dirt from the water with a long-handled net. Every week when she saw him out there cleaning the pool they rarely used, she felt guilty for not swimming more often. She'd start swimming when she returned from Hawaii, and she'd swim every day until the house sold and they moved.

"What's the temperature of the water today?" she asked from the patio.

With the net, he fished out the floating blue-and-white pool thermometer. "Eighty-four degrees," he said. He was shirtless and wore a red bandanna tied around his neck.

"Why don't you just turn the heater off. I'm going on a trip soon."

"Okay, Mrs. Kirkwood."

"Why do we keep it so warm?" she asked, realizing it cost money, a lot of money, to keep such a large quantity of water at eighty-four degrees.

"Mr. Kirkwood's orders," he replied.

She wondered if he knew that Robert no longer lived here. "I don't think it's necessary anymore," she said.

He nodded. "Okay." The net made a rhythmic lapping sound as it was dipped into the water and then lifted out, dripping with leaves. "A lot of excitement across the street," he said.

"Excitement?"

"A lot of people. Police and fire trucks and everything. Was somebody killed over there, or what?"

"I don't know." The lapping of the net reminded her of the lapping of oars. Canoe paddles. "I don't know what's going on over there," she said.

"Something sure is," he said.

The helicopter again, hovering the coast, puttering low over the roofs of houses. Somehow she had imagined it would all be much quieter, not so much noise and activity; people wouldn't be talking about it all the time.

"I'm going to go over and see what's happening when I'm finished here," said the pool man.

When Alix backed out of the driveway, she turned left to avoid the scene at the cliffs. She could see a white van in the distance, joining the other vehicles at the edge.

Milly's travel agency was located near the city hall and the police and fire stations, in a plaza of arches, bricks uneven with age and weather, cool shadows and little shops whose owners rarely changed. It was unlike any other part of Southern California, and when Alix parked there just before four o'clock and looked up at the green hills dotted with red tile roofs above the plaza, and through the trees down to the pewter-colored ocean below, she could imagine herself in a new life for the first time since Robert had left her. She and the children could live here at the plaza in one of the old apartment buildings shaded by eucalyptus trees. A large apartment, quirky with age, and they could walk everywhere—to the library and the bakery and the market. Even to the beach. The children would love it. They'd be right in the middle of everything.

"You look terrific," said Milly.

"Thank you." Alix sat in a chair opposite Milly's tidy desk. "I'm excited about this trip. And I also just had a great idea—I'm going to look for an apartment right here at the plaza for the kids and me."

"You're right. That's a great idea." Milly smiled at her. "I'll tell you a secret. Jim and I have been worried about you rattling around in that big house. I know how hard the past six months must have been."

"Well, they're over," said Alix, smiling back at her.

Milly nodded. "Where to in Hawaii?"

"Kauai."

"Want to island-hop?"

"Nope. Just Kauai."

Milly pulled a stack of travel brochures and folders from a desk drawer. "How about a stop in Maui? Won't cost extra."

"I've been there. And to Oahu, Molokai and the rest. Just Kauai this time."

"I thought you'd been there, too."

"Yes; Robert and I went there on our honeymoon." Why had she chosen the one island she had gone to with Robert? The other islands she had visited with her parents and Lucy when she was young. They reminded her of spring vacations and her mother telling her not to stare at people on the beach and to put shoes on for lunch and terrible sunburns and the smell of Noxzema. The fact was she and Robert had a wonderful time on their honeymoon and Kauai was the only Hawaiian island of which she had happy memories. "Kauai is my favorite," she said to Milly. "I just want to lie in the sun and not be a tourist." She thought of the white-hot South Pacific sun and said, "Sometimes I think my body requires sun the way other people's bodies require food and oxygen."

"I know what you mean," said Milly. "I'm beginning to feel that way myself. I think if I had to stay home in this weather I'd lose my marbles. Where do you want to stay?"

"Lihue Surf, a room facing the beach, for one week."

"One reservation . . ." Milly stretched out the word "One" as she wrote it down on a pad of paper, as if giving Alix the opportunity to correct her. "Lihue Surf for one week."

"And an afternoon flight out of Los Angeles."

"What day?" Milly asked, pencil poised over the paper.

"Soon. Sunday or Monday if there's anything available. I'm flexible."

Milly nodded and wrote on the pad of paper. The office was white and green, with delicate bamboo chairs and cushions covered with a green-and-white print. There were two other women in the office, one on the telephone and the other typing. Alix suddenly had an incredible longing for a job; not as something she should do because she was now divorced and on her own and had no other choice, but as something that she wanted to do, was even excited about. She thought of how it must be for Milly to wake up every morning with her day defined, with no vague, gray portions of the day that could become unmanageable and depressing. How it would be to wake every morning and have a place to go, a place where one was expected, needed.

"Are you happy?" she asked Milly.

"Happy?" said Milly, amused and faintly puzzled. She ran her fingers through her hair. "I guess I am. I hadn't thought about it."

Perhaps that was the secret, not going through life taking one's emotional temperature every five minutes the way she and Robert always did. "Happy? *Happy?*" Robert would repeat, as if she had suddenly begun speaking in a foreign language, whenever she questioned him on whether he was or wasn't, and then he would explain the exact nuances of his current state of happiness, or unhappiness. If he was happy, it was happy tinged with nostalgia, or tempered with anticipation, or fraught with alternatives and speculations. Robert's happiness menu. Maybe the only people who were truly happy were the people who never thought about being happy.

"Sometimes you remind me of those Geritol commercials," she said to Milly. "This is my wife and she's got eight kids and is vice president of the company and she sewed the living room draperies by hand—" Milly started to say something and Alix interrupted her. "But you do it in a good way. Like you enjoy everything and life is easy and fun."

"Easy?" said Milly. "What's easy when you think about it? It all comes down to little things. Like dishes."

"Dishes?"

"Dishes. Who's going to do the dishes? You've got two tired adults looking at dirty dishes after a long day at their offices and who's going to do the dishes?" Milly smiled. "Who's going to make the bed every morning was another heart-stopper."

"So who does the dishes?"

"We both do. Or the kids do them. Or sometimes we just open another bottle of wine and say the hell with the dishes."

"See—you make it sound so easy."

"Sometimes."

The phone on her desk rang and she picked it up. "Yes, Mrs. Lasky, they're all written up. We'll be open until five." She hung up and said, "Half this town seems to be headed for the sun. I think it's great that you're taking this trip, Alix, I really do."

"I think so, too. Do you know that I have never taken a trip by myself? Never in my entire life. I'm thirty-six years old and I've always traveled attached to other people—my parents, my sister, my husband, my kids. And when you travel with other people, at least the kind of people I travel with, your trip is already"—Alix searched for a word—"well, *defined*. Certain conditions are set up, restrictions, limitations. Definitions. But when you travel alone it's an adventure. Anything can happen or nothing. But it's not preordained, if you know what I mean."

Milly nodded. "My mother always told me that nice girls never traveled alone. And I actually believed her for something like thirty years." She picked up the pad of paper on her desk. "I'll check on reservations and flights and write up your ticket for you."

"Thanks, Milly."

"I'll drop it off at your house. Would tomorrow be okay? I'm up to here in paper work." She pointed to a spot just above her nose. "But I'll call you just as soon as I confirm your flight and hotel reservations."

"Tomorrow's fine."

Milly walked her to the door of the little office. "Are they still out on the cliffs?"

"When I left the house they were."

"My poor ivy."

Alix shopped her way back to the car. She stopped in the bakery for a loaf of bread. In the gift shop she bought tiny bags of spicy potpourri for her mother. She thought of buying Lucy a present, but she couldn't think of anything that Lucy might want that she didn't already have.

The plaza was built around a replica of an Italian fountain

183

which featured a seminude King Neptune surrounded by nymphs whose breasts spouted water. The children were fascinated by the water-spouting breasts, and when he was very small, Mark had asked her if her breasts could spout water like that, too. She bought a postcard of the fountain at the drugstore, addressed it to the children in care of Judson and Virginia, and wrote, "King Neptune and the ladies miss you. I do, too." Then she drew a happy face and signed, "Mommy."

She mailed the card to the children at the post office and then stopped in at the bookstore next door to browse for paperbacks to take on her trip. As soon as they were finished on the cliff she could start forgetting what had happened. Not submerging it, not denying it, but merely putting it out of the way as if it were an ugly piece of furniture she was storing in the garage, out of sight.

The black cat that lived in the bookstore rubbed against her ankles as she looked for books. She scratched the cat behind his ears and thought that maybe when she and the children were settled in their apartment she'd get a cat. The apartment was coming alive in her mind, more real than the house she was living in. She could see the cat in it, and the furniture and the rugs and what she'd hang on the walls. How it would feel to open the front door at the end of the day and go inside to this cozy place that was all hers.

As she drove home, fog drifted in over the empty cliffs, the air so damp and heavy she could hardly breathe. She thought of how the surf in Hawaii turned a gold color before the sun set, and the conch shell would be blown every night at the Lihue Surf and torches lit. All very touristy but nevertheless satisfying and right. And when the sky became gray it would rain and be done with it, not turn gray and heavy for weeks like a bad mood.

Back at home, she fixed herself two daiquiris, made a cheese sandwich with the fresh bakery bread, cut an orange in slices, and placing it all on a tray, went up to her bedroom to watch television for the evening.

20

THE DREAM ESCAPED for an instant. Was almost caught by the corner of her eye. Then lost again. Her heart was pounding as if she had run a great distance or been badly frightened. What had she dreamed? What was it she didn't want to remember?

Warren Sullivan.

He had not died. He had been asleep under the plaid beach blanket, not dead. He climbed back up the cliffs, looking for her. She was trying to pack for her trip but she kept losing the things she needed; forgot where they were kept, what they were. She couldn't find her tickets. She was looking everywhere, frantic, tearing open cupboards and drawers, looking in pockets and purses. The tickets were lost. He walked along the cliffs, calling her name. He waved and his palms were black with blood.

Alix pushed the sheet and blankets down to the bottom of the bed with her foot. The room felt hot. A splinter of pale light came through the space where the draperies didn't quite meet.

She forced herself to study her bedroom. Colors, shapes. The pale light on the carpet. The tray from the night before. The faint odor of orange peel. The ordinariness of it. Start dreaming of bloody hands and they'd cart her off to the funny farm. Think of the day ahead. Think of visiting her mother and Lucy. The drive to Brentwood. The newspaper that was waiting for her at the end of the driveway like an unopened letter. The first cup of coffee.

The morning smelled of other summers. Long-ago summers. Ocean, honeysuckle, warmth. Smells like music, bypassing usual paths of thought and feeling.

She walked barefoot to the end of the driveway, watching not to step on snails, and picked up the newspaper. In the pepper trees, mourning doves sang soft *ka-koos*. Up in the hills, she could hear the catlike shrieks of peacocks. Why did peacocks always sound as if they had been mortally wounded? Did they ever communicate calmly? Think about these things. Tangible, manageable thoughts.

In the kitchen, she put water on to boil for coffee and cut the string tied around the newspaper.

Page two, Southland News in Brief: "An unidentified male body was discovered early yesterday in the charred wreckage of a 1977 Toyota at the foot of the peninsula cliffs. The victim, presumed to be in his early forties—"

The words leaped out at her with the shock of familiarity. She spread the paper on the counter and leaned over to read it calmly. It was necessary to be calm about this and to know exactly what had been discovered.

But why did it seem more real when she read about it in the paper?

"Investigating . . ." Her eyes were having trouble focusing. Investigating? She looked for the word again. "Police are investigating the possibility of foul play." Foul play. The words had a Victorian ring, as if something rather nasty might have occurred. Foul play, indeed. It hadn't been foul at all. It had been fair.

Just six lines. She cut it out of the paper.

The front doorbell rang at nine.

"I'm sorry to bother you . . ." He smiled at her and held up his identification. He was wearing khaki cords, battered sneakers and a faded blue shirt. He was about her age. Alix looked at the ID he held up; looked at it but didn't read it. It always embarrassed her to appear suspicious and paranoid at her own front door. She gathered he was somehow connected with the police department; a police car was parked in front of her house.

"This will only take a moment or two," he was saying.

"That's all right," said Alix. "Would you like to come in?"

"No, thanks." He had friendly, easy eyes; the kind of eyes that smiled even when the rest of his face wasn't smiling. "This will just take a minute. We're checking the neighborhood to see if anyone saw anything unusual night before last. There was an accident. A car went over the cliff and a man was killed."

"Yes; I saw the fire trucks and police cars over there yesterday."

"Did you notice anything before that? Any cars or strange sounds? Anything unusual?"

"It's so foggy here at night," said Alix. "I'm afraid I didn't see anything. I went out to dinner with a friend and got home early, about nine, and didn't see anything."

"Later, maybe? Perhaps you might have heard something that didn't register at the time. Strange lights, a car door slamming, voices?"

Alix shook her head. She wanted to convey the idea that she truly was a helpful person, a good citizen, an honest and decent human being, but she simply had not noticed anything. For a second she believed that. She had not seen or heard anything across the street in the fog. A stranger had been out there in the dark, in the fog, doing terrible deeds. Foul play. But of course, foul play had not been mentioned by this attractive man with the nice eyes standing at her front door. He had called it an accident.

"Well, thank you for your time," he said.

She loved people with good manners. "No trouble," she said.

Sam was pruning the pepper trees when Alix backed the car out of the garage for the drive to Brentwood. She stopped the car and rolled down the window. "I think there's a pair of mourning doves making a nest in there. Be careful."

"Hey, Alix. That's wild." He came over to the car and leaned an elbow on the roof. He had grown a long, flowing mustache and it curled down past the corners of his mouth.

"What's wild?"

"You sitting there in your Mercedes worrying about the birds. You sound like my old lady. She's into birds, too. She went to a pet store the other day and unlatched all the birdcages and set forty-two parakeets free."

It took Alix an instant to realize he meant his girl friend or wife, not his mother. "What happened to her?"

"The petshop owner said he was going to have her arrested, but he was too embarrassed to call the fuzz and tell them he had forty-two missing parakeets. She's going to start hitting the big shopping centers next. The domestic parakeet is about to become the most common native bird of Los Angeles."

"How's the poetry going?" asked Alix.

"Getting some haiku published."

"Terrific."

"I'll bring you a copy next week if you're interested."

"Make it week after next. I'm going to Hawaii."

"Outa sight," said Sam.

"Regards to your old lady," said Alix, and backed out of the driveway.

Lucy was in danger of becoming transparent. So thin and fragile and pale that one might soon be able to see through her. Literally. She was sitting in a chair in front of a window through which late-afternoon sun streamed, giving her hair a halo effect. Her hands were folded in her lap, her legs crossed at the ankles. Where had they learned that was the only way true ladies sat? To cross one's legs at the knee was vulgar and common and pushed the calves out of shape. The same authority had said ladies never wore red shoes, they filed their fingernails in one direction only, and must go through life imagining a string attached to some part of their anatomy—their tits? shoulder

188

blades?—with the string pulled upward so they wouldn't slouch. Alix remembered. It was a charm school their mother had sent them to as teen-agers. She had been thirteen and Lucy fifteen. Two hundred dollars apiece and all she could remember was how to file her fingernails and cross her legs.

Two tears were sliding down Lucy's cheeks. Alix stared at the two tears, wondering, as she always did whenever she saw Lucy cry, how Lucy could be in such control of her tears. Her eyes never became red and puffy or her mouth swollen and bruised-looking the way Alix's did. Just two perfect tears which welled up, hovered at the corners of her eyes, and then made a slow, graceful descent down her cheeks; and at a certain point, just before they reached her chin, Lucy would brush them away with the back of her hand, like a little girl, so they would not drip off her chin, which would be messy and unattractive.

"Well," said Lucy. "I just don't know."

Their mother sighed.

"What don't you know, Lucy?" said Alix.

Lucy simply shook her head.

Conversations, personal ones, with Lucy often involved long sighing silences during which, if one was not alert and involved, one was in danger of forgetting just what it was that Lucy was mulling over and finding difficult to answer.

The clock in the hallway struck the hour. Four bongs. The silence surrounding her mother's house was so dense that Alix always had trouble believing that Sunset Boulevard was only two blocks away. Silence inside the house and outside. She missed looking out of windows and seeing the ocean. She'd never move back into town. She thought of the large, sunny apartment she'd find for herself and the children. And she'd get them the cat, and fill the apartment with books and old furniture she'd refinish herself. And she'd paint the walls white so nothing could detract from the view of the sea.

Their mother was staring at Lucy as if regarding a strange and exotic creature who had just stumbled into her house by accident. "Maybe if you could make yourself a bit clearer, Lucy," she said.

"Is it Peter or your job that's the cause of all this?"

Lucy recrossed her ankles and said, "Oh, God."

"Do you remember the charm school?" said Alix.

Lucy narrowed her eyes slightly. "What charm school?"

"The one Mother sent us to on Wilshire the summer you were going with that fellow who had hay fever."

"That was Hank, and he didn't have hay fever; he was simply allergic to roses. I mean, I remember Hank, but I have no recollection of being sent to a charm school."

"That's because you spent the entire two weeks in the john smoking cigarettes," said their mother, staring at the coffee table, which was in the path of the sunlight streaming through the window behind Lucy's chair. "Look at that. Do you see that? She did not dust in here today. I asked her three times if she had dusted in the living room and she said, '*Sí, sí.*'"

"Smoking in the john?" said Lucy.

"Mother and Daddy sent us to charm school to learn how to be proper ladies," said Alix, "and when they caught you smoking in the john they told you that you were lighting the cigarette wrong. A lady, they said, holds the cigarette and does not let it droop from the corner of her mouth while she strikes the match."

"Oh," said Lucy. "*That* place."

"Your father thought it was a total waste of money," said their mother, rearranging a silver box and a china pot of babies'-breath.

"I miss Daddy," said Lucy.

No one said anything.

Alix walked to the French doors at the end of the living room, which opened out to the garden and pool. Everything looked golden and warm and rich—the way California is supposed to look. The water in the pool shimmered in blue geometric patterns. Alix thought of all the summers she and Lucy had spent in that pool; how their hair would turn green from the chlorine and their mother would nag them to wash it after they swam, just as she did with Cindy, and their skin would turn prunelike. Their father would grill hot dogs and hamburgers for their birthday parties around the pool, and then later, when they were in their teens, they would lie oiled and inmobile, baking in the sun, summer after summer, serving Cokes and then beers to a parade of boys. Trying to please the boys, waiting on them, trying to look good for them.

"You certainly seem in better shape than I had expected," Lucy said.

"What had you expected?" Alix asked, walking back from the French doors.

"You sounded so spacy when you called me last week I thought you were on the verge of a nervous breakdown."

"Your sister does not have breakdowns," said their mother. "She has bad spells, like everyone does. Now I'm going to fix cocktails for us and then take you both out to dinner and we'll be cheerful and have a good time. All this talk about divorce and breakdowns." She shook her head. "Scotch? A martini? Lucy, have a good stiff drink. It'll make you feel better."

"I'd rather have Perrier."

"Water? For cocktails? I've never heard of such a thing. I have some lovely chilled Chablis; at least try that."

"Mother—"

"I'll put ice in it for you. It'll be diluted. Alix, what would you like?"

"Chablis sounds fine," said Alix.

"Cocktails should be an occasion. Your generation doesn't appreciate the mystique of the cocktail hour. It's a celebration of the day's end, a time to relax and discuss the events of the day. I worry when the little rituals of life are sloughed off; it's the rituals that get us from day to day." Her heels echoed on the hardwood floors as she went to the kitchen to make their drinks.

Alix circled the living room, looking at photographs. Wedding pictures in silver frames, all that was left of their marriages. Their first marriages anyway. Photographs of her father, sandy-haired, tall and thin, and of Lucy and herself as toddlers, and of Mark and Cindy. Only Mark and Cindy were still valid; everyone else was gone, grown up, divorced, canceled like stamps. All these photographs covering tables and piano and bookcases were false impressions. But weren't all photographs false impressions? Weren't they true only for that one instant the shutter snapped? Even Mark and Cindy had grown past that sunny photo Robert had taken of them at the beach last summer. Alix peered closely at the picture. They were sitting on the plaid beach blanket.

"You're making me nervous," said Lucy. "You act as though you've never seen those pictures before. God, why does she have to keep the wedding pictures out? I mean, there's something strange about it. As if the pictures were the whole point."

Alix studied a picture of their grandmother. The same grandmother who had bought the oak table in the den on her honeymoon in London. Feathery hat, long bell-shaped dress, puffy sleeves, tiny waist, and masses of dark, heavy hair pinned up beneath the hat.

"It really gives me the creeps," said Lucy.

"What does?"

"The *pictures*. All these pictures that are supposed to prove something. And she's got the wrong wedding out. That's Brian, not Peter." Lucy looked down at her hands. "Sometimes I think the photographs are more real than we are. More solid somehow."

"How do you mean?" Alix asked.

"It's like those tourists who go places and spend all their time taking pictures of each other in front of monuments and mountains and churches so that they don't have to do anything else. The pictures prove they've been there. Brian took pictures constantly. All over Europe that first summer we were married. Lucy having fun. In Paris, in Rome, in Venice, in London. You name it, there's a picture of me having fun there."

"Does Peter take pictures?"

"Not to my knowledge."

Click. Alix felt as if Lucy had slammed shut a door. The sunny living room was silent.

After a few moments Lucy said, "I didn't tell Peter I was leaving. I left him a note. Do you think that was cowardly?"

"Yes," said Alix.

"Yes?" repeated Lucy.

Alix looked at her sister—the new haircut, gold bracelets, silk dress, trendy shoes. Lucy always wore trendy shoes as if that were the acid test of something, but Alix could never figure out what that something was. "I said yes. It was cowardly and childish to leave your husband a note and run home to your mother. But I understand. Sometimes the only thing to be is cowardly and childish. It's not always a right-or-wrong situation."

"You have gotten so bloody weird since Robert left you—"

"Lucy, you didn't listen to me. You didn't hear what I just said to you."

"I heard! I heard you all right, and the point is that you think you're the only person in the world who has ever been divorced and this gives you license to—"

"Girls!" said their mother in exactly the same tone she had used when they were little. "It's cocktail hour and it is so rare that I see both my girls together that if you don't mind I'd like this to be a pleasant occasion. I want to enjoy you." She passed them their wine on a little tray and put a melting wedge of Brie and melba toast on the coffee table. "There. This is very cozy and nice. How long has it been since the three of us have been together?"

"A year last month," said Lucy. "Daddy's funeral."

"Yes," said their mother. "You're right. I hadn't realized how long it had been." She raised her glass—Scotch—and said, "A toast. To all of us."

Lucy and Alix sipped their wine.

"In spite of your troubles, Lucy, you're looking well."

"It's the blusher."

"It's what?"

"The blusher I'm wearing. It's called Tawny Rose."

"I see." She repositioned her diamond ring and then asked Alix, "How is the house coming along?"

"There's a couple who seem interested. They're from Shaker Heights. He plays the violin."

"In the symphony?"

"No. Thursday nights with friends in a string quartet."

"Well, I was going to say, I don't know how a musician could afford your house. Unless it was a rock-and-roll star. They seem to have all the money these days, don't they?" She passed the plate of Brie to Lucy.

"Rock stars, Mother," Lucy said. "Rock-and-roll is old-fashioned. I mean, there are no rock-and-*roll* stars anymore." She shook her head at the plate of cheese. "No, thank you."

"If you don't start eating, you're going to get sick. I don't know what I did wrong. Both my daughters look undernourished."

"Mother, you just said I looked fine and now you tell me I look undernourished. I mean, it's been a very, very difficult couple of days. On the way to Kennedy my cabdriver tried to proposition me. He kept saying he'd be happy to drive me all the way to L.A. and that I reminded him of this girl he loved in the eighth grade named Theresa O'Mallory. And then on the plane the stewardess said they had run out of steak and would I mind having Spinach Supreme instead—"

"Why *did* you leave Peter?" asked Alix.

Lucy looked startled, as though Alix had just asked an unspeakably intimate question. "I told you—he is an insensitive man. I mean, I told you that, Alix." Lucy constantly addressed everyone by name, as though she were selling something.

"But that's a masculine condition. A human condition," said Alix. "I'm asking you specifically why you left Peter. What exactly did he do that was so insensitive that you could no longer live with him?"

The air in the living room suddenly had a quality that had not been there before, as if a match could burst into flame without being struck.

Lucy carefully placed her wineglass on the table next to her. "Well, not that it's any of your business, Alix, but it had to do with the bedroom."

Their mother cleared her throat and cut more cheese.

"Oh, not sex," said Lucy. "It was about the bedroom *walls*. I had the bedroom painted chocolate on Wednesday. That's what it was called on the paint can. Chocolate. And it looked sensational, but Peter came home and went berserk. Maybe it's not a question of being insensitive. Maybe he's too sensitive. Maybe he's crazy. But a grown man going berserk over the color of walls, for God's sake—I couldn't take it." She twisted the bracelets around on her arm. She had little-girl arms, thought Alix. Thin and awkward.

"So you left him with the brown walls," said their mother.

"Chocolate, Mother."

"What's the difference?"

"Depth. Brown is flat."

"Oh."

"Alix, stop looking at me like that."

Alix was thinking of Peter, the brother-in-law she had never met, and how it was possible that she would never meet him. He might float out of Lucy's life the same way he floated in, and all he would be to Alix would be a name she had heard discussed or mentioned in a letter.

"Chinese?" her mother was saying to her.

"Chinese what?" Alix asked.

"*Food.* Are you in the mood for Chinese food?"

"Fine."

"Are you sure you don't want to spend the night?" Her mother collected their glasses and the plate of cheese and melba toast. "I hate to think of you alone on the freeway after dark."

"I'll be fine."

Her mother paused with the tray, crumpling a cocktail napkin in her free hand. "What was it? Something I heard or read today made me think of you. Made me worry about you. And it slipped my mind with all the excitement of Lucy being here."

"May I help you with the glasses, Mother?" said Lucy.

"No, thank you, dear. I'll just leave them in the sink and put the Brie away." She returned from the kitchen a few moments later and said, "I just remembered. I read something in the *Times* this morning about an accident on those cliffs by your house. A car went over and a man burned to death."

"Ugh," said Lucy. "What happened, Alix? Did you see the car go over?"

"No. The police said they thought it might have happened in the middle of the night."

"The police? The police questioned you?"

"They didn't *question* me; they were just checking to see if the neighbors heard anything."

"Was it near you?" her mother asked.

"Across the street."

"Dear God."

"A man was stabbed to death in the laundry room of my apartment building last winter," said Lucy, putting on a jacket that matched her dress. "Can you imagine? In the laundry room putting his dirty clothes in the washing machine, holding one of those little tiny boxes of Tide."

"Let's drop this depressing conversation," said their mother. "I'm sorry I mentioned that accident. Now, does anyone have to use the john before we leave?"

"Mother," said Lucy, "I am thirty-eight years old. If I have to go to the bathroom I am perfectly capable of recognizing the fact."

Alix followed her mother and her sister out to the navy-blue Buick, thinking that relationships within a family never changed. She and Lucy could grow up, leave home, have children of their own, divorce, grow old—and yet their relationship to their mother, to each other, would remain as fixed as the silver-framed photographs.

21

He was back the next morning.

"I'm sorry to have to bother you again," he said. He wore pressed jeans and a blue pullover shirt. The police car was parked in the driveway.

"That's all right," said Alix. It was a hazy morning, hinting at sun; on the ocean white triangles of sailboats could be seen, and the pepper trees on the front lawn were lacy against the sky. "Would you like to come in?"

"Thank you."

"It looks like it might be a nice day for a change," she said, walking into the living room.

"Yes." He sat in a chair and she sat on the couch, facing him.

Below, from the family room, came the sounds of Juanita's weekly battle with the vacuum cleaner.

"May I get you something? A cup of coffee?" said Alix.

"No, thank you."

Juanita thumped up the stairs with the vacuum cleaner. "Oh,

baby, oh, baby, now baby, baby," blared from the transistor at her waist.

"Excuse me a minute," said Alix. She went out into the hallway. "Juanita, please turn off the music. We can hear it in the living room."

"What?"

"The radio. It's too loud."

"Okay, Mrs. Kirkwood." Juanita clicked off the radio and continued up to the top floor, the vacuum cleaner banging against each step.

Alix went back to the sofa in the living room. He sat comfortably, looking at the titles of the books in the bookcase, at ease inside his own skin. What was the fine line between confident and smug? One so sexy and the other so sexless. "Well," said Alix. "I'm sorry—I don't know your name."

"Lieutenant Calloway," he said. "John Calloway. And you are Mrs. Robert Kirkwood."

"Alix Kirkwood."

There was something solid about Lieutenant Calloway, healthy and square. Though she never understood why the term "square" was used for such people. Round would be more appropriate. Smooth, whole, no angles or sharp edges or small, hard corners.

"We've identified the body that was found in the Toyota across the street," he said.

"Yes," said Alix. "I read about it in this morning's paper."

"I hope it didn't come as a shock."

"I beg your pardon?"

"Warren Sullivan. You knew him."

"Vaguely. I met him at a party recently."

"Sunday."

"Sunday, yes. It seems longer ago than last Sunday."

He had taken a small blue spiral notebook from his pocket and was reading his notes silently. After a moment he said, "Your next-door neighbor, Mrs. Drew, told us that—let's see . . ." He frowned at his handwriting. "Yes, she said that her husband had gone to college with Mr. Sullivan. He called them a few weeks ago and told them he had moved to Los Angeles from—" He frowned at his notes again.

"New Jersey."

"Right. Thank you. He had moved here from New Jersey and they invited him to dinner last Sunday. That's when you met him." He looked up at Alix and she nodded. "And after dinner he walked you home?"

"Yes," replied Alix. She wished she were wearing something other than her oldest pair of jeans and a sweater that had begun to unravel at the wrist. She had planned to spend the morning sorting through boxes in the garage, and had dressed accordingly. She imagined herself sitting here with this man and pulling at the yarn until the entire sweater unraveled. "Are you sure you wouldn't like a cup of coffee?"

He smiled. "Positive. I never drink coffee."

"Oh." She clasped her hands together to keep from plucking at the sleeve of her sweater.

"Did Mr. Sullivan mention any problems to you? Was he depressed? Anyone he was mad at? Anything you can think of that he told you would be very helpful to us."

"His ex-wife. He was mad at her."

"Yes?"

"I don't know if that means anything, though. My ex-husband is probably mad at me, too." She realized she was sending him signals. "Why don't you drink coffee?"

"Just never acquired a taste for it." He wrote in his notebook. His hair was very thick and glossy, like a child's. She wondered who pressed his jeans. A wife? A girl friend?

"Would you like some tea, then?"

"No, thanks." He put his notebook in the hip pocket of his jeans. "Maybe a glass of water?"

He followed her into the kitchen. Overhead, the vacuum cleaner rolled and thumped through the bedrooms. Alix struggled with an ice tray.

"Don't bother with ice," he said.

, "No trouble. Really." She held the tray under hot water. "They're supposed to pop out, but they never do." She shook a few ice cubes loose from the tray and one fell to the floor and slid across the room. He picked it up for her and pitched it into the sink.

"Thank you," she said.

"You're welcome."

· She put a couple of cubes in a tall glass, filled it with water and handed it to him. He smiled at her; easy, relaxed. She knew very few men who were easy and relaxed. At the moment she couldn't think of even one. Robert didn't relax even when he was asleep. He talked in his sleep and sometimes made odd sounds as if he were strangling. She wondered what kind of noises John Calloway made in his sleep.

He was sitting on the same stool Warren Sullivan had sat on six days earlier. Alix sat opposite him and moved a salt shaker back and forth in patterns across the top of the counter. The faucet was dripping. She ignored it. ·

"What an interesting job you must have," she said, as if she were at a cocktail party making small talk.

He looked amused. "Yes."

"Do you enjoy it?" What did people talk about these days?

He was giving her question thought. "Enjoy?" he repeated, and was silent for a moment. "I think I'm too involved to enjoy it. But interesting, yes. Usually very interesting."

The faucet dripped. Close by, someone was mowing grass with a power mower. Little beads of moisture were forming on his glass and she noticed that his hands were calloused and rough, as if he did carpentry work or gardened.

"Is that what you wanted to be when you were a little boy—a policeman?"

"No; I wanted to be a sailor."

"And?"

"And I got married too young, right out of high school, and that took care of going to sea. For a while anyway."

Married. "What do you mean?" she asked.

200

"When I got divorced I bought a boat. Now I'm a part-time sailor."

"A boat," she said. She made an arc with the salt shaker. So who pressed his jeans?

"It's a thirty-foot power boat. Old. It was built in 1929 and falling apart when I got my hands on it."

"Do you use it a lot?"

"I live on it. It's docked in San Pedro."

"That must be fun. Is it?"

"Yes." He looked toward the sink. "Your faucet's dripping," he said, and got up to tighten it. "What did you want to be when you were a kid?"

"A dancer. That's what I wanted to be when I was a big kid, too."

"What stopped you?"

"I don't know. I guess I didn't want it badly enough." She moved the shaker in circles. "Or I was too tall. Or too pregnant. Or not good enough. Probably I just didn't want it badly enough." That was the truth. She hadn't wanted it enough.

"Well," he said, and stood up. "I didn't mean to use up so much of your time . . ."

"That's okay. I wasn't busy."

"Thanks for the water."

"You're welcome."

They walked into the hallway.

"Did Warren Sullivan spend the night?"

"Did he what?"

He looked uncomfortable. "I'm sorry, but I have to ask you this question."

After a moment Alix said, "I understand."

"Did he?"

"No."

"Do you remember what time he left?"

"Shortly after he arrived."

Their eyes met. She sounded so vehement that he smiled. "You didn't care for Warren Sullivan, I take it?"

"No."

"And you never saw him again?"

"No."

He took a card from his pocket and handed it to her. "If you can think of anything . . ."

The card had his name and then beneath it, in smaller letters, "Police Department" and two telephone numbers.

"The first number is the station and the other is my home number."

"Your boat number."

"Right," he said with a smile. "Any details you might remember, just give me a call."

"I'm sorry I can't help you more," she said at the front door.

"Thanks for your time."

She looked at the card in her hand. "I'll call you if I remember anything."

She watched him walk to his car; a policeman in uniform was sitting behind the wheel.

In the hallway mirror she glanced at herself and wished again she hadn't dressed to clean out the garage this morning. She went to the foot of the stairs and called up, "Juanita, you can turn your music back on."

The vacuum cleaner clicked off, and Juanita came out of the master bedroom. "You want something, Mrs. Kirkwood?"

"You can turn your music back on if you like."

"Okay," said Juanita, turning the little radio on again, her rubber sandals flapping across the carpet back to the bedroom.

In the kitchen, Alix took the article from the morning's paper out of the junk drawer, where she had placed it along with yesterday's Southland News in Brief item. The junk drawer also contained pennies, thread, sea shells, candle stubs, torn tickets, one piece of bubble gum, an empty Scotch tape dispenser, a used flash bulb, and a PTA notice of a garage sale that had taken place last fall. She took both clippings out of the drawer and put them on the counter. The headline of this morning's article read: CLIFF VICTIM IDENTIFIED. She looked at the item from yesterday's paper. "An unidentified male body . . ." *God.* Why would she have cut it out if she didn't know the identity of the body? What if that policeman had seen it? Feeling stupid and shaken, Alix lighted a match to the clipping over the sink and then washed the black feathery ashes down the drain.

Today's article stated that Warren Sullivan had been identified by tracing the license plates of the car, and his identity verified through dental records which had been located with the cooperation of his former wife, Marjorie Kales Sullivan, who lived in Stonehaven, New Jersey, with the victim's two children, Warren, Jr., age twelve, and Margaret, age fourteen.

It was upsetting to read about the children. She didn't want to know their names and ages; it made them real and vulnerable. Knowing the names and ages of Warren Sullivan's children gave him a dimension she didn't want to think about, couldn't think about.

She imagined Marjorie Sullivan attending her classes, doing her homework, fixing supper for her children. And calling up the dentist for Warren's dental records and having to explain that he had been found dead at the foot of a cliff in California, his body burned black and faceless, unrecognizable. Only his teeth remaining.

She didn't want to think about his teeth either. Or his ex-wife sitting alone in her house in New Jersey. Or his children. These were details she couldn't handle. Just details. Don't think about them and they'll eventually go away.

The last sentence in the article read: "Police are continuing their investigation of the accident." No mention of foul play today. Why did no one, not the paper, not Lieutenant Calloway, mention the fact that a bullet had killed Warren Sullivan?

The phone rang. Folders and papers covered her bedroom floor. She was writing lists, getting organized.

"Do you believe this?" BK's voice was as shrill and abrupt as the ring of the telephone. "And of all people—your friend Rudolph. What do you think happened? Maybe he was ending it all because you spurned his advances. He did advance, didn't he?"

"No," said Alix, sorting lists into labeled folders and sitting cross-legged on the floor. Juanita was scrubbing the bathroom and the smell of scouring powder was familiar and clean.

"What on earth was he doing down here? Why *our* cliffs? Why didn't he just jump off the Marina? Had he tried to see you again?"

"No," said Alix. She opened the folder labeled "House" and wrote "Window washer" on one of the lists inside.

"Maybe he was lurking about the neighborhood trying to catch a glimpse of you. Do you think that was it?"

"I don't know."

"It really is incredibly peculiar. But it must have been suicide, don't you think?"

"I don't know what happened, BK."

"Yes, but speculate! What do you *think* happened?"

"I have no idea."

"You sound so calm about all this. Your date just threw himself off a cliff in front of your house. Doesn't that shake you up just a little bit?"

"He wasn't a date. He was a man I met at a party." She added "Yogurt" to the food list.

"The most attractive man came around this morning," said BK. "A police detective. He said they were questioning everyone who had been at the Drews' Sunday night."

"Yes, I know."

"He's been to see you?"

"Yes."

"He is attractive, isn't he?"

"Yes."

There was a pause and then BK said, "Are you all right?"

"Yes."

"All you say is yes and no. Maybe you're in shock."

"I told you he wasn't my date last weekend."

"What?"

"I mean, I've answered other than yes or no."

"Oh." Another pause. "Look," BK finally said, "we're having a lazy Saturday at home around the pool and Sidney's puttering in his garden and I think you ought to get out of the house and come up here and see us. The sun is out and it'll be good for you."

"Well, I was about to go shopping—"

"Listen," said BK in a whisper, "I need you up here. The girls have arrived and I've got to have somebody on my side."

"I'll drop by on my way shopping," said Alix. "In about an hour?"

"Terrific. And in the meantime—just don't think about it."

It took Alix a moment to realize what it was that she wasn't supposed to think about.

"Ya drive me crazy . . . yeah yeah yeah . . . hear me now crazy," from Juanita's radio.

Alix looked up window washers in the Yellow Pages and arranged for someone to come the following Saturday to clean the windows. She changed from her jeans and unraveling sweater into a skirt and blouse. She found an old toothbrush under the bathroom sink and showed Juanita how she wanted the grouting scrubbed.

"Pour a little Clorox on the tiles and it's easier," she said.

"It'll melt the stuff between the tiles," said Juanita.

"No, it won't," said Alix. "The only thing it'll melt is the dirt. And by the way, somebody will be here next week to clean the windows. I won't be back from my trip yet, but you can handle it. Tell them to send me a bill."

The phone kept ringing. Betty Lee said she'd be by later with the Shoemakers, who were very, very interested in the house and had she found the keys to the garage yet? Lucy called and said things were getting tense between her and their mother and could she come down and spend a few days? Milly called next and said everything was set for Alix's trip, reservations on a Monday flight at one-thirty, and she'd drop off the tickets later that afternoon.

Alix picked up the list for "Hawaii: Clothes" and left the house before the phone could ring again.

22

SIDNEY AND BK LIVED in carefully organized disorder. A studied clutter of chrome, leather, glass, plants, books and cats; the house built on the edge of a hill. A fifty-foot drop into a canyon directly beyond the patio and pool, with a view that encompassed the entire Santa Monica Bay and inland all the way east to the mountains beyond Pasadena. On clear nights there were glittering lights as far as one could see; the beach cities' lights rimmed the dark half moon of ocean to the west. Now it was early afternoon and the sun was hot and bright on the top of the hill.

"It's a whole other climate down there," BK was saying. "You live two miles away and it's like you lived in England or someplace."

Sidney smoked a cigarette. On the patio table were three Design Research plastic mugs filled with coffee, an ashtray, the morning papers, *Newsweek, New West, The New Yorker* and *Sunset,* plus a pair of dark glasses and Sidney's watch. A few feet away, next to the pool, Sidney's daughters, Melody and Shana, lay stretched, half nude, glistening with oil, on Brown Jordan chaises, their eyes shut and their faces turned to the sun.

"Girls, don't get burned," said BK.

"If Melody gets burned," said Shana, "maybe she'll get rid of some of her zits."

"Shut up," said Melody, her face still pointed to the sun and her eyes closed. "Shut *up*. Daddy, do something about Shana."

"Shana, leave your sister alone," said Sidney. He hadn't shaved that morning and it looked as though his skin must itch in the hot sun.

"Mommy says that the sun is the best thing for zits," said Shana. "I'm just repeating what Mommy says."

"Shut *up*," said Melody.

"Come on, girls," said Sidney. "Cut it out."

Shana sat up. "I've gotta have a Fresca or something."

"Well, go get one," said BK. "You know where they are."

"Get one for me," said Melody to her sister.

"Get it yourself," said Shana, and went through the sliding glass door into the house. She closed the door behind her and made a face at her sister.

"What I don't understand," said Sidney, "is why that guy was down here. Didn't he live in the Marina? What was he doing here?"

"And in the fog," said BK. "If it had been sunny maybe . . ."

Alix shrugged and watched one of BK's cats stretch, slowly, gracefully, as if he were doing it to the music of a harp.

"I just can't stand not knowing what happened to Rudolph," said BK. "Was it an accident? Was he just mooning around, looking at the view—but of course there wasn't a view, with all that fog. Maybe he was spying on Alix. Or do you think he might have committed suicide?"

"Rudolph?" said Sidney. "I thought his name was Warren."

"An expression, Sidney. A figure of speech."

Sidney scratched his chin, which made a sandpapery sound. The glare of the sun was giving Alix a headache. She tried on the dark glasses that were on the table, but they were too large and slid down her nose.

"*Think,* Alix," said BK. "Wasn't there something he said to you last Sunday that you could link to this? Was he depressed?"

"I have no idea if he was depressed. We didn't really talk that much." Alix stretched out her hands and felt the hot sun on them. She could see the buildings downtown, thirty miles away, rising up through the smog.

"There aren't any Frescas left," said Shana. "BK, we need more Fresca."

"Have something else," said BK.

"Everything else is gross."

"Oh, God, I'm so thirsty," said Melody.

Sidney rotated his shoulders backward and forward.

"How's your back?" asked Alix.

"Lousy," he replied. "It went out again last month when I planted the tomatoes. It was so bad I couldn't even tie my own shoelaces."

"I'm sorry," said Alix.

"Yeah, well, I do exercises and take pain pills. I'll live."

"How's this?" said BK. "Warren Sullivan is supplying coke to his entire building in the Marina; all those swinging singles. And he's diluting it with something. Let's say Ajax."

"Why Ajax?" said Sidney.

"Well, it has to be white powder, Sidney. He couldn't cut coke with green or blue scouring powder."

"What are you talking about?" asked Sidney.

"This is a hypothesis. Warren is into dope. He's ripping off the cocaine users at the Marina and—"

"BK, it stinks," said Sidney, and then to Alix, "She saw one TV documentary on cocaine and now she's some kind of expert on the drug scene."

"Mommy always keeps extra cases of Fresca stored in the garage," said Shana.

Alix looked at the cover of *Sunset*—a group of lean, tanned, smiling people sharing a meal on a picnic bench—and wondered why *Sunset* people always looked so much happier and better adjusted than people in other magazines. Or in real life.

A large black-and-white cat jumped up on the table and spread himself out carefully over the magazines and newspaper, avoiding the ashtray and coffee mugs. Alix ran her fingers over his sleek fur and thought that next week at this time she would be in Hawaii, where no one had ever heard of Warren Sullivan and she would be as lazy and warm as BK's cat.

"Get this damn cat off the table," said Sidney.

"He's not hurting anything," said BK.

"I'm going to Hawaii on Monday," said Alix.

"Oh, Alix, how terrific!"

"There are cat hairs in everything," said Sidney.

BK picked up the cat and held him in her lap. "Are you going alone?"

"Look, there's cat hair in my coffee," said Sidney.

"Sidney, the cat is off the table."

"Yes, I'm going alone. To Kauai."

"Have you told Robert?" asked Sidney.

"Why should I tell Robert?"

"In case something comes up."

"Nothing's going to come up."

"Well, he ought to know where you are. What if the house sells while you're gone?"

"Okay, Sidney. I'll call Robert and let him know I'm going to Hawaii."

"I think it's great you're getting away," said BK. "Why don't we celebrate? Stay for lunch. We'll take a swim and then open a bottle of wine. Have a bon voyage party—"

"Thanks, but I've got to go shopping and run errands."

"Okay, we'll have a welcome home party instead."

"Great."

"BK, there's no bread for lunch," said Melody from her chaise. "And we're about to run out of potato chips, too."

BK looked at Sidney and then down at the purring cat in her lap. "Your father will take care of it."

"I've got to get back to my tomatoes," said Sidney. "I've planted them all along the side of the house this year," he said to Alix. "Sixteen plants, four varieties. Beefsteak, Tiny Tim, Big Boy and Ace."

"We'll have tomatoes up the gaziggy," said BK.

"What's a gaziggy?" asked Shana.

"Mommy has a neat recipe for tomato chutney," said Melody. "Maybe she'll give it to you."

"BK, what are we going to do about lunch?" said Shana.

"What are we going to do about lunch?" said BK. "I'll tell you what we're going to do about lunch. You and your sister are going to get off your fat little fannies and get on the fancy bicycles your father bought you and you're going to ride down to the store and buy something for lunch. That's what we're going to do about lunch, Shana."

Smog hung over the downtown buildings, grew heavier and browner toward the mountains to the east, and disappeared into fog along the coast. Alix drove down the hill from BK and Sidney's house, thinking about cat hairs in Sidney's coffee and the brown filth that was called air which they all had to breathe. Were BK and Sidney happy? What did they talk about when they were alone?

Inside Bullock's, the clean, perfumed air held promises of order and perfection. In the air-conditioned calm nothing was peculiar or quirky; there were no personalities, no history. All this newness soothed her.

She sprayed her wrists with half a dozen new scents, studied lipstick and eye shadow shades as if absorbing paintings in a museum, ran her hands over buttery soft leather bags, leaned on shiny glass counters and stared at jewelry.

Today she loved the salesladies, snobbish and impersonal. She loved the dedicated shoppers with their bright enameled surfaces, their expensive shoes and perfect haircuts and skirt lengths. As if the more perfect the exterior, the less vulnerable the interior.

She bought silk underwear trimmed with white lace. Bras with the substance of handkerchiefs, nightgowns that were frilly and innocent. She bought a canvas shoulder bag with a silver clasp, and T-shirts and shorts and a tiny bikini and flowery, gauzy sundresses.

She was going to Hawaii.

She'd get a job and find an apartment.

She was in charge of things.

A list of messages was waiting by the phone when she returned home at four that afternoon. Lucy, Milly, and the children. She dialed the number in Phoenix immediately.

"I miss you, Mommy," said Cindy, her voice both sweet and whiny. "Mark threw up last night, but Grandma says it was because he ate nine of those little packages of Fritos. He told Grandma that was all he ever ate at home. Fritos and jack cheese."

"Is he okay now?"

"I guess so. Grandpa took him to the movies a little while ago, so I guess he's not dying or anything. Grandma's going to take me out to dinner tonight. Just the two of us, and I'm going to wear that new skirt you bought me. You know the one with the red and blue dots on it?"

"Yes. Be sure to wear the navy-blue T-shirt with it."

"Okay."

"Guess what. I'm going to Hawaii on Monday."

"Hawaii? Is Daddy going with you?"

"No. I'm going all by myself."

"Why don't you ask Daddy to go with you? You can't go all the way to Hawaii by yourself, Mommy."

"Why not?"

"I don't know. You just can't. I'll worry about you."

"I'll be fine, darling. Don't worry about me."

"When are you coming home?"

"In a week. And then it'll just be two more weeks until you and Mark get home, and, Cindy baby, I've got all kinds of wonderful plans for us. How would you like to live at the plaza? You could walk to the bakery and the library and all the stores by yourself."

"That sounds okay."

"And maybe we'll get a cat."

"What kind of a cat?"

"Any kind you want."

"I miss you, Mommy."

"I miss you, too, darling, but we'll all be together in just a couple of weeks."

"Would you get me one of those necklaces in Hawaii that's made out of little white shells?"

"Sure. What do you think Mark would like me to bring back for him?"

"I don't know. What he needs most is a new fish bowl. Jimmy just wrote to him and told him he's got five more guppies and he's all excited. Maybe you could just wait until you get back and then buy him another fish bowl."

"Okay, and I'll send you lots of postcards."

The doorbell rang.

"I love you, Mommy."

"I love you, too. Somebody's at the door; I've got to hang up. Be good and I'll see you in a couple of weeks. Give Mark a kiss for me."

The doorbell rang again. Alix could feel the impatience of whoever was waiting for her to answer the door. "I'm coming," she called from the hallway.

Milly was wearing her jogging shorts and a T-shirt that said RUN FOR YOUR LIFE. "I've got your tickets."

"Come on in."

"We can't believe what's happened." Her eyes were red, as if she'd been crying. "You did hear about it? About Warren?"

"Yes. I read about it in this morning's paper."

"It's so odd. It just doesn't make sense." Milly sat on the sofa, patting the cushions with an awkward, unthinking motion of her hands. "Doesn't make any sense at all. Why here? We feel somehow responsible."

"Responsible?"

"Yes, because it happened *here*. Until dinner at our house he'd never been down here. Jim had to give him directions. He had no idea how to get here. What I'm saying is he had never been to the peninsula before in his life until last Sunday and then a few days later he *dies* here. It just doesn't make any sense."

"I know," said Alix.

Milly had begun to cry. "Do you have any Kleenex?"

"No. But I'll get you some john paper." Alix went down to the guest bathroom and tore off a handful of tissue.

"Thank you," said Milly, and blew her nose. "I feel especially awful because I said such nasty things about him to Jim after Sunday night. And now I keep thinking that if we hadn't invited him down here to dinner he might still be alive." Tears ran down her face. "It's so *final.*"

"Yes."

"Weren't there any clues? Didn't he say something that might make a little sense of this? Maybe he committed suicide?" Milly's forehead was knotted in frown lines, as if the answer was accessible if she thought long and hard enough. "Do you think that was it? Do you think he was depressed about his divorce and everything and committed suicide?"

"I don't know, Milly."

"Didn't he say anything to you? How he felt or maybe he thought it was nice down here and wanted to come back and—oh, hell, I don't know—look at the view or something? Didn't he say anything when he walked you home that night?"

"Nothing that could be connected to this," said Alix. "He really didn't say much."

Milly was shredding the toilet paper into little blue strips. "This has really gotten to me."

"Let me get you a drink or something."

Milly shook her head. "No. Thanks anyway. I've got to run my two miles." She picked up the folder with the airline tickets inside. "You're booked on a one-thirty flight on United, arriving in Honolulu at three-thirty local time, and then a four o'clock flight to Kauai, arriving in Lihue at five fifty-five. And I've got you a single room with a lanai facing the beach at the Lihue Surf for six nights and seven days."

"Perfect," said Alix, and wrote out a check for the airline tickets.

"I'll have one of the kids bring in the mail and paper every day."

"Thanks."

Milly stood up from the sofa. "And let's hope when you get back this will all be solved and forgotten. Well, maybe not forgotten, but at least we'll know what happened. God, I hope so. Do you have a ride to the airport?"

"My sister will be here and she can drive me."

The rubber soles of Milly's Adidas made a squashing noise on the tiles in the front hall. "If you need a ride at the last minute, let us know and I could get away from the office for an hour or so."

"Thanks, Milly."

"Have a good time."

She had to call Lucy back. Unpack her new clothes. Eat something. She had forgotten to eat all day. She dialed her mother's number and Lucy answered.

"Mother's calmed down," said Lucy. "I thought I'd drive down tomorrow morning instead."

"What was wrong?"

"Wrong?"

"Between you and Mother."

"Oh, everything. Nothing. I don't know. I'm just beyond the stage where I need to be told what to eat and how much sleep I should get and what's wrong with my marriage. . . ."

Alix hooked the phone on her shoulder and took a bottle of white wine from the refrigerator. "Look, I'm going to Hawaii on Monday for a short holiday. Would you mind driving me to the airport? You could either come back here and have the house while I'm gone or go on to Mother's from the airport."

"Hawaii? What are you going to Hawaii for?"

"I told you. A holiday."

"You mean all by yourself? You're not going with anybody or meeting anybody there?"

Alix took a wineglass from the cupboard and filled it to the top with wine. "All by myself, Lucy."

"That's weird."

"Nonsense. I'm very excited about it. You'll take me to the airport?"

"Sure. But I think it's strange. I mean, what fun is it to go to Hawaii all by yourself?"

"What time will you be down in the morning?" Alix asked.

"Late. But before noon."

"See you then. Give my love to Mother." Alix hung up, switched on the little TV set on the counter and sipped her wine.

The local five o'clock news team was under thirty, very attractive, well dressed, and given to joking about their athletic prowess and domestic problems.

Today in Los Angeles: A woman was killed when she lost control of her car at 10:30 A.M. in Glendale. Six hundred homes lost electricity for an hour in the Silver Lake area. A dawn raid in Hermosa Beach netted drugs worth over a million dollars street value. A three-year-old boy had been missing from his Hollywood Hills home since noon, and a massive house-to-house search was under way. Mr. and Mrs. Leonard O'Brian of Thousand Oaks had trained their dachshund to answer the phone by knocking the receiver off the hook and then barking into it; two brief barks meant no one was home, prolonged barking meant the O'Brians were home and would shortly pick up the phone themselves. The identity of a man whose body was found early Thursday in the charred wreckage of a 1977 Toyota at the foot of the peninsula cliffs had been determined through dental records.

"Tonight police announced that a murder investigation is under way. The victim, Warren Sullivan of Marina del Rey, was apparently shot to death before his car went over the cliffs and burned. Police have ruled out suicide."

215

Alix sipped her wine. A murder investigation.

There would be low clouds and early-morning fog along the coast, continuing through Monday. The Dodgers would play a doubleheader at home Sunday. A band of militant vegetarians had picketed McDonald's and was scheduled to make similar demonstrations in front of Big Bob's, Love's, and Jack-In-The-Box during the coming week. Fourteen policemen on horseback and twelve employees of Lion Country Safari had successfully captured the ten-month-old baby lion who had escaped early Friday, in a canyon south of Laguna Beach.

Alix turned off the television set and poured herself another glass of wine. A murder investigation. She found some saltines in the cupboard and as the evening light faded she sat in her kitchen and sipped her wine and nibbled on saltines and wondered what they were going to investigate.

23

EARLY SUNDAY. She couldn't sleep. She lay in bed and thought: I have killed a man. It occurred to her that she should feel guilty, but she didn't. She used to feel guilty about always forgetting to buy Robert's jam. She had felt guilty for stuffing old newspapers into the drier. For not using the pool more often. But she did not feel guilty about killing Warren Sullivan.

The newspaper came at six-thirty. Through the open bedroom windows she could hear it hit the end of the driveway. The Sunday *Times*. Coffee. The little rituals of life. She washed her face and dressed in shorts and a T-shirt and went downstairs.

Page three of the Sunday *Times:*

Police are investigating the apparent murder of Warren Sullivan, whose body was discovered Thursday in the wreckage of a 1977 red Toyota Corolla. An autopsy has revealed that the cause of death was not the crash and subsequent explosion of the Toyota, as originally believed, but a bullet found in the victim's right side. Mr. Sullivan, an insurance salesman for Penwick Insurance Company of Westwood, was last seen alive by Shirley Grossman of

Long Beach, who had purchased an insurance policy from him the morning of June 23, the day before his body was discovered at the foot of the peninsula cliffs. Ms. Grossman has told police that Mr. Sullivan was in good spirits the morning of the 23rd and had told her he would call her that evening. Police did not elaborate on the nature of the call, but did indicate the call was never made. Justin G. Merritt, president of Penwick Insurance Company, said that Mr. Sullivan's death was a great loss to the company. Memorial services will be held Monday in Stonehaven, New Jersey.

Next to the article was a photograph captioned: "Warren Sullivan with his ex-wife, Marjorie K. Sullivan." Warren was wearing a short-sleeved plaid shirt, his arms folded over his chest. He looked sullen and pouty. The woman standing next to him had very short dark hair, was slightly plump and was wearing what appeared to be a bathing suit top. Had she given the paper the photograph? What was she thinking at this moment? Was she getting ready for the memorial service? Did his mother also live in Stonehaven, and if so, what were she and Marjorie talking about? Alix studied the photograph, both repelled and fascinated by it.

It was barely eight-thirty when the doorbell rang.

"Good morning," said Lieutenant Calloway without explanation, simply standing there in the doorway smiling at her. Instead of the official police car, an old dusty Ford was parked out front. Pressed jeans again. Same sneakers.

"Good morning," she said. "Would you like to come in?"

"Yes, I would. Thank you."

In the kitchen he looked at the *Times* spread out across the counter. "You've read about it?"

"Yes." She turned on the kettle. "Would you like a cup of tea?"

"Yes. Thank you." He watched her take the teacups down from the cupboard. "The coroner's office didn't give us the autopsy report until late yesterday. This is the first murder we've had around here in years. We're not even equipped to handle it. Los Angeles sheriff's department is taking over today."

"Taking over?" She found a box of Lipton tea bags in the cupboard behind the spices.

"The lab work, for one thing. We'll continue to help with the investigation, but they're in charge."

"Is that frustrating?"

"A little," he said.

The water came to a boil and she filled the cups. "Would you like to sit outside on the patio?"

"Damnedest case I've ever worked on," he said, following her outside.

"How about some breakfast? I've got eggs. Or cereal? There's cornflakes and Grape-Nuts."

"Nothing, thanks. I've already eaten."

The glass-top table was gritty with dust. Alix went back into the kitchen, returned with a sponge and wiped off the table. He held the cups up while she sponged.

"What was this guy like?"

She looked at him, the sponge black with dirt in one hand, her other hand on her hip.

"Warren Sullivan—what was he like? I can't figure him out. There's no handle to this. No hook to grab on to, to hang all this on."

"He was . . . I don't know. Boring." She took the sponge back into the kitchen and left it in the sink.

"What do you mean?" He sipped his tea, his rough hands cradling the china cup.

"Just that," she said. "Boring. He was not very interesting. I really can't tell you much about him. I met him at the Drews' dinner party, he walked me home afterward. That's all."

"The dinner party." He squinted up at the sky. "And then he's found murdered right across the street. What was the connection?"

"I'm sorry—did you want sugar in your tea? I didn't even think to ask you."

"No; this is fine. I don't use sugar."

They sat without speaking for a few moments. A mockingbird strutted across the lawn to a sprinkler with its stiff-legged gait and dabbed for water. The air was warm and the gray sky was bright.

"The honeysuckle smells so good," he said.

"Yes, it always reminds me of summers when I was little."

It felt comfortable to sit on her patio with John Calloway early on a warm Sunday morning. It shouldn't, but it did.

"I keep thinking that you know something you don't realize you know," he said. "There was some link between Sullivan and someone at that party. You were there. You spent time with him. It might have just been small talk, but you talked to him. Somewhere in your head there's a word you heard or a look you observed that could be the one clue we're looking for."

The comfortable feeling began to thin, turned to impatience. He caught the feeling as she moved in her chair, rearranged her cup and saucer.

"I know you're sick of all this—"

"Yes."

"Try and think of it as a puzzle. What was it about Sullivan that caused him to be murdered? What had he *done*? This was not a random killing. It was very carefully planned and executed. But *why*? Here you have an ordinary guy. Divorced. Two kids. College graduate. Decent job. No quirks, nothing. As far as we can find out, he doesn't have a girl friend. Or boyfriend. Or friends even. He's just a lonely, ordinary guy who moved to Los Angeles a month ago. Sunday night he goes to a dinner party on this street. Four days later he's found murdered on this street. *Why?* He's never been here before that dinner party. What happened at the party? There were eight guests and the Drews. Who else did he talk to?"

"Everybody, I guess. I don't really know. I just didn't pay that much attention."

"I feel like I'm up against a wall. There are no possibilities. Nothing to go on. No hunches. If he had been found at the Marina we'd have more to work on. But the fact that he was found out here makes a damn sure connection to that dinner party. But *what* connection? Nine suburban neighbors and only one knew Sullivan before the party, as far as we can find out, and Jim Drew hadn't seen him since 1962." He looked at Alix. "You're my only hope."

"What do you mean?"

"That clue, that *something*, is in your memory, your sub-conscious. I'm sure it is. Can't you just *try* . . . ?"

After a moment she said, "I'm sorry."

"I know," he said, suddenly gentle. "I know. It's our problem, not yours."

They drank their tea. There was the flat, popping sound of a game in a nearby tennis court. Sounds of Sunday traffic along the road in front of the house; sightseers, churchgoers, joggers, a motorcycle. She sorted out the sounds in her mind, labeled each one.

"The sun will be out soon," he said.

She nodded. "I just made elaborate and expensive plans to go to Hawaii for a week. And now the sun's coming out in my own backyard."

"When are you going?"

"Tomorrow."

"First time?"

"No, we used to go every year when I was little. With my parents and sister. But it's my first time alone. I've never gone anyplace alone. I've always traveled with my mother telling me what to wear and what to say; or my husband, who wrote out itineraries every time we took a trip, complete with arrival and departure times, points of interest, and recommended restaurants; or my kids, who throw up a lot when they leave home. But this trip is all mine. One week of doing what I want to do."

"Which is?"

"Oh, just lying on a beach and soaking up sun. Reading. Nothing exciting, really. The important part is doing it on my own. The fact that it's never foggy in Hawaii is a fringe benefit." She smiled at him. "Have you ever been to Hawaii?"

"No. Catalina's about as far as I've gotten. I take my boat over."

"Often?"

"As often as I can."

"When I was about thirteen my parents rented a boat and took us to Catalina—"

"Chartered."

"What?"

"You charter a boat, not rent one."

"Oh. Well, they chartered a sailboat and hired someone to sail it and we went over for a couple of days. My sister threw up all the way to Avalon and then all the way back. My mother was convinced she was doing it on purpose because she hadn't wanted to go; she wanted to stay home and see her boyfriend." Alix laughed.

"What's so funny?"

"My mother that weekend. She dressed all in white; white blouse, white sweater, white slacks, white sneakers, even a white scarf to tie around her head so her hair wouldn't get mussed. I think she heard somewhere that white was supposed to be nautical, but she looked as if she were going to perform surgery. And she acted exactly as if she were home in Brentwood. I mean, the same cocktails and food, and she even brought her own monogrammed sheets and towels. Everything was the same except we were on the water and she had on all these white clothes. And then there was Lucy moaning down below on her bed—or I guess it was a bunk?"

He nodded.

"But then, later, my father took me ashore and we went hiking way up in the hills, and oh, it was beautiful. Really beautiful, looking down at that blue bay and all the funny little houses sort of stuck to the hills."

"The light is different there. Colors are brighter."

"Yes. My father talked about that. The water was an incredible shade of blue. And there was another shade of blue that a lot of the houses were trimmed with. I really loved it there. I always meant to go back, but . . ." She shrugged. "I don't know. I never did. Someday, though . . ."

"Would you like me to take you sometime?"

She looked at him.

"On my boat, when you get back from Hawaii."

"Yes," she said. "I'd like that, I'd really like that."

"Good." He stood up. "When this case is over I'll be getting some time off."

He helped her carry the cups into the kitchen. "And the weather will have broken by then."

"That sounds wonderful." It did sound wonderful.

"We'll work it out," he said.

"Yes," she answered. Everything was going to work out.

24

A CAR PULLED INTO THE DRIVEWAY and tooted the horn. Lucy. She pulled a canvas satchel from the back seat. "Hello!" she called as she came up the path toward the front door.

"Lieutenant Calloway, this is my sister Lucy," said Alix.

"Hello," said Lucy, radiating charm and energy. Unbelievable, thought Alix, how completely Lucy changed around men.

"I'll call you next week," Calloway said to Alix, and headed for his car.

"My God, isn't he attractive. Where did you find him?" said Lucy, still standing at the front door.

"I didn't," said Alix. "He simply appeared on my doorstep."

"I don't believe it."

"He's a policeman, Lucy. He's investigating that accident across the street. Though now it seems that it wasn't an accident."

"It wasn't?"

"No." Alix took Lucy's canvas satchel and carried it down to the guest room on the lower level, Lucy right behind her.

"Well, what was it, then?"

"A murder."

"A *murder*?"

"Yes." Alix opened the closet door and checked the number of coat hangers. "The dresser drawers are empty if you want to use them."

"Right across the street. Aren't you scared?"

"Of course not." Alix opened the shutters.

"When that fellow was stabbed to death in my building there was a little circle of blood on the concrete floor next to the washing machine and the maid was afraid to go down there, so I did the laundry and I could never go near that spot where it happened without searching out the circle and looking at it. Like if I faced it right away it wouldn't bother me so much. Do you know what I mean?"

"Yes."

Lucy unpacked a pair of jeans, a shirt, a nightgown and a robe from the satchel and hung it all in the closet. "You must be frantic to get out of this place."

"Frantic?" Alix repeated, the word conjuring up images of mazes and hysteria. "No, not frantic."

"Anxious, then."

"Eager," said Alix, realizing that Lucy's grasp on life excluded the subtleties of words, shades of meaning. "Anxious implies anxiety."

"Oh, spare me one of your dissertations on the proper use of words," said Lucy, running a tortoise-shell comb through her hair. Alix could not remember ever seeing Lucy use a plastic comb. "My point is simply that it can't be easy living out here all alone in the suburbs in this big house without a husband or the children. I mean, it can't be easy. *with* a husband and children. You can't say it's fun, can you?"

"No," said Alix, "not fun."

"Well, that's what I meant." Lucy unbuttoned her shirt. "I want to go back with some color," she said, and hung the shirt in the closet, refastening the top button so it wouldn't slide off the hanger.

Neat, organized. Lucy would never lose anybody's socks. Robert had married the wrong sister. Except that he couldn't stand Lucy.

"Not a tan," Lucy was saying, "just some color." She stepped out of her slacks, shook them, aligned the creases and folded them over a hanger. "Nobody gets a tan anymore." She closed the closet door. Her bra and panties matched, a blue-and-green abstract design.

"Nobody gets a tan anymore?" repeated Alix. She was thirty-six years old. Why did Lucy still make her feel dumb? Out of things. The little sister. When she was eighty-five years old she'd still be Lucy's little sister.

"Not unless you want to get skin cancer," said Lucy, "or look twice your age."

"Oh." She was twelve years old and Lucy was describing her first French kiss. She didn't want to seem dumb or out of things then either. She wanted to yell, "He did *what* with his tongue?" but instead she had very coolly looked Lucy right in the eye and said, "Oh, really? He did that?" Cool. Above all she was very cool. "But the sun isn't out," she said.

"The haze," Lucy replied, taking off her underwear, rolling bra and panties into a ball and then tossing them into the canvas bag. She stood naked in the middle of the room with her hands on her bladelike hips. "Sometimes the sun filtered through hazy clouds is more potent than pure sun. Haven't you ever heard that?" She took a silky one-piece bathing suit from her bag. "It's something to do with the way the rays of the sun are slanted or reflected." From her makeup case she took a tube of Bain de Soleil. "Towels?"

"In the bathroom. Take a bath towel."

"Aren't you going to change?"

Alix was thinking how much Lucy was like their mother.

"It'll do you good to lie around the pool," said Lucy. "You could use some color."

The resemblance increased as Lucy grew older. She even sounded like their mother. Looked like her. The way she held her head, chin tilted up and pushed slightly forward. Rising above distractions, anything that went wrong. For reasons Alix didn't fully understand, this resemblance made her feel closer to both Lucy and their mother. As if the similarities connected all three of them, proof they belonged to each other. Attached them to something greater than themselves. Was the whole greater than its parts?

"Aren't you going to put your suit on?" said Lucy, pinning up her hair in the bathroom.

"Yes," said Alix, and paused in the doorway, watching Lucy fix her hair. "Remember how Daddy used to say 'okey-dokey' instead of yes or okay?"

"And 'doggone.' Remember that? So much nicer than shit or fuck. Doggone it."

"Yes."

"Do you have any magazines? Or this morning's paper?"

"In the family room."

"And some wine?"

"In the fridge. I'll bring it out to the pool."

"Remember when you sent away for the bust cream and we spent hours rubbing it into our chests?" said Lucy, and laughed, a raucous, uninhibited laugh that Alix hadn't heard since they were teen-agers.

Alix turned over on the chaise. "And one day Mother found us rubbing it in and she thought we were up to something kinky."

"I shall keep this a secret from your father!" Lucy said in a fine imitation of their mother, and poured more wine into their glasses.

"And then when we explained what we were doing, she said, 'I fail to see the need for bosoms at your age!'"

Again Lucy's raucous laugh. "That's right! Oh, Alix, that's right. I'd forgotten how she always used to call them *bosoms*."

"I was so jealous when yours started to grow finally," said Alix, warm and giddy in the hazy sunlight. "And when you got your period I thought I'd die of jealousy."

"Remember that booklet Mother gave us? I think she sent away for it. Or maybe it came in a Modess box. Anyway, the opening sentence was, 'There is nothing to become alarmed about.' "

"No. It didn't really say that, did it? You're making it up."

"I swear!" Lucy's hair had become unpinned and her face glistened with suntan gel. " 'You are now a woman. There is nothing to become alarmed about.' I swear it said that."

"I remember the part about the importance of remaining dainty and feminine during That Time of Month. I could never figure out exactly what that was supposed to mean."

"I still haven't figured it out," said Lucy, and finished her wine. "Dear God, we're going to be hung over tomorrow."

"I am going to Hawaii tomorrow," said Alix, enunciating each word carefully.

"Bon voyage," said Lucy.

"Thank you very much."

"And aloha."

Alix closed her eyes. Aloha. Ciao. Ciao, Warren. Patterns formed against the orange light coming through her eyelids. Formed, merged, split, dissolved. The plastic strips of the chaise could be felt beneath her towel. The garden smelled decadent. Honeysuckle, star jasmine, mock orange. Heavy as perfume. The pool filter whined. Across the street the ocean rolled in against the cliffs.

"Aloha," Lucy said again. "Every summer, remember?"

"Spring," said Alix. "Spring vacations."

"Right." A splashing sound as Lucy poured more wine. "And you'd spend the whole time asking, 'How many more days, Daddy?' like they had taken us to Siberia or someplace. And then we'd get lectured about how fortunate we were."

Alix was watching a tiny silver plane, five minutes into its ascent from Los Angeles Airport, float higher and higher in the pale sky.

"Faster than a speeding bullet," she said.

"More powerful than a—a what?"

"A locomotive."

"Right. The Lone Ranger rides again!"

"No, that's Superman."

"I always liked the Lone Ranger better. 'Who was that stranger?' 'I don't know, but he left a silver bullet.'"

Fifty silver bullets, eleven ninety-five.

Who was that stranger? Nobody. Garbage.

Hey, Lucy, listen to this one. Hands down the best story of the day.

"Was he here long?" said Lucy.

"Who?"

"The fellow you found on your front doorstep. The cop."

"No, not long." Alix smiled. "What did you think of him?"

"Very, very attractive, like I told you. I would surmise," said Lucy, having difficulty with the word, "that he is probably a very nice lay."

"A nice lay?"

"Or do you already know that?"

"No. Not yet."

Lucy propped herself up on the chaise, leaning on her elbow. "Not *yet?*"

"He's taking me to Catalina when I get back from Hawaii."

"*Catalina?*"

"Yes. On his boat."

"I nearly died going to Catalina on a boat once. Do you remember that?"

"Yes."

"Be sure and take Dramamine before you go." Lucy sat up, oiled her legs again and sipped her wine. "A real boat, with beds and everything?"

"I believe they're called bunks."

"Hmmm."

"Yes. Hmmm."

"Will this be the first time since Robert?"

"First what?"

"Oh, *Jesus*, Alix . . ."

"I don't know. I mean, I don't know what's going to happen. Oh, Lucy, it's been so long. I feel . . . I don't know. Nervous. Like my first date, when I was so nervous I couldn't chew—"

"You couldn't what?"

"*Chew.* This fellow who was about thirteen or fourteen invited me out and he bought me a hamburger and I was so nervous I couldn't chew or swallow. My mouth wouldn't work. I was afraid I'd get crumbs all over my lips or choke or something."

"This time don't swallow, dummy!" Lucy shrieked, and then laughed uproariously.

Alix imagined Calloway's boat and the motion of the water and what it would be like to lie there with him. A nice lay, Lucy had said. Yes, John Calloway would be a very nice lay. A fantastic lay. She remained perfectly still, thinking, thinking about how very much she wanted to sleep with John Calloway.

"You know what's nice?" said Lucy.

"What?"

"Not to have to worry about dinner. You know how you always have to think about dinner if a man is around? Men are so concerned about their meals. Have you ever noticed?"

"Yes."

"Mother even mentioned it the other night. She said that since it was just us girls, maybe we could nibble something rather than going to the bother of cooking or getting dressed to go to a restaurant."

"Mother said *nibble*?"

"Really." Lucy rubbed more Bain de Soleil on her arms. "So we nibbled on cheese and fruit."

"Robert used to think he would faint, literally faint dead away, if he didn't have three balanced meals a day."

"*Balanced meals?* That sounds just exactly like Robert." Lucy oiled her face. "Only Robert would use an expression like that. I mean, I have never understood Robert's appeal. He was attractive, I guess, but so preoccupied with what he ate and how much exercise he got and his clothes. He was a very tense man, Alix."

"Is."

"What?"

"He *is* a tense man. He isn't dead, so he *is*."

"Do you miss him?"

Missing Robert was suddenly such an extraordinary thought; it seemed as though she hadn't missed him for years. She couldn't remember what it even felt like to miss Robert. "No. I did in the beginning. But not anymore." Alix sat up on the chaise. "Do you suppose they talk about us like this?"

"Who?"

"Robert and Brian. And Peter."

"They don't know one another."

"I mean to other men. Their male friends."

"I have no idea." Lucy pulled herself up from her chaise, stood unsteadily for a moment by the edge of the pool, then dove in.

Click. I have no idea. What had she said wrong? It was after five and the imperceptible shift had taken place between afternoon and early evening. The weight of shadows had changed. The breeze shifted and blew from a new direction; off the sea, cooler. Lucy came out of the pool, wrapped herself in a towel, and pinned up her hair.

"Well," said Alix, "I guess I'd better go in and pack."

"Yes," Lucy said, and helped her gather up the glasses and the empty wine bottle.

"I'm sorry I missed the children," said Lucy, sitting in the middle of Alix's bed, watching her pack. Her hair hung wet and straight from her shower and she wore a short white robe. She was eating an orange, pulling apart each section as if she were to be graded on neatness.

"I'm sorry, too," said Alix, cutting off the tags on her new underwear. "They're growing up so fast."

"They're good kids."

"Yes." She folded three bras. "When are you going back to New York?"

"Day after tomorrow. There's a meeting early Wednesday morning I have to be back for."

Alix put her new sandals in plastic bags.

"I lied," said Lucy.

"About what?"

"The walls. The bedroom walls."

"Oh." Alix tucked the sandals in the back of the suitcase.

"I might do crazy things. As a matter of fact, I did have the bedroom painted chocolate and Peter did have a fit, but I mean, I wouldn't have left him over something like that." She arranged the sections of orange in a petal design. "It was much more complicated."

Alix took her robe from the hook behind the bathroom door. "How was it more complicated?"

"Other people were involved."

"Other people?"

One of Lucy's long silences and then, "Men."

"Oh."

"Not mine."

"Oh?"

"Peter's."

"Oh, Lucy . . ."

"AC-DC, as we used to say."

"Yes."

"He claims to be impartial, but I suspect he actually prefers men."

Where are the ordinary men? thought Alix. Just once let us find a man who is whole and uncomplicated. She thought again of John Calloway.

"I had thought that I was more sophisticated," said Lucy, getting off the bed and pacing the room. "I thought Peter and I could handle this situation. But one night last week he didn't come home. My sophistication gave in to my imagination." She stood at the window, looking out at the ocean. "I couldn't handle it, I just couldn't cope." She had begun to cry, forgetting how tears looked dripping off her chin. "We have a dear friend named Larry who works with me, and it finally dawned on me just how dear a friend Larry was to Peter. I mean, we've gone off skiing on weekends together, and Larry's always around on Sundays when we stay in town. Can you imagine? Can you imagine going through something like this? I feel crazy. I mean, Robert was unfaithful, too, but at least the competition was only half of the human race."

Alix looked at her sister for a long moment without saying anything, and then went into the bathroom. From under the sink she took a small cosmetics case and began to pack it with toiletries and cosmetics.

"Everybody knew about Robert," said Lucy, standing in the doorway.

"I've been wondering who told Mother."

"Alix, it wasn't a secret or anything. It was common knowledge that Robert was screwing whatever he could get his hands on. As long as it was female."

"I think I'd have preferred Mother not knowing about it." She filled a small plastic bottle with shampoo.

"For God's sake, don't tell her about this. She won't understand."

"But neither do you."

Lucy's mouth became a thin line. "I do understand. I'm having certain difficulties with all of this, but I *understand* the situation very well. I mean, I'm aware and open and have read a great deal about the subject and I respect Peter's honesty in facing his problem, though he doesn't consider it a problem. Which it isn't, of course. It's a preference. A sexual preference is not a problem."

Alix put a bar of Neutrogena in the cosmetics case and thought that Lucy's ideas were as trendy as her shoes.

"So," Lucy continued, "the problem is mine, not Peter's. It is I who cannot cope with this situation."

Alix cut them both a wedge of cheese. She looked through the refrigerator for things that would spoil while she was away, and threw out an opened can of juice and a half loaf of bread. "Do you love him?" she asked Lucy.

"Do I what?"

"Do you love Peter?"

"It's not really a question of loving someone; it's a question of establishing a meaningful relationship, which is what I find so difficult with Peter. I mean, how can we establish an atmosphere of mutual trust when I'm so upset about, well, Peter's sexual preferences?"

"Love," said Alix. "What about love?"

"You ask these simplistic questions, Alix. No. If you want to know the truth, I don't love Peter. I never did, really. But I thought we'd make it together. I mean in a broader sense than just in bed. I thought if we were together we'd manage. We wouldn't be lonely."

In the distance a car honked. Somewhere a dog barked. The refrigerator hummed.

"And now?"

"And now . . . I don't know. I'll be forty in two years. You think that only happens to other people. Grownups. I wonder when I'm going to start feeling like a grownup." Lucy hooked her hair behind her ears. "I guess what I am is scared."

"Yes."

"Are you?"

"I was, but now . . ." Alix paused and thought. "I guess I can't think of anything to be scared of."

Lucy looked at her as if seeing her for the first time that day. "That's strange. That's really *peculiar*. How can there be nothing to be afraid of?"

"I don't know. I can't explain it."

"Maybe you're just numb," said Lucy. "I mean, Daddy died hardly a year ago and then Robert left. . . . Maybe you just couldn't take any more, so you turned off. Your emotions went dead. That's what's going to happen to me one of these days. I'll look at Peter and I just won't care anymore."

"There's a difference."

"In what?"

"Between not caring and not being scared."

"I don't know." Lucy took a bite of cheese. "You make it sound

234

like a value judgment. Like not being scared is somehow loftier, more noble, than not caring."

"Lucy, that's nonsense."

"No, really; that's how you make it sound, Alix. You've always done this. You've always looked down your nose at me. You and Daddy. You and Daddy always had so much in common and talked to each other all the time and everybody always thought I was silly and unstable and not as smart as you. . . ."

Alix stared at her.

"It's true, Alix. That's exactly the way it was."

"Oh, Lucy . . ."

She wanted to tell Lucy that nothing was exactly the way it appeared, that truth was open to interpretation. Definitions were not as simple, as logical, as commonly assumed. But she didn't know how.

25

"I'M NOT GOING TO PARK," said Lucy.

"That's all right," said Alix.

"I mean, it's such a hassle to park. Do you mind if I just drop you off?"

"I said it's all right. I don't mind. There's no reason for you to see me off."

"I'd like to see you off, Alix. I just don't want to park."

Alix sighed and looked out the car window at the Pacific Coast Highway. Golden Nugget restaurant, with the "$2.00 Early Bird Dinner," Straw Hat Pizza, Taco Bell, health food stores, car lots, mortuaries, Life Style furniture, antiques, wicker furniture, water beds, the orange and aquamarine triangle of the House of Pancakes. And occasionally a glimpse of the ocean. She thought of the long flight over that ocean, the hours she would spend listening to the hum of the engines, staring out the tiny window at the water below, the clouds.

"Thank God there's not much traffic," said Lucy.

"We have plenty of time," said Alix. "It only takes twenty-seven minutes."

"Twenty-seven minutes? What are you talking about?"

"Nothing. Nothing important."

"I never realized it before, but out here everybody turns distance into minutes. Back East people talk about distance in terms of miles. Did you ever notice that?"

"No, not really." Alix opened her new bag with the silver clasp and checked to see that she had her airline tickets, took out a bottle of Binaca, shook a few drops on her tongue, combed her hair and put on more lipstick. She was wearing new clothes, underwear, shoes, print dress; every inch of her felt new.

"You ass," said Lucy to a driver in front of her, and then passed him. No one on the road ever drove at a speed to suit Lucy. "He pulls out in front of me and then proceeds to go under the speed limit. I mean, certified morons are being issued driver's licenses these days."

"Lucy, there's plenty of time."

"That's not the point."

"I know." She wanted to say something to Lucy about Peter, but didn't know how. Or what. She thought of how Lucy always started her sentences with "I mean," as if perpetually trying to define herself to others. She thought about the details of this trip. The luggage, tips, meals, getting from place to place. Being a stranger. She had always been taken care of, protected, shuttled about like a piece of luggage when traveling with her family or Robert. This trip was a metaphor. She was thirty-six years old and she was free.

"God, I'm excited," she said.

"Well, be careful of your skin," Lucy replied. "Really, go very slowly on the beach or you'll be burned to a crisp. Do you have a hat?"

"No," said Alix, smiling.

"It's nothing to joke about, Alix. You could get sun poisoning if you're not careful, let alone just ruin your skin and look like you're about ninety years old by the time you get home."

"I'll buy a hat. I promise."

"And some of that stuff that blocks out the rays of the sun."

"I'll get some."

"Oh, shit," said Lucy as a car cut in front of her without signaling.

"It doesn't matter," said Alix.

Lucy drove leaning slightly forward. At every stoplight she clicked her nails on the steering wheel.

They were almost to Century Boulevard and the airport. Alix looked at her watch. Twenty-five minutes. She was neither here nor on her way yet. As if anything that was said wouldn't count, or really mean anything.

"People don't drive like this in New York," said Lucy.

"Do you remember how Daddy always used to hum when he drove?" Alix said. "He wasn't even aware of it. I pointed it out to him once and he told me he never hummed. I wonder why he didn't realize it."

"You remember the weirdest things, Alix. I mean, you really pick up stuff that is strange. I don't remember Daddy humming when he drove. I think you imagined it."

"No. He always hummed the minute he got behind the wheel."

They were at the airport. "This is a much better airport than Kennedy," said Lucy. "You've got all those numbers and colors to remember at Kennedy."

"You don't have to go all the way around to get to United," said Alix. "You can cut through the first road to the left."

"I'll go all the way around. I can't stand trying to cut through four lanes of traffic."

"There's a light there now. It's easy."

"Well, I'm used to going around. We have time, don't we?"

"Yes." Alix looked at her watch again. "My flight doesn't leave for another hour."

"You do understand about my not parking."

"Of course."

"You can check your bags through at the curb."

"Yes."

"I hope you have fun," said Lucy. "Get some rest. Meet a man."

"Meet a man?" said Alix. It was like hearing an old tune, one

238

whose lyrics she had almost forgotten. "I don't think I want to meet a man. I just want to lie in the sun and be alone for a while. Isn't that strange, Lucy? Think of all the years our lives were dedicated to meeting a man."

"Well, it isn't as if you don't have any irons on the fire. I mean, there is that cop."

"Yes. There is that cop."

"Well . . ." said Lucy. They were in front of the United terminal.

"I hope things go okay for you." Alix touched Lucy's arm.

"Yes," said Lucy, and kissed her on the cheek.

Alix could smell Calèche and the expensive smell of Lucy's makeup. She wanted to tell Lucy she loved her, that sometimes love was a matter of shared pasts. Shared blood and histories. But she didn't know how to say it without making Lucy uncomfortable, or risking the closeness she suddenly felt toward Lucy. "Take care," she said.

"You, too."

The car door slammed and Lucy disappeared into airport traffic.

Alix checked her bags through to Kauai, went to the ladies' room, combed her hair again, looked at herself in the mirror, then found the gate for her flight. Gate number 10. Thirty minutes before she could board. She could see the plane, huge, glinting in the gray Los Angeles light, capable of magic. Of getting up into the air, all that bulk and weight and space, and hours later landing in the sweet soft tropic air of Honolulu. Once Robert had tried to explain to her how a plane could get up into the air; a perfectly simple scientific phenomenon, he had called it. But it was magic, no matter how much Robert explained.

She picked up her boarding pass and realized she was smiling —at nothing, at everything. She smiled at strangers. At the gray-haired man standing outside the ladies' room, holding a woman's coat and purse. At the plump young couple with their arms around each other, wearing matching Hawaiian shirts. At the woman in a pink pants suit sitting next to her, who kept saying to her husband, who was silently smoking a cigarette, "Cut it out, Seymour, just cut it out. Don't start in. I mean it, Seymour." Alix smiled at Seymour. And at the man who walked up to Gate 10 pulling a skateboard to which he had attached his suitcase.

She'd arrive in Lihue at five fifty-five. She could go down to the beach for a swim before dinner. For dinner she'd have fresh fish. Maybe she'd order room service. Eat dinner curled up in her robe in her room and afterward she'd sit on her balcony and watch the sun set and then the torches lit along the beach and listen to the drums and music.

A voice over the PA system asked, "Would Mr. T. Buchanan please come to the information desk?" The woman sitting next to her said, "Seymour, I mean it. Cut it out. This is a vacation, for God's sake." A woman came out of the ladies' room and took her coat and purse from the man who had been holding them for her. Alix sensed that she herself was being stared at and she looked up. Lieutenant Calloway stood in front of her.

How strange to see him in public like this, out of context, was her first thought.

"I missed you by ten minutes," he said. "I tried to catch you at home."

"I don't understand." She stood up.

A voice over the PA system again asked for Mr. T. Buchanan. The couple in matching shirts kissed.

"Let's find a place to talk." His hand was on her elbow.

Alix hesitated. The waiting room was crowded. The woman in the pink pants suit stared at them.

"I've got to talk to you, Alix."

She realized he had never called her by her given name before.

"Please," he said, his hand gentle on her arm.

26

AN AIRPORT BAR, similar to the one she had sat in with Robert eleven days earlier, after they saw the children off. Round Formica table, the PA system announcing arrivals and departures, the cool, neutral temperature of all airport bars. The dim blue air smelled of luggage and liquor and cigarettes.

Calloway ordered drinks, a daiquiri for her and a beer for himself. His usual easiness was gone; today there were edges and corners. His eyes avoided hers.

Why? What could he know?

He took his blue notebook from his pocket and set it on the table as if that were the reason he had to talk to her. There was nothing personal about this. The notebook had acquired information which he had to discuss with her. It was all in the blue notebook. She had a vision of the notebook suddenly acquiring tiny antennae and gathering information on its own.

He cleared his throat, his eyes focused somewhere over her left shoulder. "I'm afraid something's come up."

What? What could have gone wrong? "Something's come up?"

He nodded and opened the notebook. An arriving flight was announced. At another table someone laughed. The bar was filled with the droning noise of a public place. Calloway turned pages in the notebook with a snapping sound. Alix realized she was holding her breath.

He found the page he was looking for and began to read in a monotone: a computer readout, nothing personal. "A realtor, Betty Lee, came to see me at the station this morning and stated that she had information regarding the murder of Warren Sullivan. She wanted to report something seen by the teen-age children of clients who were interested in buying your house." He paused.

"And what was seen?"

"A red Toyota parked in your garage on Wednesday afternoon."

Alix sipped her daiquiri. Silence hung between them like an object, requiring their attention.

Over the PA system came the announcement for her flight. "United Airlines flight number one ninety-three departing Los Angeles for Honolulu is now ready for boarding at Gate Ten."

Their eyes met for an instant and then Calloway continued to read in his computerlike monotone. "The teen-agers looked into the garage through a small window by the side of the house. The boy, Ronald Shoemaker, said he was checking for space in the garage for a workshop when he and his sister saw the vehicle in question. They thought nothing of it until yesterday, when they heard their parents discussing an article which had appeared in the newspaper stating that Warren Sullivan's body had been discovered in a red Toyota."

Their eyes met again and held for a long time. She took a deep breath that came out a sigh.

"The car. That damned car," she said at last.

"Alix . . ." From the look on his face she realized he had expected a denial, an obvious and innocent explanation.

He closed the notebook and put it in his pocket; he cleared his throat again. "I have to advise you of your rights."

"But that was the whole point."

He looked at her, puzzled. "What was?"

"My rights."

"Look, Alix, don't tell me anything. Get a lawyer. Please, just don't say anything."

"He raped me." The words like stones. Edges defined, weighted, real.

Calloway stared at her. "Oh, Christ."

Then reached for her hand and held it. "Oh, God, Alix."

The boarding announcement was being repeated. "United flight one ninety-three is now boarding at Gate Ten. All passengers with boarding passes . . ."

She thought of sun and silence and a long stretch of beach. Lying on that beach and soaking up sun and not having to explain or justify or speak at all. One week of being free and on her own. A chance to be silent, to prepare herself for whatever it was she had to face now. Just one week.

She gripped Calloway's hand. "One week," she said. "Let me have the week. I'll come back; I'll have to come back: my kids are here. Where would I go? What would I do? Another week won't make any difference. Not to the police. But it will for me. Just once on my own, just one time—"

He looked down at the table, at their hands, his face closed. "Alix, I can't do that."

"Of course you can! You missed me at the house; what if you missed me at the airport, too? Fifteen more minutes and you would have. A traffic jam, that's all it would have taken."

He was silent.

"One week," she said. "Just one week. I'll be back. You can trust me. Trust me for a week."

"*Trust* you?" His face undefended, unguarded; the shadows and lines suddenly vivid.

"Yes. You can, I swear to you. I'm trusting you now. I'll tell you everything."

"Alix, don't."

"Then later. When you need for me to tell you everything. I

promise. Please—you were late, you missed me at the airport. My plane had already left." She was still gripping his hand. "Please trust me. Let me do this."

In his eyes, the angle of his shoulders, his silence, she could feel the tension. How many years of being a good cop?

She forced herself to be quiet. To give him a chance to think, to understand. She stared at him in the silence. Dear God, how she wanted to get on that plane. Had to. Just one week.

Finally he rose. "Wait here a minute. I have to make a phone call. I'll be right back."

She didn't say anything. She nodded.

Then waited. She felt suspended with waiting. As if the waiting itself were a means to an end. Or maybe the end itself. Now what? Whom was he telephoning? What happens next? How was one arrested? She tried to remember what happened in films, books, on television. What if she made a run for the plane? Ran shrieking through the airport that she couldn't take any more?

She finished her daiquiri. Why was Calloway taking so long? She thought of her new clothes folded and packed in her suitcase, waiting on the plane for her, tagged for Kauai. The expectant feeling inside the plane now; the preparations for a long flight over the ocean, for drinks, meals. Everyone safe, enclosed, ready to begin a journey, an adventure.

Over the PA system: "Final call for United Airlines flight one ninety-three departing Los Angeles for Honolulu . . ."

The waitress cleared their glasses from the table. "Another daiquiri?" Her voice was kind, as if she thought Alix had been abandoned.

"No, thanks," said Alix, and looked once more at her watch. Calloway had been gone for five minutes now. "Where are the public telephones?"

"Just outside to the right. You can't miss them."

"What do we owe you for drinks?"

"They were paid for."

Alix walked out of the bar to the waiting room. To her right was a row of public telephones. Three persons were using them.

She stood staring at the three strangers talking on the telephones.

Calloway was gone.

One week.

She took the boarding pass out of her purse and ran for the gate.

All Futura Books are available at your bookshop or
newsagent, or can be ordered from the following
address:
Futura Books, Cash Sales Department,
P.O. Box 11, Falmouth, Cornwall.

Please send cheque or postal order (no currency), and
allow 25p for postage and packing for the first book
plus 10p per copy for each additional book ordered up to
a maximum charge of £1.05 in U.K.

Customers in Eire and B.F.P.O. please allow 25p for
postage and packing for the first book plus 10p per copy
for the next eight books, thereafter 5p per book.

Overseas customers please allow 40p for postage and
packing for the first book and 12p per copy for each
additional book.